AND US SERIES BOOK 1

KISSES, LIES & O's

by

WILLA DREW

Moving Words Publishing

Join the mailing list for updates and follow Willa Drew at

willadrew.com

If you like this book, please consider giving it a review, so others

can enjoy it as well.

PRAISE FOR WILLA DREW

Willa Drew's writing style blew me away.

Highly recommend this author and book without a doubt!

My first book by Willa and it won't be my last!

I look forward to reading other books by this author in the future. Because I went into this one with hope and promise, and it absolutely delivered! Now it's your turn!

This is a great story written by two clearly talented authors. The characters have been put front and centre of this book, with their story and development being what it is all about.

This is the first time I have a read a book by these authors and I enjoyed the collaboration. The book flowed well, seamlessly moving through the story.

I am glad I stumbled on this book and these authors, and I will definitely be adding them to my list of authors to keep my eye out for.

The authors did a wonderful job of writing the characters in a way that I felt connected to them right away.

THE AND US SERIES

What starts out as a lie, turns into a passionate and heartfelt romance story about finding oneself and love.
Told in dual POV, this series spans a year of Sarah and Nick's lives against the backdrop of major holidays and ends with a guaranteed HEA.

Kisses, Lies, & Us
Passions, Hopes, & Us
Distance, Love, & Us

If you like friends-to-lovers, secret identities, movies, soulmates, and a right person wrong time new adult romance the And Us series is for you.

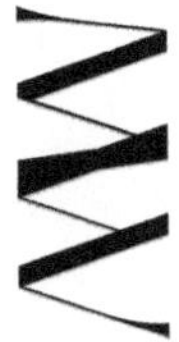

Published by: Moving Words Publishing

www.movingwordspublishing.com

Cover: A Fabulous Production

(@afabulousproduction on Instagram)

Artwork: María Peña

(@me.me.pe on Instagram)

ISBN: 978-1-957897-18-9

Second Edition: March 2025

CONTENTS

For those who believe in second chances

PART 1

CHRISTMAS EVE

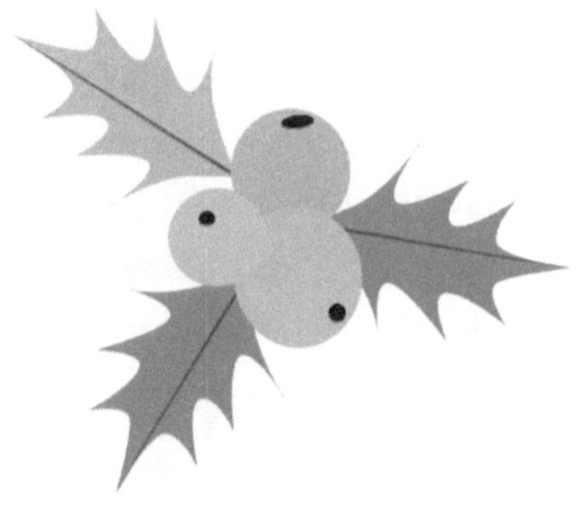

ONE

NICK

The truth is—I tell lies all the time. What's one more?

I twirl the fake ID my friends gave me for my birthday. It's my face all right, but according to the black block letters on this driver's license, my name isn't Nick, it's Shawn. The address is also not mine, nor the age. I'm newly nineteen, and Shawn's twenty-one. Old enough to drink but not too old for those inclined to question.

I catch the bartender's eye for the third time. A tingle travels down my neck.

She reaches over in front of a woman my mom's age, lays a snowflake-shaped coaster on the bar to my right, and places a fancy pink cocktail with a paper umbrella on it. Glossy green leaves frame the name tag on the pocket of her white resort uniform. The sprig of ivy is the only nod to Christmas Eve. The tag hangs down at an angle, making it hard to read her name, but it begins with an S.

"And what can I get for you?" She hands a glass of sparkling water to a server who appears and disappears to my left. Her voice rings over the smooth jazz. My pulse beats in my ears and dampens the chatter of a couple dozen patrons scattered around the small dimly lit bar.

"Old Fashioned." Dad's been ordering them at every place we've been to this week. This whole trip turned into him showing off that he's landed on his feet. He spends every day trying to get back into Mom's good graces. Bonding time with me doesn't appear to be on the agenda anymore.

"Is that your ID?"

I slide the laminated card her way, and she flicks her eyes between the photo and me. The one-corner-of-the-mouth smile I learned from my brother plus the direct eye contact should project enough confidence to calm any suspicions. I vibrate like she raised the bass in my chest to high but don't lift my eyebrow or move into full-on flirting. That'd be too much.

"Visiting from Chicago?"

"Yep."

One of those preppy professional-service smiles reveals white teeth that amplify the glow of her sun-kissed face. Lots of hours spent at the tanning booth to get that shade, I bet.

She beams even wider, and I see that one of her canines on top is crooked. You have to pay attention to notice, but now that I do, her whole image changes, and the film of affluence the resort transferred onto her disappears. The tightly wound string inside slackens.

The bartender hands my fake back. Her fingers are cold and . . . damp? I run my thumb over the ID to remove what I hope is water and slide the card into the pocket of my jacket.

"Sorry." She catches my gesture and wipes her fingers off on a bar towel, reinforcing the humanity behind the uniform. I relax into my seat. "Buffalo Trace or Woodford Reserve?"

What the fuck are those? I flip my phone over. Me, Nick, has no idea what she's asking about, but the twenty-one-year-old Shawn should have an answer.

"Whatever you think's best." Another thing I picked up from Dad. He's been throwing the phrase around, and Mom thinks he's matured. I hope he did. For her sake.

The bartender nods and turns around. While the bulky shirt doesn't reveal much of her body, the black pants hug her butt, and she'd get much better tips displaying that thing to the customers. She stands on her tiptoes to get a bottle with amber liquor from the glass shelf. I should stop staring at how cute her nose looks in profile, or wondering what she would look like in a less bulky top, or looking at her pants. I shift in my seat and try to ignore the flare of heat at the base of my spine. Definitely not looking at those. It's a slippery slope.

I force my eyes away from her bouncy ponytail that matches her whole sunny persona and survey the rows of bottles. The bar has no Christmas trees or Santas, going with a snow theme instead. Along the shelves with multi-colored jewel cases containing alcohol lies white fluffy material pretending to be the snow that doesn't exist in LA. A string of large snowflake-shaped lights glows above the top of the bar.

There aren't many things I'll miss about Chicago, but snow on Christmas might be one. I'd have to get used to people walking around in shorts, flip flops, and light sweaters. No matter how festive it is, nothing screams "Christmas" to me in LA.

The white sleeve of her uniform slips and reveals her tiny wrist when she moves to get a short tumbler with a line design cut across the bottom. Something James Bond would use. Many steps above the red plastic cups I drink cheap beer out of back home.

She grabs three bottles and sets them next to the glass. It's like I'm watching Mom's favorite British baking show, wondering what's next. I lean in. First, a bit of clear liquid goes in, then water, some dark stuff from a small container with a yellow cap, and a dash from an even tinier one with an orange label. The text on them is too small for me to read to find out what they are. I assumed cocktails could be convoluted, but this looks a bit like my chemistry class. She stirs the mixture with a silver spoon that has a long skinny handle, places one gigantic baseball sized ice cube into the glass, and pours Woodford Reserve over the ice.

Everything she does is self-assured and practiced. She shaves a bit of orange and lemon peel, folds them, runs them around the rim of the glass, squeezes a twist of mist over the whole thing, and places them in next to the ice. The scent of citrus hits my nostrils and sends me back to Yiayia slicing lemons from her garden for Psari Plaki. The bartender's tan fingers match my drink but it's her crisp uniform, the glass, and the garnish that make this scene look like everything I'd expected from an overpriced bar at a high-end resort.

"Enjoy." I almost believe she means it. I bite the inside of my cheek as she moves the glass my way.

Ah, here it is. This would be the money shot: her hand setting the drink down as if it's in front of the viewer. The bar top can't be wood. I'd change it to something more reflective, maybe acrylic, so I could play with the lights and reflections.

I narrow my eyes and see the camera moving in as her hand pushes forward with the drink. The contrast of the amber liquid, tan skin, white cuff of the shirt, and touch of yellow and orange from the fruit peels work together to make the shot dramatic. I could underscore this scene with some sick beats as the glass comes toward us, and then something slow as we pan to it.

"Something wrong with the drink?" She leans closer and the foliage moves on the tag, revealing her name.

Sarah C.

"Sarah, right? All good, thank you."

Another trick of Dad's. "Call them by their names," he told me yesterday, "the staff appreciates it." The staff. My stomach churns. People like him who come to places like this have staff, listen to smooth jazz, and order drinks you need a degree in mixology to make. He forgets Mom is the staff.

She's been cutting people's hair for the last ten years.

How do I drink this? I take a deep breath and rotate the glass. I've come too far to disappoint Sarah. Am I supposed to sniff it, like Mom does with her wine? I can't remember if Dad did anything special with his. I raise the drink to my lips.

The liquid burns my throat, but I think I hide it well. Lying's always come naturally to me. I get that from Dad, too.

I take another gulp. Pretending. One more gulp. Fibbing.

Sometimes I forget who the real Nick is.

And another one. It burns less with every swig, but I hate the taste. Bitterness coats my tongue. I can't drink any more. The glass, however, I love. Maybe I'll buy one like it for myself one day and drink beer out of it.

Why didn't I order a beer and enjoy something I liked instead of pretending I'm sophisticated? For the sake of who? The middle-aged crowd around me? The sunny Sarah, with her big grin and bright blue eyes? Eyes that are checking me out. No. I shake my head. Checking the fancy, Old Fashioned-drinking Shawn out.

Would she like me if I didn't pretend? If, for once, I was just me?

The fake ID can shield the real Nick from potential fallout yet let me be...well, me. Minus the right name. I straighten, my brain lighting up at the idea. The little piece of plastic, the small lie offers a chance to not be afraid to be Nick. Be myself.

"Sarah?" I begin my experiment.

From this point on, I vow to only tell the truth.

To this girl.

For this one night.

My heartbeat tries to outrun the tapping of my foot. Bartenders are like shrinks—they're supposed to listen and keep your secrets. Right?

Two

Sarah

AND I THOUGHT TONIGHT would be boring.

Pull a double on Christmas Eve, compliment a few drunk lonely men, and make some good tips so I can pay off my overdue cell phone bill. Maybe get back to the apartment and the swinging Christmas Eve party my roommates are holding before someone starts having sex in my bedroom. The plan was simple.

Enter this guy. He's a plot twist in the film noir that was supposed to be my evening. He's all sorts of tall, dark, and handsome dressed in a black jacket and a red T-shirt that's calling to me like a beacon in this sea of winter white.

I swish the martini shaker and watch out of the corner of my eye as Shawn takes a sip of his drink. Did he notice I put a little extra bourbon in? Probably not. Months of bartending to figure out how to pour the perfect shot, but no one notices. They just want to name drop when ordering their fancy drinks. The silver cylinder almost flies out of my grasp, I rattle it so hard. I grit my teeth and restore my customer satisfaction smile. Sometimes I wonder if they even know what it is they're drinking, or if it's just the latest fad.

Shawn rubs the condensation off the smooth tumbler of his Old Fashioned. Up and down. His strong fingers wrap around the crystal. Lucky glass.

Really, Sarah? It's been a bit of a dry spell but c'mon. It's just fingers. And who under forty orders an Old Fashioned?

Old Fashioneds aren't in right now. It's all about gin these days. One celebrity goes viral selling gin, and their millions of fans follow suit. But maybe I should change my lead character's drink from a rum and coke to an Old Fashioned? Make Wesley seem more worldly. Hmmm. Need to think about that.

Sure. I've been *thinking* about Wesley and my opus for two months now. How about writing for a change? That screenplay isn't going to finish itself.

Unlike this martini. I can make 'em in my sleep. Plop, swish, pour.

I turn on my signature smile and focus on delivering a perfect martini to the next customer. In return, I get the glassy-eyed response from the woman sitting next to Shawn. Seeing me, but not seeing me. To her, I'm just another California blond. That's me, your sweet, valley-girl bartender, here to listen to your woes, offer a kind nod or encouraging word as you spend your evening getting pickled at this swanky resort my poor broke ass couldn't afford to eat at, never mind stay.

Except I'm not sweet or from the valley. No one here notices or cares that I grew up far away in the great white north, as Californians like to joke. No, really, never heard that one before. It was like a daily mantra when I first got here and people remarked on my accent, or rather lack thereof. It's plain Canada to me, where the maple syrup is sweet and people can't look you in the eye when they lie to you. Not like here.

But Shawn's brown eyes didn't look away. The sparkle I see there almost makes me believe he cares enough to know my name.

"Sarah?"

Shawn *did* want to know my name. I sway his way. "Yes, Mr. Old Fashioned."

He swings his head, and I watch his dark hair flop over his forehead. "You're never going to let that go, are you?"

"Well, I call 'em as I see 'em and you . . . you dug your own hole, Mister." I bite my lip.

"Seriously, what can I do to change my reputation here? I'm desperate. Give a guy a break." His puppy-dog eyes urge me to give him anything he wants. I grin.

Holy crap. What is wrong with me?

"Fine. Give me something to work with here." I roll my eyes but flash him my real smile. Will he even notice the difference? Hey? Did he just raise an eyebrow at me? I'm seeing things now. "What's your favorite song?"

It's like he struck gold. Or I did. He sits up straight, and I have to look up. The skin on my neck heats. Wow, he is tall. I like tall.

Evens out my short. One side of Shawn's mouth curls. Cute. So cute.

"That's a big question. I mean, one song for all time? Too many options." His gaze locks on mine, and his pupils grow as we enter a staring match. "You have to narrow down the playing field a bit. You can't put my latest fave and the Beatles in the same category."

I laugh. I actually laugh. Air rushes into my chest, and I'm giddy. Where did this guy come from?

I place my arms on the bar and lean toward him, waiting to see if he checks out my cleavage. I'm pretty sure he was eyeballing it earlier. They all check out my chest. Maybe I should give him the benefit of the doubt and chalk it up to an attempt to read my nametag. Yeah, right.

Shawn's eyes never leave mine. The bar behind him falls out of focus. I might need to sit down. "Okay, then. Favorite Christmas song."

Now he laughs. Crinkles form at the corners of his eyes, and the sparkle is back. "Oh, I asked for that, didn't I?'

"Yup." Who am I to disagree?

Tapping his finger—the one previously feeling up his glass—against his bottom lip, Shawn makes a face like he's concentrating hard. Goosebumps rush across my clavicle. I love that he's taking this seriously. He's taking *me* seriously.

"Well, you know, I like the classics. I'm gonna stay in my lane. *Little Drummer Boy*, wait for it"— his grin is infectious—"*Peace on Earth* by Bowie and Bing." He slaps his hand on the bar, pleased with himself. "Two geniuses of their genres coming together to create magic. That's Christmas to me."

"Who are you?" My mouth takes over.

The light in his eyes dims. No, no, we were having fun. Ignore my stupid question, keep talking about Bowie. I clutch the edge of the bar. My brain scrambles, trying to bring back the sun. "I love Bowie too."

"Just a k . . . guy from Chicago here for the holidays visiting my dad." He rubs the fine layer of stubble on his chin. Would the short hairs be soft, or scratch my fingers? "I'm waiting for him to finish up a meeting."

"The windy city, eh? Enjoying the warm weather?"

"I guess. Doesn't feel like Christmas, though."

"Where I grew up, we always had a white Christmas. We'd go skating on Boxing Day."

Shawn scrunches his nose. "Boxing Day?"

He's peering at me like I have two heads.

"Keep forgetting you Americans don't celebrate Boxing Day. In Canada, where I'm from"—I point at my chest, but his eyes don't stray— "it's the day after Christmas. You get to lounge around stuffing yourself with leftovers, watching movies, or, if you're like my mom, you throw your kids out into the snow to burn off the sugar they inhaled. I think she wanted some peace and quiet."

Why am I still talking? I pick at a snowflake-shaped coaster. I just shared more with Shawn in two minutes than I did the first six months I lived with my roommates. And I'm pouring the liquor, not drinking it. Yet. One of the perks of this job is sampling new products our boss acquires so we can recommend them. The new Japanese and Belgian beers I'm bringing to the "so you're alone on Christmas too" celebration—the impromptu party my friends Siobhan and Claudia are throwing for out-of-towners—looked promising. Is there even such a thing as a local in LA?

"I can roll with that. Not the sugar, it's not my thing, but the movie part, for sure. I'm either watching one or filming one."

"Well, you're in the right town." I wince at the vinegar in my voice. Really, Sarah, you gotta get over this. It was one bad move. How were you supposed to know it was a scam? Not everyone in Tinseltown is a liar or a crook. Newbies, like Shawn here, start off decent, straightforward, and honest, and he might even stay that way. I shrug. For most of us, this town eventually chews us up and spits us out like yesterday's trash.

"That's my plan. Move here."

Should I burst his bubble? Warn him? Nah, not my place. Shawn has family here. They'll look out for him.

"Hey, Sarah, where d'you want this?" Ryan's holding another box of the wine I asked him to bring from the storeroom. Is it number eight or nine? I'm losing count. I massage my temples. Hope we have enough to last the rest of the night.

"There is fine." I point to the other end of the bar, where the last unopened bottle sits.

"What else do you need help with?" Patience has never been Ryan's virtue. The man can't seem to sit still. "I need to get back to the floor. The VIP group needs attention."

Shit. I survey the dwindling crowd. Standing here just chatting with this Shawn guy isn't good for my tips.

"On my way," I shout to Ryan over my shoulder and give Shawn my best apology smile.

I top off the guy who's drinking Veuve like it's water, which is great for the bar, but my skin crawls as he licks his lips while not so subtly staring down the open collar of my uniform. My stomach rolls. His attempts at flirting irritated me before Shawn showed up but are ridiculous at this point. I pull the material closed and hoof it down to Ryan to help him unpack the box.

This Icellars Winery red is popular lately. Glad something from my hometown can make it in LA. I leave two bottles on the bar as my coworker stacks the rest underneath.

"Got a live one there?" Ryan turns his stoned smirk on me.

"What?"

"The hot kid." My partner for the evening nods in Shawn's direction.

"Him? He's not a kid." Not with that five o'clock shadow.

Ryan narrows his eyes at me like he's got a secret. "Only guy here under fifty. Besides me."

"What's your point, Ryan?" He's a little too aware of my LA loser streak. You could say, he got the ball rolling. We had a thing when I first started—another one of my mistakes. I was so green when I moved out here. All bright-eyed and bushy tailed. Good thing the thick skin grew quickly.

Still, unlike every other aspect of his life, Ryan is pretty mature about being friends. I think. He doesn't seem to mind that I'm basically his boss.

"All I'm saying, I've seen that look before." His eyes dart down the bar to Shawn. "Is he eligible to join the Sarah Club?"

I follow Ryan's gaze. Shawn's honey brown hair flops over his eyes as he studies the half-empty glass he's no longer drinking. Flutters dance at the base of my throat. Good taste in music. Check. Doesn't take himself too seriously. Check. Hands big enough to wrap around my waist. Check.

"Why not?" I scrunch my nose. "Could be fun."

"Attagirl." Ryan grins at me. The same grin that got me in trouble the first time. Good thing it holds no power over me anymore. "Get back on that horse. Ride, baby, ride."

I punch Ryan lightly in the stomach as I turn and saunter toward my target.

"Hey, Shawn." He doesn't react. I reach over and touch his hand. He startles, tugs on a red cord, and takes out an earbud.

"Talking to me?"

The whirl spreads to my diaphragm. "Yes. My shift's ending. Wanna ditch these old folks and hang with some people our age?" The offer is out of my mouth before I have a chance to overthink it.

He pulls the other earbud out and lowers his head, looking at me. The whir falters. Why isn't he saying anything? Should've buttered him up first. He must have plans already.

"Got something in mind?" Shawn asks.

He's interested. My stomach does a little flip. Maybe this Christmas won't suck after all.

"Yeah, my roommates are having a party. The more the merrier." Please don't say no. Please don't say no.

"Sure."

And just like that, I won't be the only single girl at the party tonight. Of course, he's only coming because it's better than hanging out with this crowd all evening. But still. My lungs expand.

"Great. Give me ten to finish up and change."

"Okay. I'll wait here."

As I turn to go, Shawn scans my body with another raised eyebrow, and I can tell he likes what he sees.

Three

NICK

What happened? We were talking, like really talking, and she walked away. But what should I expect? It's not like this is a date. The girl has a job to do.

The new wave of Muzak they're pumping makes my ears want to bleed. To drown out the smooth jazz, I put my headphones in and cue up the Oldies Christmas playlist I put together for Mom's holiday party at her hair salon. Bing's pum-pum-pums croon and blend with Bowie's wish for peace on earth before the music moves into five different versions of Irving Berlin's *White Christmas*. People hear White Christmas and think of Bing Crosby, but there are so many other worthy renditions. Does Sarah have a favorite one?

I can't stop staring at her. She doesn't stare back but her from-under-the-lash, let-me-check-you-out glance is not so subtle. That's some special treatment. No doubt about that. She ignores the blatant flirting from the grey-haired man she keeps topping off with some bubbly drink. The perv's at least twice her age. Santa Claus is Coming to Town by The Jackson 5 starts up in my ears. I bend over the drink I'm not going to finish. A pleasant haze settles over the bar. How much wasted booze is that?

At the other end of the bar, Sarah attempts another sneaky eye-rake. I can't read lips, but I bet the conversation she's having with the surfer dude she's been bossing around is about me. She better be saying something good cause I'm not playing around. What she got was genuine Nick Stavros. No fakeness in sight.

Louis Armstrong sings about sharing in *Zat You, Santa Claus?* Or was I too eager? Going on about Bing and Bowie. Should have chosen Bieber. He's Canadian. Or anything from the twenty-first century? Something she might like, instead of revealing what Mom calls 'my old soul.' I bounce my knee. Am I losing my touch? Although the touch has never been me, it's always been whatever the girl was looking for.

Like my last girlfriend, Mackenzie. She wanted a hockey player with anger issues and aggressive make out sessions, preferably somewhere the right people would see us. Nicky, being the people pleaser extraordinaire, obliged. It did get me access to her dad's video editing studio. No complaints here.

The music slows and Joni Mitchell regrets giving up her baby in River. A feeling I don't understand. My soul remains calm. Never had a girl I lost my shit about. Not playing innocent here. I have needs and they got met. Mackenzie wanted what I had to offer, and if we helped each other in and out of the bedroom, it only made our relationship more beneficial. No feelings were involved. We both knew what we wanted and got exactly that.

Until I wasn't a hockey player anymore. She ditched me for my former teammate Clark, who was aggressive without any acting. That hurt way less than the puck I caught with my face. I trace the scar it left on my cheek. No regrets. I appreciated the relief of not wasting my time on a girl I had nothing in common with. Asking her dad to work at his camera shop was not as hard as I thought, so even without Mackenzie, I got access to all the filming equipment I needed.

Damp fingers on my hand. I look up, and Sarah is in front of me. Her eyes search mine. What did I miss? Is she expecting a reaction? A response? I tug on a red cord and the festive music disappears.

"Talking to me?"

"Yes. My shift's ending. Wanna ditch these old folks and hang with some people our age?" She stumbles over her words, they come out so fast.

Well, well. The internal standing ovation I'm imagining boosts me up more than the cheers from the bleachers after a hard check against the boards. The real Nick is not so bad at flirting. Good to know. I remove the second earbud and give her my full attention. Dad expects me to stay close since we're leaving as soon as his meeting is over. But that could be hours. And anything Sarah has to offer is so much more . . . alluring for anyone with functioning senses than hanging at this overpriced mausoleum.

"Got something in mind?"

"Yeah." Her mouth turns upward. "My roommates are having a party. The more the merrier."

Party isn't what I had in mind. Something one-on-one would be better, but beggars can't be choosers. The point is, it's still spending time with her.

"Sure," I say.

Her eyes light up at my words. "Great. Give me ten to finish up and change."

"Um, okay." I look around the room. "I'll wait here."

Sarah rounds the bar and sways her hips as she passes by the pool. To work here she has to be at least twenty-one, but I'd swear she's my age, if not younger. She's even tinier than I thought, yet all sides of her look the right contrast of big and small. She'd fit perfectly in my hands. Heat flares across the tips of my fingers and I tuck them under my thigh before they decide we should follow.

She disappears behind a white door. I put a twenty under my glass and plug the earbuds back in. It's Mariah Carey wailing the chorus to *All I Want for Christmas is You*. How fitting.

I scratch the stubble from not shaving since we've arrived in LA. Was that a pity invite? But when she touched my hand—I don't know. The heat travels to my chest and pools there. Something's happening between us.

Either way, it's better than staying here waiting for Dad to finish schmoozing some big-name studio exec, hoping this screenplay sells. I wanted them to drop me off at the beach or the

Griffith Observatory but according to Dad, there's no need to sightsee because I'll get a chance to visit every tourist trap when I move here. I huff. Instead, I was the third wheel on a trip down memory lane for him and Mom.

A hand on my shoulder startles me.

"Shawn?" Sarah's touch is warm and gentle.

My stomach sinks. Shawn. That's me. I forgot I wasn't me—stupid fake ID.

What was I thinking, using it? Oh, right, needed a cool LA story to tell my former teammates. Haven't had the nerve to use it back home yet, where someone might recognize me. The guys used my high school yearbook picture. They find it funny to tease me, say I look like Shawn Mendes. There are worse dudes to be compared to. His songs are not my go-to, but his collaboration with Bieber was decent. And who am I to say no to a good fake? At least the last name is clever: Rosstav—an anagram for my real surname.

"Sorry it took me so long."

She's changed. And I like it. The damned heat resurges.

The bulky white uniform top is gone, replaced with a much more form-hugging but equally white top drawing the eye to her skin even more. One side of the collar slides down and exposes her tan shoulder and the strap of her bra. The shirt is short enough to reveal a swath of taut midriff, and I ball my hands to keep from touching her.

Her hair is no longer in a ponytail. A smooth gold sheath is gathered over the shoulder that's still covered. And then there's the bottom half of her outfit. The cutoffs are so tight. I've never been this happy to see someone wearing shorts in December. White fabric tennis shoes and a bulky blue sweater draped over her messenger bag complete a look I wouldn't see in Chicago after the first of September.

"Ready to go?"

Am I ever. I push off the barstool and follow. As we leave, I take in the view. She looks even better in denim. I bury my hands in my pockets to cover my reaction. Yep, I'm going to like living in LA.

"Let's take my car."

"Sure."

She taps the remote in her hand, and the headlights on a dark blue car flash. Looks like a Beemer. An old one. Still has that snub-nose look. Yep, there's the blue and white propeller logo on the hood. I skim the cold metal lines of the fender. Can this get any better? She drives a convertible.

I fold myself into the passenger seat, not quite enough space for my long legs, but this ride is worth it. Her car is all sorts of right. Not Mom's embarrassing minivan, a true old-school convertible. I crane my neck to inspect every inch of the interior. Is it too cold to put the top down?

Kelly Clarkson blasts a high note of *Silent Night* as Sarah starts the car. Her hand shoots out and turns down the volume. "Sorry, I like to feel my music."

I like this girl. "Totally get it." I lift my red Beats earbuds—the only item I never leave the house without. "Same. Mom says I'll regret it when I'm her age and need a hearing aid, but that's for the old N . . . me to worry about." Fuck. I almost slipped. This was too close.

"D'you live with your mom?"

The first instinct is to embellish, to fall into the comfort of my old Nicky habit, and lie about a place of my own. That'd be easy. But tonight is about the truth. Let's test the waters.

"For now."

"That's smart." She doesn't seem bothered. "The best way to save money if you can do it. I did too, until my move to LA."

I uncurl my fingers and rub my sweaty palms on my jeans. That wasn't bad. Actually, it was good. Felt good to tell the truth.

Sarah shifts the car into first, and it jerks.

"You drive a manual?"

"My dad insisted I learn, and then I liked it. Old Betty here and I have been together for a long time." She pats the steering wheel before shifting gears again.

"You named your car?"

"You haven't?"

"I . . . I don't have a car." I relax into the seat. Not trying to talk my way around lies is freeing. Way to keep this honesty ball rolling.

"Oh. Sorry. I always assume everyone has a car. It's essential in LA."

"I'll put it on my 'move to LA' list. You drove this here from . . ."

"Toronto. Yup. See?" She points to the dashboard. "The speedometer's in kilometers."

Not gonna resist that invite. My pulse quickens. I bend over to look at the speedometer—and her—closer, but it's my nose that gets a treat. She smells like strawberries as I breathe her in. Blood rushes many places at once. Sarah's scent is the only part of her I can access freely. The rest of her is not mine to enjoy. It doesn't make me want her any less.

I lean in more, but that only makes things worse. The closeness is torture. Sweet, sweet torture. This pain I can take. Or end, if she'd be interested. If I closed the distance between us, my mouth would land on her neck, and I could draw a map with my kisses from the soft hollow under her ear over her jaw and to her lips.

My stomach rumbles.

Did she hear it? I hope not. Even though the only edible thing I've had since lunch five hours ago were the free pretzels at the bar, and I tend to care about food as much as a hungry hippo, right now I don't want anything to distract me from the exposed skin that I'm becoming obsessed with.

Maybe the drink on an empty stomach is to blame for how attracted I am to Sarah and how carefree and comfortable it is to be around her. I tear myself away and rest my back against the cool leather of the seat. Maybe it can chill my fevered fantasies. I wish.

Another rumble, but it's not my stomach this time.

"Was that you again or me?" She pokes my leg. I catch the white of her teeth on her lower lip. "I'm starving. Mind if we stop for something to eat first?"

Is she kidding? If I can't have her, I might as well be fed. The salad with chicken strips Mom insisted I order at lunch left me hungry before we left the swanky restaurant. Starving doesn't even cover it. Play it cool.

"I could eat." It's the truth.

"I know a food truck with the best tacos. It's near Griffith Park. Have you seen the view from the observatory yet?"

Baby, I've seen it all is what the sophisticated Shawn would probably say.

"Haven't seen much of anything." My uncensored words are flowing now.

Her mouth turns down a little at the edges. I've screwed up. I clutch the grab handle. I knew this was too good to be true.

"That sucks. LA has so much to offer." She's not mad. "When I first got here, I wandered around awestruck for weeks. I can give you a tour, if you like. How long are you in town for?"

I hate my dad. Why do we have to leave tonight?

"I'd love that. But my dad rented a house in Santa Barbara." The rental is the same house the four of us spent our last Christmas in together as a family. Mike and I had fun learning to surf. Of course, that was before. Before the truth came out and banished my big bro, Mom, and me to Chicago. The weight I've been carrying on my shoulders for ten years presses down.

"We're going there tonight and flying back home the day after Christmas."

"Oh." Does she sound disappointed, or am I imagining it? She drums her fingers on the steering wheel. "Too bad. Maybe next time."

"Totally. I'm hoping to move here next summer."

She rewards me with another smile.

FOUR

Sarah

THE TACO TRUCK IS here. I don't even have to look, because the moment we pull up, the smell of meat and fried something permeates the parking lot.

Wasn't sure it'd be here on Christmas Eve. They've decorated it, but the style is the polar opposite of the sleek elegance of the Diamond Club. The blow-up Santa Claus has a 'Ho-ho-ho, Merry Christmas' light running across the white of his beard. Snoopy lies on top of a mailbox that accepts letters for Santa. Spanish lyrics spill from the tiny speaker at the window framed by red and green candy cane lights. The song drones on about going to Belen. Wonder where that is? A red poinsettia plant stands on the table wrapped in red and white striped plastic. It's gaudy but festive at the same time.

The menu is in Spanish and English, but I don't need to look. Shawn is examining it with an occasional side-glance at me.

"Need help? The meats are listed on the left." I point to the panel above us.

"What's in it, apart from meat?" He shuffles left to right.

"Depends on what you want, but they can add or take away pretty much anything."

"What are you getting?" Uncertainty laces Shawn's voice. He sidesteps to let two teenage girls pass through. Both of them spend more time looking at Shawn than at the menu. The nerve. I squint at them. I'm right here.

"Taco de cabeza." One of the girls catches my glare and gives either some appreciative nods or her impersonation of a bobblehead.

"And what meat is that?"

"Braised head."

Shawn rubs his jaw. "Seriously? Like the brains?"

"No, the head of a cow." His eyes budge. "It's slow-roasted until the meat is fall-apart tender."

"Nope. Not making it sound any better."

I try not to smile. "Don't yuck it until you try it. Claudia, one of my roomies, is from Mexico. She introduced me to this place and got me to give it a chance. I'm addicted."

"Yeah, but no. Not today." He appears nauseated instead of intrigued. "Anything less adventurous?"

"Define adventurous." My eyes take their time climbing from his chest to his neck, on to the face I wouldn't mind seeing every day. The view is delicious. "What d'you usually eat?"

"Burritos."

I'm almost afraid to ask. "From?"

"Taco Bell?" His pained expression makes me want to brush away the wrinkles on his forehead.

"Right." I pinch the bridge of my nose. Not much to work with here. "How about carne asada?"

"Is it spicy? I don't do spicy."

So, Mr. Perfect does have flaws after all. Makes him even more real. My throat catches. I'm in trouble here. "It's chopped beef. You can't go less adventurous than that."

"Three of those then." He looks relieved.

"They are large. Like, really big." I hold my hands a foot apart.

His eyes twinkle. "Not a problem."

My cheeks heat. It's burritos we are talking about. Still, I can't hold his gaze. The girls are waiting for their food, but thankfully their phones get their full attention.

"Dos tacos de cabeza y tres burritos de carne asada, por favor." I show off the Spanish Claudia taught me.

"Algo para beber?" The all-business girl at the front is testing the limits of my knowledge.

"Shawn?" He comes up and ducks under the awning to join me. "D'you want anything to drink? An horchata or a lemonade?"

He looks at the glass bottles with colorful liquids and the whirling cold drinks behind the girl in the truck.

Shawn's face scrunches. The last time I saw a grimace like that was on Ryan's face when the freezer failed and he had to dispose of the rotting shrimp. "Nah. Better not."

I chuckle. Looks like the burritos are as far as he is willing to go today. Not going to push my luck.

"No, gracias," I say to the cashier.

"That'll be $27.50." She switches to English. "Your order number is one-six-five. Shouldn't take long."

I open my messenger bag to find my wallet when a long arm stretches around me, placing bills on the counter. A hint of leather and citrus follows.

"No, I got this."

"We should split, at least." I stare at the toned muscles that strain against his black jacket. My mouth goes dry.

"No way. We're using your gas. This is on me."

He has manners. I'll forgive his lack of adventurous side. Can't remember the last time a guy bought me dinner. My stomach rumbles. I'm starving.

The wind picks up while we wait for our number to be called and the blow-up Santa sambas to the beat of a new song blaring from the speakers. With Shawn as my plus one I might join the dancing at the party in my apartment. Good excuse to wrap my arms around him, especially after some liquid courage.

"Hey." I elbow him gently. "I have some beer in my trunk. Perks of the job."

"Yeah? I could do with a beer." He stuffs his hands in his pockets and his gaze falls to the ground. It's the first time he's not looked me straight in the eye.

"Me too."

I get a shy smile, but he's still face down.

Those chicks giggle and glance our way. No, gawk Shawn's way. I cock my eyebrow at them and step closer to him. Another couple approaches the cashier, and Shawn moves out of their way, bumping into me.

"Sorry," we both say at the same time. I don't move, enjoying the warmth of his body seeping through the thin fabric of my shirt. I'm getting warmer, and not just because he's protecting me from the cold, but because my cheeks are heating up. So are other, less visible parts of me.

"Number one-six-five. Your order is ready. Number one-six-five."

"It's us." The protective wall of Shawn is gone, and I already miss it.

I've barely buckled up before he opens the bag of food perched on his knees. "Hey, not so fast. I promised dinner and a view."

"But this smells so good." I love his goofy pout.

The engine roars to life. "Patience, Mr. Old Fashioned, patience."

"Fine." His exaggerated sigh brings a grin back to my lips. "It better be worth it."

I shift Betty into a lower gear as we make our way up the canyon hill to the observatory. Shawn asks to drop the roof, and he's hanging out over the side of the car filming our ascent on his phone. He looks more comfortable now that he has headroom.

With the top down, my hair gets in my eyes. I tuck an errant strand behind my ear. It's impossible not to smile at the glee on Shawn's face as we speed along. The whirling in my chest returns, but it's lighter and invigorating. I feel better than I have in months, enjoying showing off the city I now call home.

The observatory is lit up green and red, but the place is deserted. I swing into a coveted front row parking spot, and the LA skyline sits before us like Van Gogh's Starry Night come to life. Twinkling lights map out the gridlines of the streets of my town.

"I'll get the beer." I pop the trunk and jump out. "Ale or Lager?"

"You choose." Shawn tosses over his shoulder. More flutters bloom under my ribs. See, not pretentious. I had a half-hour lecture on the benefits of pale ale from the last guy I hooked up with. I catch myself. Not a hook-up here, Sarah, remember?

Shawn takes the Yellow Diamond Belgian Pale Ale, and our fingers brush. Little shivers run down my spine. It's chilly up here with the top down. And my mouth is dry because I'm thirsty. Nothing to do with this guy in my car. None whatsoever.

Shawn is halfway through his first burrito. This guy can eat. I mean, I have a pretty healthy appetite, but he makes me look like a lightweight.

The radio plays the latest song by my fellow Canuck, Bieber.

"Have you"—Shawn swallows the bite of burrito interfering with his words—"have you seen it? The video? Worth watching cause of Colin Tilley. He directed it."

I have no idea who that is, but my own mouth is too full of delicious braised beef cheek to comment, so I nod in agreement.

I try not to groan at how good these tacos are as he opens his second burrito. Why don't I eat here more often? Right, no money to eat out. Outside of work, ramen noodles are the only food groups in my diet.

If it weren't for my job, I don't know how I'd get by. Free food, occasional free booze, and access to the pool are just some of the perks that keep me working at the resort. Then there are the VIPs who think big tips give them the right to squeeze my ass, the lack of benefits, and the irregular hours. And it's only been getting worse lately. I exhale the grievances. No need to spoil this moment.

My last bite is even better than the first. Good food, spectacular views—Griffith Park never disappoints—and great company.

Shawn takes a swig of his beer and wipes his lips with the back of his hand, then catches himself and grins at me in apology. I hand him a napkin.

"Thanks, sorry for the mess." He squeezes the bottle between his knees. I try not to stare at his long legs crammed against the glove compartment and focus on him snatching the last burrito from the bag on the dashboard.

"I see the burritos are a disappointment."

"They're effing fantastic." He elongates fantastic like the longer he makes it, the tastier the food.

I like how real this feels. He's not trying to impress me. No, "Oh I know so and so—he'd totally read your script." Or "You'd be perfect for this job opening down at the studio." Maybe this is what I needed all along: to date someone from out of state.

Not that this is a date—way ahead of yourself, Sarah. He leaves in a few hours anyhow. Didn't he say he'd be back this summer? "Why move to LA?"

"School. I wanna be a director."

"Huh? Director of what?"

He drops his burrito into the wrapper. "Movies, theater, television."

"Ah, got it. Lofty goals."

"I'd do shorts too. Gotta start somewhere. Already shot a commercial for the camera shop where I work. It even ran on our local station. And I shot several videos for a local acapella group." Shawn stops eating while he talks, his food forgotten. "The one I loved the most was doing a documentary on how different kids get to school. It was for a school project, but I made it into a short instead of writing it. Months of filming, weeks of editing, and a fifteen-minute film was the result. Loved every minute of it. Doing that every day would be living the dream." Each word grows into a path he sees ahead.

I like his passion. His eyes shine like the bright lights of LA below us. I was that hopeful once.

"What dream brought you to LA? I mean, assuming it wasn't to tend bar." He takes a bite of the burrito.

"I wanted to write the movies you're going to direct." Wow. I never admit that.

"It's a plan." His puppy-dog eyes catch mine, and my insides go liquid. "Are you working on anything now?"

And I feel the weight of failure descend. "I'm writing a screenplay."

There. I've admitted it. Months of writing in coffee shops and on my breaks at work. Or I was, until all my inspiration dried up.

Shawn watches me with interest. "Awesome. What's it about?"

I've come this far. Might as well tell him. I straighten. Unlikely I'm ever going to see him again. This is why people tell strangers things.

"It's a modern-day *Magnificent Seven* meets *Footloose*."

"Yul Brynner or the remake with Denzel Washington?"

This guy does know his movies. "Yul, of course."

"Of course." There's that grin again. So cute. "What's the setup?"

"It's set in small-town America. Wesley—that's my hero's name—he's new to town and discovers the locals are being bullied by the mayor. Businesses must pay protection money; nothing happens unless the mayor approves it . . . that kind of thing."

"I like it." He licks a finger, and I try not to drool. "Is there action?"

Right, guys always want action. "Well, I saw it as more of a drama. Using the law to oust the mayor. But I haven't quite figured out that part yet."

"That might work for the overarching theme." He fidgets in his seat and turns toward me. "But what if you add a ticking time bomb?"

"What'd ya mean?"

"Say, you build to a scene where the mayor's goons are coming by one night to collect the monthly protection money from" —he looks around—"the taqueria in town. And the owner wants to make a stand."

My mind races. "Okay." I like where this is going.

"Okay? That gives you some good 'preparing to defend the restaurant' sequences. But it's the night of the big showdown. Goons show up, Yul, I mean—what's his name again?"

"Wesley."

"Right, Wesley and his crew, along with some of the locals, are all hanging out in the restaurant, acting like it's a normal night, regular patrons." I put my elbow on the armrest and soak up his words. "Owner says no, goons threaten, white hats rise, and pandemonium ensues."

"By concentrating the action in that one small space, I create tension, Quentin Tarantino-style."

"Exactly." Shawn's practically vibrating, and I'm feeding off his energy. "You can do a one-roll scene where it starts from one punch"—he hits the air in front of him, and it looks real, like he's done some punching before—"and the blood flies in slo-mo, and the camera follows it. The spatter lands on another guy, and he joins in, hits someone with his elbow in the process." He keeps illustrating the moves, although the kick looks like a knee into Betty's dashboard. "Can be a chain reaction where all the good guys and the goons are interconnected. And you can speed up and slow down as the camera moves around the room."

Doesn't he need to breathe? Not that I'm going to interrupt him. This is gold. The movie plays out in my head. I'm more of a feelings and tension person. Adding a fight scene can be the spice I've been missing to kick the story back into gear.

"Could be the pre-fight shot has everything in order." He's using the napkins, food containers, and balled-up foil to construct a scene around the gear shift. "But the final shot is the good guys covered in blood. And food. With the bad guys left lying all over the place, the restaurant in disarray." Then he pauses and looks at me. "What's the *Footloose* connection?"

"Oh, you know, the daughter of the mayor meets Wesley, instant attraction. Holly, that's a working name, joins their side." Maybe Holly could meet Wesley in the restaurant, a meet-cute over a drink. I narrow my eyes and picture the cozy booths and the colorful interior. Yeah, that could work. "So, I tell the story from inside one location. That's my unique perspective."

"Yep. The restaurant as a character or your omniscient narrator? Lots of close, tight shots highlighting the action." He makes a square with his thumbs and forefinger and pretends I'm the subject his fake camera is focusing on. What would it be like to be the center of his attention? Every caress of his eyes sends heat rippling through me.

I take a sip of my beer to try and cool down. It's all I can do to not reach across and kiss him.

FIVE

NICK

HER MOUTH AROUND THE rim of the bottle should not conjure every indecent scenario of what else that mouth could be doing—starting with kissing. Kissing that smart, smart mouth of hers. I press my lips together, trapping a different kind of thirst she unlocks. A chick who likes the right *Magnificent Seven* and gets Tarantino. If she likes hockey, I might be in love.

What? Where did that come from? I shake my head to get rid of that thought.

Sarah frowns. "Something wrong?"

"No, no, I was just thinking." My cheeks ignite, despite the cold. "I didn't expect this. When I went to the bar, I don't know . . . I thought tonight would suck, but it doesn't. It's great." C'mon. Stop talking.

"I agree. I'm having fun, too." Sarah grins. With those lips.

My wishful thinking spreads warm tendrils down my neck. "D'you mind if we get out and check the view?" The truth, remember? "My legs are getting a bit numb here."

"Crap, sorry, I forget not everyone is Thumbelina size." The apologetic smile she gives me forms tiny wrinkles around her mesmerizing blue eyes.

Not just blue—I lean in—there are specks of gold and a dark rim around the pale irises. The air between us prickles with something invisible but nonetheless tangible. My gaze skims the curve of her cheekbone and the smooth plane of her forehead. Her skin glows even in the dim light of the car.

Is it soft?

Is it warm?

I have to know.

My finger is like a moth drawn to her flame. A lock of her hair grazes her temple, and my resistance caves. I brush the silky strand behind her ear. The tentative contact both jolts and sooths. More. I need more.

I cradle her cheek in my palm, and my thumb grazes the upturned slope of her nose, the shadows under her eyes, the soft hair of her eyebrows. She feels hot against my icy hand, matching the heat rising in me, desperate to escape and spread around her, draw her in.

Touching her, tracing her features is more amazing than hours of kissing Mackenzie, yet not enough. I want to taste and savour, run my mouth along the gentle curve of her chin, permanently etch my hand against her neck, explore every freckle and line. What I desire is right there.

My gaze drops from her eyes to her lips. Parted. A trace of her smile lingers, only to morph into a long sigh. Sparks spread like wildfire from my hand to my heart. My pulse skyrockets. I gulp. Did I do this to her?

Drums blare in the tiny gap between us. Dad's ringtone. Fuck. It's like he knows I'm experiencing a moment of bliss and needs to take any joy from my life. My stomach sinks. He's better than a cold shower. I pry myself away from Sarah and fumble to find the earpieces dangling on my chest. The music stops as I grab one of them and plug it in. "Yeah."

"What about not leaving the resort area do you not understand?" Dad never shouts. But this is the first time since he remembered he has a son that he sounds like a parent and not a pretend friend. He doesn't give me a chance to answer. "I leave you alone for one minute to close an important deal, and you pull this. I assume you're not in the bathroom."

"No, I left."

"You left. The resort? How?" Dad's tone sounds like my coach between periods when we're down three-zip. In the background, Mom's voice is feeding him lines that he ignores, asking if I'm okay. "Where exactly are you now?"

I clench the hand he made me tear from Sarah. "Griffith Observatory."

"This is how you spend my cash? You were supposed to grab a soda and wait for me. I shouldn't have given you the money." I imagine him saying it through his teeth. "Nicky," he booms.

My breath catches. I look up at Sarah when Dad says my name. She examines her nails and pretends she's not listening to my side of the conversation.

"You are supposed to be a grown-up. How can I trust you if you do shit like this? You could've at least texted me before you left the resort."

"What d'you need?" Not going to tell him he's right and I could've texted.

"For you to be where you were supposed to be. Now we'll be late. We're on our way to pick you up."

"I'm in the parking lot. The place is closed. Won't have to look hard."

"How the hell did you even get there?" Dad sighs. "Never mind, park your ass there and don't move. I mean it. We'll be there in twenty." The line drops.

"Message received," I say to the dead air.

I jerk the earbud out and stare straight ahead. Fuck. I'm my own worst enemy. If I want Dad to let me live with him next year, I better get my fake Nicky vibes back on. Money to rent an apartment in LA isn't in my budget. I shove my phone into my pocket, and pain shoots through my hip. I wince and move to ease the cramp in my leg.

"Still wanna get out of the car?" asks Sarah.

"We better. That was Dad. He's coming here to pick me up."

My body complains about sitting curled in the small space for too long as I unfurl. Out on the asphalt of the parking lot, I raise my arms, bend my elbows, grasp my hands behind my head and stretch to my full six-feet-four-inches. This year I got one inch over my brother, although he outweighs me by at least fifty pounds of MMA- and gym-crafted muscle.

The gym is something he's been dragging me to ever since I quit hockey last year. The sport was too expensive and traveling around the country with the team too much of a strain on Mom timewise, never mind financially. She had to either reschedule her weekend clients or lose some of her business. The whole thing was pointless; I'm not good enough for a hockey scholarship, despite her hopes.

Quitting made sense, giving me the time I needed to get more hours at the camera shop to save up for what I really want to do. In the last year, I've managed to get my hands on some decent used video equipment. People coming into the camera shop trade in their old stuff for new, and one of the perks of working there is I get first crack at them. Before moving out here, I've got to upgrade to a professional camcorder. Last week, a used Canon XA11 came in, but I don't have enough cash yet. I hope no one snaps it up before I can afford it.

I didn't think about the other expenses of living in LA. A car wasn't on my list of pre-move needs, but I'm adding it, along with picking up an extra shift or two a week. My chest tightens. Maybe I can put up some flyers to get some work as a videographer. I kick a stone and send it flying over the edge.

The city below stretches out before me, full of possibilities. I envy it. Don't get views like this in Chicago. I lift my chin and absorb the sky meeting the horizon. The newness of the freedom this place offers drowns my worries and hesitation.

The breeze rustles the leaves. Even though it's evening, it's still in the mid-sixties, and not wearing a heavy parka half the year is something I'm looking forward to next winter. I'll be leaving my cold-weather gear behind in Chicago for when I visit. Not going to miss hats, scarves, boots, and gloves.

I crack my neck, tuck the dangling earpieces under my shirt, and shift my attention to enjoy a better view. Sarah perches her butt on the hood of her car, the wind tossing her hair across her back, the lights of Los Angeles twinkling below. I swallow.

She half turns and mesmerizes me with her stare. I drink her in.

Sarah flicks a blond strand of hair off her face, and my finger tingles at the memory of doing that. I suppress a groan. Dad might've ruined the moment, but my want for her hasn't gone anywhere. I bite the inside of my cheek. Starting something with the quarter of an hour I have left in her company is pointless. Might as well take in the city that's going to become my home.

"Gonna join me?" she asks. Even from here I can see she's shivering. With her sweater in the car, that thin shirt can't protect her from the gusts of wind that blows around at this height. I shake off my jacket and move toward her. She needs it more.

Six

Sarah

Hot damn.

Shawn stretches after getting out of the car. Is that a little trail on the squares of his abs under his shirt? My breath grows shallow. I can't tear myself away from the view. Nor do I want to. Those long, toned arms could pick me up, support me, no problem. Bet the view is better from his six-foot something vantage point. Images of what I could do to him reel through my mind.

My body accepts the challenge and goes on high alert. My stomach tenses with anticipation. My skin grows tight with want. I might be drooling.

Can I jump his bones in this parking lot?

No, Sarah, don't go there. I clench my fist. His Dad is on his way to pick him up. He's going to spend time with his family. Christmas, remember? Families spend time together. At least, they're supposed to.

Every time I called Mom these last few weeks she asked me to come home for Christmas. I can't afford the flight, and it'd take too long to drive there and back. My shoulders slump. I know if I go, I may never return to LA. The crack that formed in my chest when I arrived here aches. Mémère is right: if I have a dream, I have to give it everything I have. That means sticking around, at least for a few more months. I have one more chance, one last avenue to get my start in the business. I sit straighter. If that doesn't pan out, it's back to Toronto and my family.

I turn away from Shawn and face the Hollywood sign.

At least Toronto isn't far from Chicago. Shit. What am I doing? Must. Slow. Down. This is simply a lovely evening. Two lonely souls keeping each other company. I shouldn't ruin this like I do everything else. It would be nice to have at least one pleasant memory of LA. I won't spoil it by giving Shawn my number. That way, he won't disappoint me when he doesn't call.

Men are men wherever you go, assholes don't have a zip code, and I ran into my fair share back home. Tending bar at nineteen teaches you pretty quick how to handle drunks, fools, and know-it-alls. As long as I kept my heart out of the situation, I was fine. I know how to have fun and when to draw the line. My heart rebels with a pang.

Yet all that didn't prepare me for the different breed of men in LA. It's like every guy I meet went to the "screw 'em and use 'em" school of dating.

Learned my lesson. I stay in control and shut things down before they escalate.

I glance at Shawn. I could ask him for his number. Maybe text him, or we could video chat when he's in Chicago. And he'll have a friend in LA?

Who am I kidding? I'm not imagining us being friends. I'm already writing a play-by-play of how we'll make out, how we can . . . the guy hasn't even kissed me. The memory of the heat of his hand confirms the reality of his intentions. He was going to kiss me before his dad called. I could feel it. I still feel it. The longing I have under control stirs. The pressure beneath my ribs builds. We could be making out in my back seat right now, if only we had more time.

The cool breeze brings some relief to my burning body, but my hair is in disarray. So much for taking care to brush it out and arrange my outfit to show off my assets, making him wait extra long for me.

I pick at the fringe of my shorts. Why isn't he up here with me already? I still my fluttering heart, turn to the passenger door, and move the mess of my hair out of my face.

"Gonna join me?" Another gust of wind or the anticipation of his answer makes me shiver.

Shawn takes off his jacket, ambles over, and plops himself beside me on the car, making poor Betty shake.

"Here." He drapes his jacket across my shoulders, and his crisp scent hits me. A cologne? No, that's my bar clients. Something citrusy but woody at the same time. Subtle. A shampoo?

Whatever it is, the scent is not like the overpowering per-fumes that hide the decay of LA. I inhale, and my body betrays me. I lean his way. A tiny bit. Closer. Another inch. Close but not close enough. Still no contact. Maybe I'm wrong.

His arm brushes against mine. Maybe I'm not wrong.

Goosebumps erupt where my skin touches his. The light move I could've discounted as accidental changes into him pressing our arms together. For warmth? Or he might be trying to get his long frame comfortable on the hood. Fever tiptoes across my collarbone and infects my other side. I tremble. This is not real. I'm reading too much into it. If only my imagination would be this active when I sit in front of a blank page of my screenplay. I sigh.

"It's nice up here," Shawn says.

"It is nice." Is he feeling it, too? Although it's better than nice. The fever is all-consuming now. It's hot. I'm hot.

"The view's better than in the movies."

The view? I don't give a damn about the view right now. I want the movie part, the romance scene in Act Two, Wesley and Holly giving in to their attraction to each other. I want those hands to touch me again. I want to taste those lips that have been teasing me all night.

Need to get my mind out of the gutter. I cross my legs and stare at the stupid view. I brought him here to see the sights, not shoot a love scene. I inhale the cold night air, hoping it can suppress the feverish urges that have no place here. Focus on the leaves, the trees, the shimmer of festive LA. Look around you, Sarah. This would be a perfect location to shoot a love scene.

"Yeah, I used to come up here all the time." My arm is melting where we're touching, but I don't want to move. I squeeze my thighs together. Lie. I want to move—closer.

I shift so that my pinky grazes his. My hand looks so small compared to Shawn's. His shoulder looks so inviting. I could tuck myself in there just fine, lay my head on his chest, his chin resting on my hair. Like sheltering underneath a strong oak tree, him protecting me from the storm, from the big bad world with its lies and betrayals.

He accepts the invitation, sliding his long fingers in between mine. Adrenaline rushes through my blood. His hand is cool and dry; his touch is light, as if he's afraid I might break. My heart is racing. Can he tell?

For a moment, a blissful moment, we do nothing but hold hands. I . . . I can't explain it, but it's like I'm under a spell. How can that be? He massages the top of my hand in a slow circle, just grazing the skin. Is there a defibrillator nearby? I might faint.

"What am I looking at?" Shawn breaks the silence, but his voice is soft, like a gentle rain on a summer's day. Maybe he sings?

"Oh, well, the black part without the lights is the ocean." Lame, Sarah. "Over there is the Santa Monica Pier, see the Ferris wheel? And of course, the Hollywood sign." I point toward the center of the city. "That's the Staples Center. Sorry, now it's Crypto.com Arena, where the Kings play. That's LA's—"

"Hockey team." He looks at me sideways. "D . . . Do you like hockey?"

I giggle. Like I giggled when my crush Jimmy in 8th grade asked me if I liked reading, because he liked reading too. "Um . . . Torontonian here. Hockey's part of who I am. Even played for a few years."

Shawn is beaming like he just won the lottery. "So cool."

"You?"

"Me?" He points to himself, making a show out of it. Goofball.

I lean in and nudge him with my shoulder. "Yes, how about you?"

He does that thing again, putting his finger against his scrumptious looking chin. Only men who shave every day typically do it for me, but Shawn is nothing like them.

"Blackhawks beat the Leafs any day." He chortles.

He knows my team. My lungs refuse to expand. Breathe, Sarah.

"I play a bit." Shawn gives me a sideways look, as if trying to make a decision. "No, played. Gave it up last year. A puck hit me in the face once. That's how I got this."

He twists to show me a small scar on his left cheek, hiding in his stubble. My fingers act of their own accord; I reach up to inspect. He leans down to my level to give me a better view, and I swallow. I'm back to being a teenager. The temptation to touch him pushes other thoughts out. His lips are right there again, right in front of me, asking, no, begging me to kiss them.

Spurts of his hot breath tap on my cheek, and my hesitation fades. I erase the remaining distance between us and brush my lips against his.

There's no indecision from Shawn. He's right here in this moment with me. A skim of his hand at my waist and I explode—nothing holding me back from tangling my fingers in his soft, silky hair. I find the base of his neck and tug him to me, taking more.

Sturdy arms are pulling me closer, caging me. He holds onto me like a precious thing. Must handle with care. I happily mold myself against him, letting his strong, solid body warm me. I tilt my head back giving him more access to my mouth.

I can't stop the moan from escaping. He feels better than any dream I've ever had.

I never want this to end.

SEVEN

NICK

THE SCAR IS SUCH a great excuse to get her closer. I hated the violence of hockey, and that was the clear sign I'm not a good fit. That puck hitting me was barely an injury. I had much worse, but lifting my shirt and showing her the scar on my back might not be a good move. She can discover it later. My stomach tenses. What later?

I wish there was a later.

If that were an option, I'd make my move right now, instead of feeling like a teenager. I stop tapping my toe. I am a teenager, but it's like I'm fourteen again, never kissed a girl and afraid I'm going to regret making the first move. I huff. That phase didn't last. Who makes the first move, or the second, doesn't matter. It's what happens after—if you want to spend time with each other, if you have something to talk about, if you can be your real self and not a pretend version the other wants to see—that matters.

I've never been good with girls. There's this tension—not the physical tension, that part is easy—but the what ifs, the secrets, the pretense. The memories taste bitter on my tongue. After a date, I long to be alone in my room where I can be me, where I don't have to think through every word and action to make sure I play it right.

Tonight, I feel none of that. I'm not the hockey hunk whose conversation is centered around the trendy stuff or who'd rather say nothing than make a fool out of himself. Tonight, with Sarah, I'm the over-sharing movie nerd, who's afraid of spicy foods, has no car, and can't stop pulling his phone out to shoot the sights. My breaths are easy. I'm light and bursting. Like I'm in one of my dreams, and can float, fly over downtown LA with Sarah by my side.

She gets me. I get her. And I don't want to ruin it by taking it further. Damn. I'm lying to myself. I very much want to take it further, so much further. I fidget. Not getting closer but unable to move away. How unfair it is that the only time this happens to me is with someone who doesn't even know my name.

The words are forming in my mouth. My tongue ready. *There's something I need to tell you. The ID I gave you was a fake. I'm actually Nick. I'm nineteen. I'd like to have your number.*

Her lips brush mine, and the words dissolve.

Heaven.

The world falls away.

I let go, because we fit. Freaking fireworks.

It's the barest of kisses, but every cell in me comes alive. My heart stutters. When it restarts, the beat grows into a pounding, a roar, a torrent of rapid pulses that are about to burst out of my chest. With every palpitation I get closer to Sarah, I sense and smell her more. I absorb everything she gives me, and the tenderness is more arousing than any hot-and-heavy make out sessions I've had with Mackenzie. How is it even possible?

Her fingers are doing something to my scalp. Another wave of fierce heartbeats crashes through me. They are driving me crazy. Nope, Sarah's fist tangled in my shirt pulling me down to her is what's driving me crazy.

I've got to touch her too, but I don't want to spoil this. If I just reach out and . . . damn, her skin is soft. My thumb tingles at the feel of her. I love this top, so easy to slide my hand around her waist, up her back, tug her closer.

Sarah lets me.

I cradle her in my arms and don't push, don't ram my mouth into hers like some cheesy movie scene. No, I take my time. I kiss her how I want to kiss her.

Slow. Trying. Tasting. Taking.

What I want is to protect her from the chilly wind whipping her hair about. Does she read my mind? She tucks into me, where she belongs, giving me better access to her, opening for me. Her mouth is on mine, and it sends my heart back into overdrive.

A moan. Her moan. It doesn't touch the cool air outside our lips but sounds inside me. It's her voice, but it's my moan, too.

It enters my soul, and for the first time in my life, I understand what all the romantic bullshit is about. Because it's happening to me.

The physical attraction was there the moment I saw her, and I love that part, too, but this. This connection, the link to another person I never knew existed. The ache. The realization I was the walking dead before this.

What would I do to make this last? Anything. I swear, anything. My soul is hers.

A car horn blasts beside us, and I jump away from her. It's Mom and Dad—perfect timing, as usual.

I know I should leave, but the pull between us is too strong for me not to go back to her. My heart zooms in on Sarah. She's the perfect sunset I'd stare at every day. I bracket her face with my hands, drinking in the sight of her. I give in to my craving and kiss her again.

Dad's yelling something.

"I think your dad's upset," she whispers against my lips.

I want to say I don't care. "I gotta go," I whimper instead.

She pulls away, and the separation from her skin hurts. This is wrong. She gives my chest a gentle nudge, and I step backward, milking every moment to keep her in my sight.

Another horn blast.

One last look at her beautiful face, hair floating around her like a halo. Click. I capture the reel forever in my mind. Her mouth opens as if to say something, then closes. She raises her tiny hand and waves at me. Click. Click. Click. I turn away and sprint to the car.

Mom and Dad halt their arguing when I slam the passenger door and slump into the backseat. Dad's face is illuminated by the dashboard, making him look like a villain in a cheesy horror flick.

"What was that?" He switches his attention to me. "You left the resort for some random chick?"

I see red and slam my elbow into the car door. "Don't call her that. The place was a dead zone. I haven't seen anything in LA from my list."

"For fuck's sake, Nicky. Don't break my car." Mom puts a hand on Dad's arm and he takes a breath. "I told you, you could sightsee later." His voice goes down a notch. "This was a waste of time. What were you thinking, dragging me to this goddamn mountain?"

His true colors are showing. The swearing he's bottled up all week makes an appearance. I open my mouth to reply with the expected Nicky response, but nothing comes out. I clench my teeth and massage my elbow. Nick doesn't have to say anything. Nick has a right to have a good time however he wants. "She was showing me the sights."

"Showing you something, all right." Dad glances in the rear-view mirror. "And where's your jacket? I just bought you that."

Fuckety-fuck, as my brother would say. I smile, kinda liking the idea that she has something of mine. Gives me the perfect excuse to see her again.

"You spoiled youth don't understand the meaning of hard work."

Good one, Dad. I want to tell him about Mom pulling off eighty-hour weeks. How dare he choose to forget the years he spent in prison, sitting on his ass reading ten hours a day? Even I've been working since I was fourteen. Calling me out on not working hard is rich coming from him.

But I don't say that. I still need him for my LA plans. The plans that now include not only moving to LA, going to college here, and getting a car, but also finding my way back to Sarah.

"I work for this money," Dad keeps spouting. "It's not like it grows on trees."

This crap again. I pop in my earbuds. The Carpenters sing about home being the best place for the holidays. I close my eyes. LA's going to be my home.

Goodbye, Chicago. Goodbye, fake Nicky.

The woman sings about the sunshine and friendly faces.

I see Sarah . . . shit, I don't know her last name. Doesn't matter. I know where she works, know her favorite food truck. I'll find her. Sarah's going to be my girl. Not Shawn or Nicky's girl. No. Nick Stavros's girl.

Karen Carpenter gets it. You can't beat home sweet home. And I've found my home. Sarah is her name.

PART 2

VALENTINE'S DAY

EIGHT

Sarah

A SCREAM IS TRYING to claw its way out of my throat. I hate flying under normal circumstances, but this? My right hand squeezes the zipper of Shawn's jacket, my left grips the armrest between me and the woman who looks as pale as the snow I left behind in Toronto. I shut my eyes.

I want to live. I want to live. I want to live.

Mom's heart won't survive if I die a week after my grandmother. With three generations of Côté women dead in one week—who'd run the bakery then? My brothers? They'd burn the place down in the first month. Another jerk shakes the cabin. I open my eyes and stare into the tear-filled face of my fellow passenger. She puts her hand over mine, and we cling to one another.

"Due to technical difficulties, our plane is making an un-scheduled landing in Chicago's O'Hare Airport." A woman's voice crackles through the cabin. "Please remain seated and await further instructions." The message isn't instilling much faith.

The plane lurches, sending my right shoulder into the hard plastic between the plane's windows. A shower of yellow masks on strings falls around us like decorations at the world's worst surprise party. Can this really be happening? If it weren't for the fact that my heart is bursting out of my chest, I could fool myself into believing I'm in a movie. I catch the all-too-real plastic mask dangling in front of me, push it over my nose and mouth, and slip the elastic over my head. The bag does not inflate, but I can feel the oxygen flowing. I breathe a little easier.

Shawn's jacket hugs me. My security blanket, a constant since he placed it on my shoulders the night I learned what a book-worthy kiss is like. I jam one fist into the pocket his long fingers once warmed. It gives me the illusion our hands are together. Almost.

A sharp edge scratches my skin. I pat the inside of the jacket. A hidden compartment? My fingers dive into it and come out with a plastic card. It's a driver's license. His driver's license. The ID he showed me at the bar when we first met. The black print beside his picture reads Shawn Rosstav. I roll my eyes. That's his last name. The cabin gets brighter. I've been googling every variation I could think of, but the correct letters unscramble the pile of Scrabble tiles that have been rattling in my head. I had the Russian -tov instead of -tav and was missing the extra s.

I stare at the expressionless face—one I've been conjuring in my head since our Christmas Eve together. Warmth spreads from my hand straight to my heart; the pounding quiets to a manageable beat. I'm calmer. Either it's the effect of seeing him, or the oxygen is helping, because I don't think about death anymore. I wish I could move the hair out of his eyes, see the pools of chocolate brown that peered into my soul. If only he were smiling here, because I'm beginning to forget what his silly grin looked like. But I won't forget the kiss. It's there for me to read about any time I want.

The scene with my main characters, Wesley and Holly, kissing in the parking lot of the restaurant has every emotion of my first kiss with Shawn. The soft caress of his lips over mine, the shared breaths, the longing that spreads through my chest and stomach every time I think about it. The memories looped and pushed until they transformed into words, igniting the page with our shared passion. I hope my script is good enough to get me into the Starlight Foundation Future Filmmaker competition—the last chance I'm giving myself to make it as a screenwriter in LA. With the oxygen mask in the way, I can't give his surly face a kiss like I'd want to in real life, but even looking at him reminds me there's good in this world.

A different noise rumbles under the plane—the release of the wheels. I glance at the pitch-black sky outside, searching for the lights of the city, and brace for the landing.

"And here's your food and your hotel voucher. You'll need to proceed to the baggage claim and then follow the directions to the shuttle area. It'll take you to your hotel. We rebooked you on the 11:40 a.m. flight to LA tomorrow. Check-in closes forty-five minutes before departure." The woman in the navy Air Canada uniform repeats the same spiel I heard her deliver to the two passengers in line before me. I don't want any food and, with the adrenaline coursing through my veins from the emergency landing, I'm not sure I can sleep either. I wish I could just rent a car and drive.

At least I don't have to pay for any of this.

I follow the signs to the baggage claim, texting Siobhan as I go.

Me: Not going to be home tonight. Stuck in Chicago.

Of course, my carousel is on the other end of the cavernous room. I brush past gangs of passengers standing in small groups, bored or tired expressions clouding their faces. I'm not the only one who isn't excited to be in Chicago tonight.

A pair of red Converse shoes attached to long lean legs stretching from an airport seat paints a cool contrast in the sea of puffy black coats and solid gray boots. I need to write this down for a potential opening scene. It'd be a good way to draw attention to whoever is wearing them—say, the main character. I strain to complete the image but can't see the man's face. Oh well, that's what my imagination is for.

This is what I do. I create imagery, characters, scenes, tell stories. Always have. If only I could make a living off it. The dream. My dream. The one Mémère was sure would become my reality. The knife her death thrust into my heart burrows deeper every time I think of her and widens the hole I'll live with for the rest of my life.

I miss her so much already.

I open the Note App and type the scene with my thumbs. A text notification pops up.

Siobhan: Chicago?

Me: Emergency landing. All's well. But not getting out until tomorrow

Siobhan: Sucks.

Me: I know, right?

Siobhan: Want me to let work know? Don't mind covering your hours.

My pulse speeds up. The thought of missing my shift at the resort tomorrow threatens to restart the panic attack I narrowly avoided during the landing. Mrs. Marino is a decent boss, and her assurance I could take the time I needed to attend the funeral was genuine. When I told her about my grandmother's unexpected death, she sent me home in the middle of the shift and paid me for the whole eight hours.

Ryan agreed to pull a double and skip the afternoon of surfing he had planned. That told me a lot more about how much he cared than the awkward side hug with a single pat in the middle of my back. That was a week ago, and I can't afford to lose any more hours. This flight drained my account and without my next paycheck, no way I'm making my portion of this month's rent.

After the funeral, I spent a few extra days in Toronto to adjust to my new reality. No more Mémère. I still can't grasp the concept. I want to call her and tell her about the problem with my plane and how I prepared for the worst. She'd laugh at my fear of flying and say the reward was worth the risk.

Me: Could you? Thanks.

Siobhan: Are you kidding? One of the biggest tip days of the year? I'll have those love-starved fools eating out of the palm of my hand.

Shit. That's right. It's Valentine's Day tomorrow. The image of my little brother, Taylor, fake gagging when he watched Meg Ryan and Tom Hanks kiss on top of the Empire State building sums up my feelings about the date. I swerve around a young couple and their toddler as they struggle to get the little boy to move.

Me: Enjoy $$$$$.

Me: Maybe the new guy can help.

Siobhan: Two days on the job and I already hate him. All teeth, no brains.

"Attention passengers of American Airlines Flight 247 from Los Angeles. Your luggage will now be available on carousel ten." I cringe at the announcement ringing through the room. LA won't let me forget about itself even when I'm in Chicago.

Most of the people from my flight rim carousel number nine like ladyfingers on Mémère's sought-after strawberry and cream icebox cake. That's what I get for sitting by the toilet at the back of the plane. I was happy I could get a ticket at all. The dude beside me is blasting his music so loud even I can hear The Weeknd singing about not sleeping and find myself humming along. Reminds me of Shawn and those red earbuds of his.

I take off Shawn's jacket, fold it over my purse, and adjust Pop's lucky Maple Leafs hat. The royal blue details complement my eyes, like they matched his. A quick way to make my eyes pop when I don't feel like putting on makeup.

Is my luggage ever going to show up? Grief, lack of funds, and my near-death experience war in my skull. The back of my head throbs. I rub my hand over the knitted ridges of Pop's woolen hat. Its usual calming effect is not enough. The pain erupts and floods my veins. Crappy situation or not, Shawn's ID worked its magic on the plane: his longed-for eyes were the antidote to my overactive imagination. I pull the plastic card out and stare at his face again. Like a dam, it quells the distress. The corners of my lips twitch. Can't believe it had been there all along.

If only I'd found it earlier. I bet he's looked all over for it, maybe even called the lost and found at the resort. Instead, Ryan and I spent hours scouring the internet for Shawn Rostov. Should I try to return the ID, or has too much time passed? He's probably replaced it by now. It's been almost two months.

I couldn't live without a driver's license, but he said he didn't have a car. It's not just the driving though, it's the drinking. Not a single bar or club will let me in without carding me first. It's like they think being short makes me underage by default. Do people assume Shawn's old enough because of his height? Must be nice. Lifestyles of the tall and handsome.

The gray rubber belt in front of me squeaks to life. After several rounds, I spot my strawberry-patterned suitcase—Mémère's parting gift when I headed to LA last year. She scoured half the stores in the Greater Toronto Area to find it. "It has to be perfect for my granbaby," she told me. I hurry over to grab it and crash into a cute couple who are walking wrapped up in each other.

"Watch where you're going." The big burly guy in ripped jeans hugs the girl to his chest; her pink tips contrast against his black leather jacket, better suited for the LA weather than the middle of winter in Chicago. I place my hand on Shawn's eerily similar one hanging over my purse.

With a smile for an apology, I drag my suitcase off the rotating belt before it tries to make another round. I check the tag to make sure it's mine. Yup, Sarah Connor.

"You okay, baby?" The guy presses his mouth against a pink strand on the top of her head and murmurs something in her ear before she lifts her chin to plant a long thorough kiss on his lips. I turn away and roll my eyes when they can't see me before giving them a wide berth. Get a room. The exit is far away from their full-on make out session, and I aim for it.

The thought of the kiss Shawn and I shared sends an electrified current through me. My lips tingle. I want another kiss. At least.

NINE

NICK

CAROUSEL TWO HAS A couple of familiar faces from my flight but no bags yet. The fake leather seat squeaks under my weight, and it feels good to stretch my red Converse out in front of me, even if I take up three feet of the walkway. I crave space after being crammed into an airplane seat for four hours.

Why can't Chicago be closer to LA? I plug in my red head-phones and repeat the album I've been obsessing over. The longing. The sadness. The rage. It's distressing and poetic. It's like they took the lyrics from the spongy matter of my heart.

The top menu of my screen is full of message icons. Back to the real world. I can't pretend I'm too busy to reply to people, though it isn't going to be my life for much longer. Four months and I'm free. Freedom is what I feel in the final scream of the single. I'd normally join in, but I'm in the airport.

Mom: Call me when you land. Don't stop for any food on the way; I made your favorite.

Mike: Gonna be late. Pick you up at the arrivals. What gate?

Big bro's doing his shit. Taking care of me. I could've taken the bus home. I'm not a baby. Still not going to say no—it's cold as fuck out there. Hope he remembers to bring my parka.

I open "The H Crew" group chat to see twelve new messages from my ex-hockey team and friends.

Kaz: Sound Bar or Crocodile Rock tomorrow?

Leon: Rock first. Zaf's gonna meet us there.

Clark: Valentine's Day boyzzzzz. All those lonely ladies.

Kaz: Easy picking.

Clark: *broken heart emoji*

Leon: What about your girlfriend?

Clark: What Mackenzie doesn't know won't hurt her.

Clark: Last one there buys a round.

Kaz: Who's picking me up?

Leon: Nicky, you back?

Clark: Nicky's gonna finally pop his Shawn ID's cherry. *cherry emoji*

Kaz: *beer emoji*

Leon: *three beer emojis*

Damn. Since the season started in the fall, the coach forbade partying of any kind, so no one asked about Shawn Rosstav and the fake driver's license they gifted me. My old hockey team hasn't won a single game yet this season—a fact which isn't lost on me, since I'm the only variable that changed between last season and this one. But being the best player on the Chicago Young American's team is one thing, and getting a hockey scholarship for college is quite a different story.

Even with the crappy record and no chance at the playoffs, they still have games until April, so there's no way Coach Mc-Gregor's going to approve this escapade. Drinking with the crew wasn't the worst thing to do when I had to fit in and be part of the team, but it's not like I'd see them much after June. Keeping up the pretense is frustrating and a waste of time. Clark can be the team captain and the prom king. Mackenzie was the only reason I had to wear that stupid crown last year.

A man steps over my legs, and I shoot him some daggers. I pull my legs in and shift forward in the seat. When are these bags going to show up? My stomach rumbles. Dad forgot he promised to drive me to the airport, and I almost missed my flight and definitely missed dinner.

I glance back at the messages on my phone, deciding whether to put off the inevitable or not. Picking up girls on Valentine's Day? Sounds low, even for them. Not like I expected more of the guys, but I don't want to flirt with anyone, even if it's just for show. I have Sarah.

Okay, I don't have her. But I will. Sparks of determination boost my certainty. The wannabe toothpaste model I asked about Sarah when I visited her bar yesterday probably doesn't pay attention to anyone but himself, or he might be new. I should've waited to ask other employees, like that long-haired surfer lookalike who worked with Sarah on Christmas Eve.

If only I'd had more time. Some of the fireworks under my breastbone fizzle. One day wasn't enough. I couldn't afford to be late to my interview. I couldn't mess it up. That Starlight Foundation Future Filmmakers competition might get me noticed as a director, never mind that the winning movie's cash prize is a good chunk to supplement my financial aid.

I need all the aid I can get.

Why is money always in the way? Would've been easier if we were still rich. But when Dad went to prison for tax evasion, leaving LA for Chicago ten years ago to stay with Mom's sister meant we didn't have to pay rent. For years, Mom's junior hair stylist salary barely covered our food and bills. With Mike working at his new fancy engineering job, things have been better, but that's Mike's money. I can't expect him to pay for me.

Dad's grand gesture of letting me stay at his place for my interview this week turned into temporary use of the couch in his one-bedroom apartment. Better than nothing, but for all the showy restaurants he took Mom and me to over the Christmas break, trying to prove that he is back on track after getting out of prison, he didn't apologize for skipping out on child support for nine years or offer to contribute to my tuition. I'm nineteen; the state doesn't require he supports me anymore. Maybe Mike is right, and this is an awfully convenient time for Dad to reach out to me after years of ignoring my letters and emails.

People are fleeing the carousel area, some of them too close to me and not paying attention, rushing like there's something of importance going on. I take out my headphones.

"*. . . proceed to carousel ten.*"

The announcement ends.

"Hey." I wave down the couple who were sitting next to me on the plane. "What's going on?"

"They're moving us to carousel ten."

"Attention passengers of American Airlines Flight 247 from LA. Your luggage will be now available on carousel ten. Please proceed to carousel ten." The announcement loops.

O'Hare is a fucking mess. First they say two, then ten—that's on the other side of the room. I hang my backpack over both shoulders. Do they send you to a carousel to pick up your bag if you fly first class? I'm pretty sure if you have your own plane and a pilot to get you places, someone'll load and unload your stuff. I smile at the thought. A private jet is the best choice: all the leg room and any destination I want. Sarah and I jet-setting across the world. Hello, Mile High Club. We could visit her folks in Toronto or my mom in Chicago whenever we want.

I follow behind the couple who can't keep their hands off each other and almost crash into their backs when they stop.

"Watch where you're going," the big broad-shouldered guy my height roars at someone in front of them.

"You okay, baby?" His tone is sweet as he kisses the top of his girlfriend's pink-striped hair. I look over them for the source of the commotion and see the butt of a tiny blond woman trying to drag a giant suitcase plastered with—strawberries?—off the carousel.

I have half a thought to walk around the lip-locked Romeo and Juliet and help, but before I get a chance, she's off, dragging luggage half her size. She's wearing the unmistakable blue hat of a Maple Leafs fan. Sarah's favorite team. Speaking of Canada, I gotta check and see if Chicago beat Toronto tonight.

"Excuse me." Avoiding the peep show, I circle the handsy couple and almost step on the fingers of a young boy making snow angels on the dirty olive-green airport carpet squares.

"So sorry." A frazzled woman picks him up and blocks my way through, waiting for a guy in a retro tracksuit to unfold a contraption that might be a stroller.

"No problem." I shoot her my most charming Nicky smile.

She doesn't react. Instead, she pushes the child into the seat. "I told you we should have stayed the extra night in Toronto," she says to the guy. "Sleeping in the hotel with Tobey tonight is going to be a nightmare. I hope it's worth it for you."

"I didn't know the plane was going to have mechanical trouble." The presumed husband seizes two hard-sided bags from the slowly revolving carousel and clears the way. "I wanted to be in LA for Valentine's Day. Mom was going to watch him, so we could have time to ourselves."

Another vote for a private plane and being rich. Why all the hoopla over a made-up holiday anyway? If you're in love, shouldn't every day be about it, not an arbitrarily designated one each year?

Ten minutes later, carousel ten starts up, and my bag is one of the first to show. I snatch it and head for the exit.

Me: Ready. Meet you curbside, lower level, American Air-lines.

Mike: On my way.

My ears and nose are frozen by the time Mike pulls up. The side door of Mom's minivan slides open. I throw in my hockey duffle and hop into the front seat next to Mike.

"Glad to be home?" Mike pulls away and joins the slow line of cars heading from the terminal.

"Not like I have a choice."

"Don't start." Mike's jovial greeting turns to irritation. "We don't have to fight all the time. You only have to stay in my good graces for a bit longer. I'm still your transportation and your supervision."

Yep. I rotate my shoulders to dislodge the familiar blood-boiling irritation. Definitely getting myself a car in LA. No more relying on others to drive me. Mike doesn't hear it, but he sounds so much like Dad sometimes it's scary.

"I can ride in the back if you prefer to pretend I'm not here. That way, you're free of the burden of being responsible for me." I stare out the window at a white shuttle bus jammed with coat-clad people.

"Cut it out, Nicky."

"Nick." I talk to my reflection. "It's Nick."

"Since when? All your life Nicky was good enough."

"Since I'm nineteen, and an adult about to live on my own. How hard is it to start calling me by the name I actually like?"

"Should I address you as Sir Nicholas then?"

"Fuck it. No one in LA will call me Nicky."

"They sure won't if you don't get that scholarship. We can't afford it otherwise."

"I'm moving no matter what. Even if I have to crash on Dad's couch first. I'll find the money if the competition falls through." I adjust my earbuds instead of driving my elbow into the door. "I'd rather do it there than here. I can get real industry experience, shoot something that'll beef up my portfolio."

"How dumb are you? Thousands of wannabes like you flock there every month, and if you don't get in, it means you're not welcome."

Nothing about believing in myself. I dig my fingers into the door handle. The tension permanently lodges between my shoulder blades, like it's never left. No 'go after your dreams,' or 'take a risk.' No. Mike is about certainty. He has a plan for a plan and some insurance in case any of those go wrong.

I'm too young to forfeit my chance at what I've wanted to do all my life. Slogging at a job I tolerate nine-to-five, or what's more like eight-to-six, for the golden cage made out of bi-weekly deposits in my bank account? No, thank you. I'd rather be poor and happy than rich and miserable. Not planning on being poor though. Rich and happy has always been my vision.

"Nicky!" Mom grasps my face in her hands and kisses my nose.

"You're not going to have the 'don't call me Nicky' conversation with her?" Mike scoffs as he bumps my hockey duffle out of his way.

"What's wrong with Nicky?" Mom puts her arm on my back and ushers me toward the kitchen. "You'll always be Nicky to me. I'm fully prepared to show naked baby pictures at your wedding, call you Nicky when you are my age, and force-feed you your favorite foods every time you come to visit. I've earned the right after all these years."

"Mom." I'm not an ungrateful son. She raised us on her own, and I'll let her call me Nicky all she wants. But she is the only person who gets that privilege.

"Don't Mom me." She grins. "Wash your hands and meet me in the kitchen."

TEN

I PUSH MY WAY into the hotel room and a wall of cold air hits me. I keep Shawn's jacket on and fumble with the thermostat to crank the heat. Despite most of my flight being packed into the hotel shuttle, the half-hour ride was more bone-chilling than my week in Toronto.

The room fits my hotel airport expectations: bed, desk, TV, lamp, bathroom—all awash in the beigest beige imaginable. I walk to the window and check out the view from the sixth floor, which consists of pitch black peppered with orange streetlamps. An icy design covers the bottom of the window.

When I drove to California last winter, everything I owned packed into my convertible, I brought my down-filled coat, scarf, and gloves. They spent over a year in the back of my closet. Only Mémère's hat stayed close at hand. I had to drag it all out before my flight home. Cold winters with heavy clothing is another adjustment I'd have to make if I give up and move back to Toronto. Mom would love that. She's never been to LA, but in her mind it's full of fires, gangs, and homeless people. She watches the news too much.

My fingers type an essay on unease against my knee. I can't avoid letting my parents know what happened anymore. I text Mom.

Me: Don't freak. My plane had to land in Chicago. Stuck here for the night. They're flying us out tomorrow morning.

Mom: What happened? Let me call you.

Mom: I'm calling you.

Her face and "Mom's Cell" fill my screen. Not in the mood to talk to her, but she'll call again, and again, and again. Fine. I throw my hands in an I give up gesture, as if she can see me all the way from Canada. It's easier to get it over with.

"Mom, hi."

"What happened? Are you alive? Are you injured?"

"Come on, I'm talking to you and sitting safely in my hotel room. Not a hair on my head was harmed. I did briefly think about giving up flying for good, but I need to get to LA some-how, so I might take a sedative on my way back instead." I sit on the chair by the desk and look through my bag for a charger to plug the phone in.

"Okay. You're alive. That's all I needed to know." The noise of a hockey game gets louder in the background. Dad must be watching TV in the living room. "Here's Dad."

"Hi, muffin." Dad takes the phone from Mom, and I hear the game pause. "Sounds like you've had quite a scare."

"I'm okay, Dad." I get my calm-in-the-eye-of-the-storm demeanor from him.

"You know, it's only an eight-hour drive from here to Chicago. If I get in the car now, I can be there in the morning. Bring you home, so you don't have to fly. You don't have to go back to LA." The leather of his recliner squeaks as he shifts. "There's a job and your room waiting here. No rent. Free food. You can eat bread again, and real baguettes, not whatever it is they serve in your fancy resort lacking any gluten. This could be a sign."

Dad also believes in signs. I didn't think I got that gene but lately, I've been wondering if fate is trying to tell me something.

"Maybe LA isn't the right place for you."

I rip open the cover of the room service menu and rifle through the pages as if it's the worn paper and not my dad hinting I'm not going to succeed. "Dad, we talked about this. If nothing happens by the summer, I'll consider it."

"I just want you to be happy."

I want to be happy too. My heart pings in agreement with his words, but the hollowness in my chest echoes in dissonance with the sentiment behind it. What we put behind the elusive *happiness* is not the same thing. I cover up the ache with a round of I love yous, hang up, and my ears ring. I don't remember the last time I was alone in a room. The silence weighs on me, and I turn on the TV for my companion. I surf through the main cable channels and the local ones. When was the last time I watched live programming? Streaming seasons of old shows or recent "it" series to binge-watch with Siobhan is the only time I ever turn on the TV in our shared living room.

I pick a random channel because it's a video of a girl in a hotel room, like me, except hers is stylish. Not sure I get the elven ears, but the song hits home.

Will I dream of Shawn again tonight? The familiar flutter returns, moves from my head into my chest and settles under the button of my jeans. Dreaming of him has become a regular thing. Reliving our night together, or him coming to the club to find me.

With two fingers, I strip the thin beige cover off the double bed—no need for a black light to guesstimate when the last time was the hotel washed the thing. I sink into the overly soft mattress. My spine would sigh in relief if it could. On the flat screen, a hunky guy in a tuxedo clasps a delicate necklace around an elegant model's neck and whispers, "Happy Valentine's Day," into her ear.

What a silly made-up excuse of a holiday. If you're in love, shouldn't every day be about it—not an arbitrarily designated one per year? I roll my eyes. Glad I'll be on a plane for most of it; it'll be easy to avoid.

The bright green digits of the alarm clock on the bedside table shine the verdict. Midnight. The creases in my balled paper heart betray the past futile attempts when I was still hoping to share this day with someone. How naive. Now I know the truth. It's just another day, one I don't have to participate in, and I get to skip the Hallmark holiday's moneymaking scheme. Not that I ever took part. No matter how much I liked a guy, I've yet to have a boyfriend or even a date on Valentine's Day. At least I'm not breaking my streak: no romantic dinners or fancy jewelry await me tomorrow. I bury my nose in Shawn's jacket, pull my knees up, wrap the lapels tighter around me, and let the heart-ball unfold just a tad. This is all the Valentines I need.

Honestly though, I'd appreciate a happy heart day. A smile tugs at one corner of my mouth. The high school version of the holiday wasn't too bad: the halls plastered with sappy posters were a perfect backdrop for the secret candygram delivery in second period. I rub my eyes. Best to put aside childhood fantasies. I wipe the silly grin off my face. I'm an adult now with real-world issues, like the weird noise Betty's roof makes every time I put it up. Do I wait until it stops working or bite the bullet and spend the money Mom and Dad gave me for Christmas on the repairs? LA winter rains in a convertible without a functioning roof is not something I'm interested in experiencing.

The convertible was Mémère's idea. I think she was living vicariously through me. Test driving Betty with me was "a hoot" according to her. This time I can't control my mouth. I let my lips stretch into the toothy smile she worked to cajole onto my face any time I doubted myself.

"You deserve the best," she insisted.

The salesman in the back had gripped his seatbelt for dear life while the three of us whipped around the empty parking lot, putting the car's struts to the test. Rolled into one tiny package, with warm hands, a disarming smile, topped with silver hair in tight curls, people always underestimated Mémère. My heart lights up. She was my personal cheerleader and the one to give me a shove or two in the right direction, more certain of my talents than me.

Why did she have to get sick? Why didn't she tell me the cancer had spread? Why didn't I notice? The glow inside me dims. On our Tuesday night video chats from the screen of my phone, lipstick du jour brightening her thin lips, wrinkles hidden under expert makeup, she was full of life and promised to find me a man who'd worship me like Pops did her. Like every Côté woman deserves.

Mom begged me to come home for Christmas, but I scoffed at her nervous nature and clingy attitude. The darkness that rolled over me when I found out about Mémère's death seeps in. I should have seen the signs, but she insisted I stay in LA, that fate had plans for me. I rub my stomach, guilt gnawing at me. If I'd come home, I could have seen her one last time, said things I didn't get a chance to, hugged her. My grief snuffs the remaining flickers and plunges me into the pitch black that the world is without her. I missed my opportunity.

My hands are not getting warmer. I stuff them into the pockets of the leather jacket and run across Shawn's driver's license again. My eyes fall closed, and I focus on the sharp edge of the plastic—the proof that he happened and wasn't a figment of my overactive imagination. The heat from my memories of him warms me. If I'd come home, I wouldn't have met Shawn. Did Mémère know?

A deep baritone announces the scores. "And in a nail-biter, our team squeezed by the Leafs 4–3 in the final seconds of a rough overtime." Chicago beat Toronto again. Shawn would boast about his hometown hockey team being better.

I can see it now. The warmth travels into my cheeks. His smiling eyes staring down at me, the "I told you so" escaping his lips. He leans in, kisses my nose. "Your nose isn't icy anymore. Glad my jacket is keeping you warm." His voice is soft and velvety, like it was that night. I'm surrounded by Shawn: secure and content. I can almost feel his fingers on my skin as he says "So nice to be in the same room with you. I dreamed about finding you for so many nights, and you beat me to it. Thanks for coming to—"

ELEVEN

Sarah

"It's Valentine's Day," the reporter on TV shouts over the hoots and hollers in the background. "It's not as rowdy as New Year's, but the younger crowd started the Chicago Valentine's Day tradition of bar and pub crawls early."

Realization slams into my heart like a bird into a window. I wipe the dream Shawn out of my eyes and sit up on the bed. He was right. His brown eyes stay in my mind. His words 'thanks for coming' play on repeat. I pull the driver's license out of my pocket and look at the solid black print beside his unsmiling face. The license number, the date of birth, the address. The fluttering wings in my chest pick up speed.

I have his address.

Shawn lives in Chicago.

I'm in Chicago.

Am I seriously considering this? Showing up at Shawn's house out of the blue on Valentine's Day? That's way too corny even for a romantic movie. I'd get laughed at if I wrote such a thing in my screenplay.

But . . .

A flicker of Shawn's fingers on mine flies over my hand. I close my eyes and think of those few hours together. The rightness of it. The feel of his lips on mine, his fingers tracing the small of my back. Shivers run through me. Not from the cold, but from the rising heat on my skin. The way he held me like I was something precious, someone of value—no one has held me like that before. His care wraps around me like the jacket he lent me. Goosebumps start in my pinkie and careen across my arm, up my neck, and down my spine, all control lost.

At Griffith Park, I had no doubt he desired me. It was in his kiss. My lips tingle with the lingering memory. Our embrace was short, yet its effect lasted for hours, days, weeks. But what about now? Has he found someone else to kiss? Will I be interrupting their Valentine's Day?

Sleep falls away. Thoughts of Shawn scare off any chance of it.

I roll off the bed, open my suitcase, and take out my PJs and toothbrush. In the bathroom, I turn on the shower and step into the hot water. Every tendon in my body eases under the steady beat of the misty stream. A massage that removes the tension of being stuck between the two places I still call home. I'm not cold anymore.

The collection of cute little shampoo and conditioner bottles doesn't look fancy, but when I pour the light pink liquid on my palm, the smell of strawberries fills my nostrils. It transports me back to Toronto, sunlight streaming through the window in the kitchen of Côté Fraise: flour, sugar, and cream ready to create magic. I taste strawberries and see Mémère, her fingers dyed red by the summertime fruit along with mine. She's laughing.

My lips stretch into a smile. Even the recollection of her good mood is infectious. Doubts wash away, and I'm lighter than I've been since I got the call. Is this a sign from Mémère? It was her idea to marry her strawberry sounding maiden name Fraise and her husband's Côté together to adorn the sign above her first bakery. "Nothing ventured, nothing gained." It's Mémère's voice in my head. That can't be. The bottle in my hand creaks with the pressure of my grip. I'm a rational twenty-first century woman, and I don't believe in signs.

"Take risks," she said, when we sat in the back of her bakery daydreaming about my future as a writer. The look in her pale blue eyes promised I'd be all right when she hugged me goodbye as she sent me to LA to follow my dreams. The life-giving organ in my chest caves under the strength of her conviction. Mémère knew how to live and wanted the same for me. Baking was her high; her creativity burst into textures and flavors my imagination couldn't fathom. She didn't understand my need to write, but she championed it.

"Take risks." Easy for her to say. Her risks worked out. Following a dashing Canadian hockey player with eyes like the ocean from Lyon to Toronto, opening her own business in the midst of an economic depression, raising a daughter while her husband spent more time away than home, and growing a bakery, displaying Côté Fraise on the window.

"Take risks." What do I have to lose? I raise my chin. What if Shawn forgot all about me? Then I can stop pining and move on. But he will remember me. The terrifying part is the sureness of the "meant-to-be" fate. I fear the power of my connection to this stranger.

Hair wrapped in a towel, I snap up his driver's license and my phone to search for his place. A pretty brick house with steps leading to a door with a glass insert pops up. I can imagine myself knocking on it and seeing Shawn's brown eyes gleaming with delight. Possibilities dry the threatening tears from the corners of my eyes. He'd wrap me in a tight hug and thank me for finding him. But this time, it won't be a dream.

It's been almost two months since our night together. He's been a constant in my life, in my thoughts. Have I been in his?

The house isn't that far from here, twenty minutes by car, but I don't have a car. A cab will cost money. I check my credit card balance. There's enough, barely. Am I really doing this? My stomach flips. I work out the timing.

If I get up early enough . . .

This emergency landing has knocked the common sense out of me. I need a drink. Haven't I learned my lesson on human nature in LA? What sparkles in the dark often turns to dust in the light of day. Shawn could be an illusion. He could be a serial murderer. He could hate dogs. He could be married.

Shawn could be a liar.

Yet, I know what he is. I straighten my shoulders. He's kind. He's funny. He's not like the guys I usually date. Shawn's smart, passionate—the way his eyes lit up like fireworks when talking about how he'd direct our movie. A smile curls my lips. He's cute . . . no—handsome . . . no—hot. He's . . . oh, face it, Sarah—he's what you want.

On the TV, a meteorologist dressed in pink points out the probability of snow tomorrow. "All signs point to a white Valentine's. Perfect weather for cuddling by the fireplace. It's not too late to surprise your loved one. My favorites are these fresh strawberries dipped in milk, dark, or white Morkes chocolate. Yum!" Her teeth bite into a chocolate-covered strawberry while *Morkes Long Grove Chocolates* appears behind her in red and white letters. "With a history of candy making going all the way back to 1920, Morkes Chocolates makes their high-quality confections from scratch, with all-natural chocolate, pure butter, fresh ingredients, and a lot of love."

I chuckle. Talk about signs. Mémère wanted me to meet Shawn. Now, on the way back from her funeral, I find myself stuck near his town, his address in my hand, surrounded by images and smells of her favorite fruit. It's as if she's whispering, "Go for it."

That's nonsense. It's pure coincidence.

Nonetheless, it's still happening.

Okay, Mémère, I'm listening. Certainty settles any lingering flutters of indecision. A pair of beautiful brown eyes urges me to take a chance. I set an alarm on my phone, exhale, and open the door to whatever awaits.

Twelve

NICK

The hotel room is huge, but I'm not going to complain. Sarah sits on the bed with her back to me, like she did on the hood of her car. Betty, was it? She's wearing my jacket, and her blond hair has a reddish glow in the low light of the hotel room. We're alone, and there is a door between us and the outside world. Can she hear the pounding of my pulse? I'm afraid to breathe. She found me. What I couldn't do in LA, she managed here. Did the guy at the bar tell her I was looking for her? Would I have seen her there if I'd waited?

"Sarah?" Her name leaves my lips, and I wait for her to turn, to experience those eyes looking at me and seeing me, knowing me. The drums in my ears fall silent. The room stills. Her head moves, and I admire her profile, but she's watching the muted big screen.

"You weren't exaggerating." Her voice has a trace of laughter in it.

"About?" I swallow the lump in my throat.

"Chicago being better." She points at the TV. "They beat Toronto in overtime."

I follow her eyes, and it's a repeat of the newscast from last night. "Yeah, I saw it. Sorry." I walk to her side.

"There's always next time, right? But you can still tell me you told me so."

"I told you so." My chest expands, the oxygen slowing the rampant beats of my heart. I smile and stare down at her. She's clutching my jacket around her small frame, like she's freezing. I lean down and kiss her nose; it's warm against my lips. "Your nose isn't icy anymore. Glad my jacket is keeping you warm. So nice to be in the same room with you. I dreamed about finding you for so many nights, and you beat me to it. Thanks for coming to—"

I'm cold and damp. What's going on? Oh no, I know this feeling too well. I swing my arm and hit a wall of muscle. Dammit. I open my eyes. Mike is standing over me with a half-full mug of water. "Fucking asshole." I grab the pillow from under my head and throw it his way, but he knows my maneuvers and dodges the onslaught with a quick leap to the side.

"Nothing better than a wet dream." Mike cackles at his own stupid joke. I curl my fingers into the duvet. I'm not in the mood for so many reasons. "Who's Sarah? Thought you aren't dating anyone." Mike sets the mug on the bedside table.

The pouring of water on each other's heads has been our wake-up ritual for years. I'm not mad at him for that. The childish games Mike and I play are the only thing we agree on these days, and remind me of when we were close, before everything imploded. I'm pissed at my reality because Sarah isn't part of it. I rip the bedsheets off my tense body. I scramble up, drag off my shirt, and wipe my face and hair. He didn't get too much on me.

"Hey, spill." Mike laughs at stupid joke number two. How do girls find his asinine humor charming? "Nick, who's Sarah?"

"None of your business." I give him the finger, and while his attention is on that hand, toss the damp ball of my T-shirt. It catches him square in the chest.

"Ouch." He rubs the wet spot on his chest and picks the limp material up off the floor. "Touchy subject? A girl doesn't like you or what? I can give you some pointers." His hands ball my shirt back up, and I don't let my guard down. "Mackenzie seemed to appreciate my advice. Not sure why you two split."

"Irreconcilable differences." My voice is hardly audible.

"What?" Mike curves his finger behind his ear, like Yiayia does when she's talking to us while she has the TV on and refuses to turn it down.

"Irreconcilable differences," I repeat a bit louder. My throat is itchy and dry. I gulp the rest of the water from the mug, but it doesn't help much. I need coffee. Hot. Lots of foam.

Mike looks away "Right. None of my business. Got it." I grind my teeth. How did that answer tick him off? He's been extra grumpy since his trip to visit his secret girlfriend he doesn't want to talk about. "You've got twenty minutes if you still want a lift to Mackenzie's place." Fun time is over.

"I do. Thanks." I hate being dependent on him for rides. I stomp across the room. "Meet you downstairs."

Mike walks through the door into the hallway and closes it behind him. I pick clean clothes out of the closet. My door squeaks, and a wet ball thwacks my back.

"Get out of my room," I shout. The door slams before I can do anything.

That asshole ruined another dream about Sarah. I have those a lot, but this was a new one. Maybe because of my failed attempt to find her yesterday, maybe because I can't give up on us finding each other. The thudding behind my breastbone resumes. Previous dreams were a variation of our time in LA, or me chasing her and never getting to hold her. This time, I was next to her. Touching her. My fingers tingle with the feel of her skin on mine. Another minute, and I would've pressed my lips to hers. She felt so real, so much like a flesh-and-blood girl and not a figment of my imagination. I jerk the door of my closet open. My stupid brother fucked it up.

THIRTEEN

NICK

THERE'S TOO MUCH SNOW for Mike to ride his bike, so the three of us pile into Mom's minivan. Mike is driving. Mom's in the front seat. I stifle a groan and strap myself into the back seat like the good-boy Nicky they expect.

"Did you eat any breakfast?" Mom's putting mascara on using the mirror on the visor that flips down.

"No." I cross my arms. "I'll grab something on the way."

"How're you getting to school?" asks Mike.

"Clark's picking up Mackenzie, and I'll get a ride with them." My eyes drill holes in the windshield. "I need to see her father before he leaves for work."

Mike's eyes flick to me in the rearview mirror. "As long as Mr. Tucker's okay with that."

"He is." We merge onto the highway, and Mike focuses on the icy stretch ahead. The snowplow cleared the road earlier in the morning, but it's snowing again. Only a light dusting, but it covers the cement ramp and the roofs of the cars around us. Everything is gray and gloomy. Valentine's Day this year is just that. A day.

Now we're not together, I don't have to worry about making the whole school swoon over an elaborate bouquet for Mackenzie and a dozen of the chocolate-dipped strawberries she loves so much. I tug on the seatbelt strangling me. Last year's charade was worth the crowd-pleasing "Ahhhhhhs" though. If nothing, Mackenzie likes a show. I'd do so much more for Sarah. Give her anything she wants.

"Drop me off by Morkes." I clasp the straps of my backpack, ready to get out.

"A gift for Mackenzie?" Mom asks.

"She's with Clark." I clear my throat. "You know that."

"Well, I've seen how she still looks at you." Mom shakes her brown curls. "But I'm glad you don't have any girls on your mind. Focus on school, and you won't repeat my mistakes and base your whole life on someone's beautiful eyes."

"Umm." Sarah's blue eyes have a fine gold rim around them, and I'll see them again. Sure thing. Cords around my heart loosen at the knowledge.

Mike pauses the car on the same block as the café. I say a quick goodbye then push the sliding door and jump out. The bell above the café's door dings when I enter. There's only one man ahead of me.

"So, the strawberries then. Anything else?" The cashier waits for the man in an unzipped puffy coat over a business suit to answer.

"That's it." He pays, and I slide up to the register.

"Haven't seen you here for a while." Lily, the twenty-something cashier, saw me here plenty of times with Mackenzie. "Chocolate strawberries for you as well?" She's well aware of my ex-girlfriend's obsession. I hope Clark is getting some for Mackenzie this year. Not my problem, though.

I feel her watching me closely. I shrug. "No. I'm here for breakfast. Can I get two hot croissant sandwiches with ham, cheese, and egg, and a caramel latte, please?" I should probably get something for the Tuckers and Clark. Only fair. "Oh, and a flat white, a cappuccino, and a tall decaf with a splash of milk."

"For here or to go?"

"I'll eat the food here, but can you get me a tray for the drinks?" I look around, and there are a couple of tables still open by the window. "Not too busy?"

"Don't jinx us." Her red heart earrings bob in and out of her short hair. "The rush is about to begin." She rings me up. "I'll bring it over to you when they're ready."

I nod and choose a table by the window. My jaw relaxes but the itch in my throat lingers. The steel seat is cold even through my jeans. I shiver. I better leave my coat on. The place is decked out in shades of red and pink, hearts everywhere, like the Diamond Club yesterday. This Valentine's Day would be completely different if I'd found Sarah.

My temples burn with ways to persuade her to be my girl-friend. Should I send some strawberries to her? Might need her last name. Or can I send them to Sarah the Bartender? And who do I send them from? No way I'll pretend to be Shawn again. Should've told her the truth. Maybe roses would be more romantic. My internet search for twelve long-stemmed roses to be delivered in LA offers results in many options that are half a week's paycheck. Damn, those flowers are expensive, but Sarah's worth it.

"Here you go, Nick." Lily places my food and the tray with the four drinks on the wood surface of the table. I put my phone in my pocket.

"Thanks." I tear into the first croissant; the hot gooey cheese burns the roof of my mouth. I take another bite, too hungry to care. Should've ordered three.

My cell vibrates.

Clark: Running late. Entertain Mac for me?

Not this again. I huff my disappointment. This guy is always asking favors.

Harry Styles's voice croons above me about strawberries and summer evenings. They're set on selling those strawberries, the dead of winter or not. I chew and scan the bulletin board to my right. There's the flyer I put up for the taekwondo studio Mike teaches at. I should've gone there more. Maybe I'll find a dojang in LA. More fun than going to the gym alone.

Some guy named Chris is looking for work, selling himself as a social media guru. Would he need any videos for his clients?

I could shoot them for extra income. Saving up is a priority. I pick up the second croissant, and it's not that hot anymore. Checklists spin in my brain. I've been looking at used cars. Sarah said I'd need one when I move to LA. I can't wait to drive her around town, take her out on a real date.

The last bite of breakfast is in my mouth. I reach for my coffee when my cell vibrates again. What does Clark want now?

I wipe my hands on a napkin, pick up my phone, and glance at the notification. "Congratulations" stares back at me. The restaurant disappears, and my world contracts to that single word.

Is this the email I've been waiting for? My eyes nudge my finger to tap, to reveal what's in store. My thumb trembles as I drag it across the screen. If it is, my life will change. Air goes in and out my nose, but it's not reaching my lungs. I hit the notification and open the email.

"The Starlight Foundation is pleased to offer you a spot in our Future Filmmakers Competition this summer."

I stare at the letters that dance on my phone, refusing to settle.

I reread the first sentence.

The phone clatters next to my empty plate. I recline on the flimsy chair. The metal legs squeak under my weight. I run my fingers through my hair and slam my fist on the table.

Fuck, I got in. I actually got in.

I want to jump for joy, scream, dance. Instead, I try to sit still and wait for my breathing to become an automatic function of my lungs again.

I did it.

I punch the air. Take that, Mike. I'm not a wannabe, I'm a *be*. I read the email again, digesting each word. They liked my work and thought I had vision, potential. *Welcome to the program. The competition starts in July.* I'll be part of a team making a movie.

My hands are shaking. My head is reeling. I can't believe it. I did it. One day the name Nick Stavros will be on movie posters everywhere. The titles of the films I direct—on everyone's lips.

Including Sarah's.

The thought of her lips makes me remember that it's been months since I've touched a girl. I need to kiss Sarah again, and not only in a dream. The thud that happens whenever I think about her rams into my ribcage. This is going to happen. I close my eyes and conjure up the dream from this morning. Sarah, I'm coming. Another thud. We don't have to wait till fall. Thud. Thud. Thud. Nothing will stop us.

Everything is different now. This is my shot. I down the last of my drink, grab the tray with the coffees, and rush out the door of the café to take the next steps toward the future I've designed for myself. Something *I* want for a change. Hope Mackenzie's dad understands.

I'm not changing my mind, no matter what Mom and Mike think. LA will be my home again.

FOURTEEN

Sarah

"Could you drop me off here?" I lean toward the taxi driver and point to the other corner of the intersection we're about to cross.

"At the top of the street? You sure?" She signals a right turn and gets closer to the curb. "I can take you to the exact address."

"No, thanks, here is perfect." I pay and step into suburban Chicago, or to be exact, Long Grove, Illinois.

Shawn's neighborhood is rows upon rows of single-family brick houses. They line the street before me, all butted up against each other. Most have a porch of some kind, accessed by a few stairs in the middle of each patch of lawn. Said lawns are currently divided by sidewalks dug out of the mounds of snow blanketing the area. They must have had quite the snowstorm.

And another one is on the way. I can smell the snow threatening. I glance at the cloud-laden sky; this storm better wait until my flight takes off. I can't afford another delay.

At least the trip here was easy. And quick. My tennis shoes skid across a patch of ice, but I keep my balance. With little traffic, the taxi flew along, and we got here faster than I expected. I'm too early to go knocking on anyone's door. The little café I spotted from the taxi is next to a convenience store. The windows of both are plastered with fuchsia-colored hearts—typical Valentine's Day decor. Perfect. I'll waste a little time in there.

A tall tree trunk of a guy wrapped in a bulky black parka exits the café, a tray of cups in his hands. I try to catch the door before it closes behind him but miss. The polite Canadian in me bristles. He could've held the door open for me, it's only common courtesy, but I'm in a gracious mood; he might've missed me—in too much of a hurry to deliver the fancy coffees. Better be careful, buddy, these sidewalks are slippery. Wouldn't want to spill those.

Inside the café it's warm and cozy. My eyelashes unfreeze. One wall is dominated by a bar, currently awash in a rash of ruby-red, hot-pink, and snow-white hearts. Cupid had a heavy hand. A short line of people winds around the few steel bistro tables. I join the waiting game, stuffing my hat in the pocket of my gray winter jacket. The hat almost falls out again. Damn all these extra layers. I'm not used to this anymore. Hats, and gloves, and scarves, and coats, and boots—California is looking better and better.

I'm not wearing Shawn's jacket today—a little too much to show up on his doorstep decked out in his clothes.

Wouldn't that look great? "Hi, Shawn, remember me? The random girl you kissed on Christmas Eve? So yeah, here's your driver's license back—let me rub off the drool first. Oh, and I'm not a stalker or anything. Even though I'm wearing your clothes like a teenager walking around in her high school boyfriend's letterman jacket."

Why am I doing this again? I roll my eyes. Because it's him. Because I want to believe there's something special between us. Because maybe Mémère is watching out for me. Guiding me. Warmth radiates through my chest. I can take a risk, even if it's for her sake.

Tufts of honey brown hair peek out from under the red beanie of the tall guy in front of me. They remind me of Shawn's luscious locks. The ones I ran my fingers through, soft and silky. This place is right around the corner from his house. My cheeks heat. Could it be him? That would be a coincidence, but it's not like my being in his town isn't already one.

My pulse quickens. I reach out and tap him on the shoulder. A pair of hazel eyes meet mine. Pretty, but not the ones I'm looking for. Not Shawn. My shoulders slump.

"Huh?"

"Um." I didn't think this through. "Do you know what time it is?" Nice cover, Sarah.

The dude huffs and points to the extra-large clock on the wall behind the cashier.

"Oh, thanks." I offer him my sorry-to-bother-you smile.

The tower of a man turns away, and I try not to let the disappointment pooling in my gut drown my enthusiasm. Did I really think it was going to be that easy? C'mon. Life has never been that simple. At least not for me.

My phone dings.

Mom: Happy Valentine's Day.

Mom: *string of heart emojis*

Mom: Dad surprised me with breakfast in bed.

Of course he did. I stifle an "ah." Look in the dictionary under romantic, and you'll see a picture of my dad. And not just on the big occasions, but for no reason whatsoever, he'd send her a dozen roses or surprise her with a weekend out of town. He cherishes my mom and isn't afraid to show it.

Me: Lucky you.

Me: Did he make crêpes?

A picture of a plate of heart-shaped perfectly crisp and not burnt crêpes lands in the text chain. The 'ah' escapes my lips, against my protests. Of course, Dad added strawberries today. He thinks of everything.

Dad doesn't make pancakes. I grew up on thin, melt-in-your-mouth pillows of dough browned to perfection, stacked high for Sunday breakfasts. The ideal food for a lazy morning and a surprisingly effective antidote for hangovers. I tried making them for my roommate Siobhan, but the lumpy sheets tore, the edges burned, and I threw out more than we ate. The cooking gene must've skipped a generation.

Mom: What are you having for breakfast?

Should I tell her where I am? What I'm doing? I bite my lip. Better not. She'll worry about me. I can't handle her neuroses today. She means well, but the constant stress over anything else going wrong is stifling me. Ever since the Big Disappointment, she doesn't trust anything good can happen in LA.

Mémère was the only one I told about Shawn and our Christmas Eve escapade. We giggled like schoolgirls over the details when I called her at the cottage on New Year's Day. Not that I told her everything. Still, she said she liked the sound of Shawn. Thought he had potential. Gave me shit for not giving him my number.

I'll tell Mom if . . . no, when it works out. I lift my chin. Regale her with my adventures in Chicago. A fun story I can tell to make her laugh and show her that good things do happen outside the safety of Toronto.

Me: Grabbing something at a café.

Not a lie.

Mom: Dad says have a good flight. His offer still stands. Call me when you land.

Fifteen

Sarah

I ORDER A CROISSANT and a hot chocolate, complete with marshmallows. My stomach rubs its hands in anticipation. I deserve a treat. The chocolate covered strawberries in the display case look delicious. Should I buy some for Shawn and me to share later? No, too much.

I check the time. Still too early. I select a seat in front of the window by the door; the legs of the steel chair squeak as they scrape across the concrete floor. I shove my suitcase under the table. There's a bulletin board on the wall with a flyer for a lost cat, an ad for a taekwondo studio, and a resumé of someone looking for work: "Chris is proficient in social media." Good luck to you, Chris.

What other job options do I have? I'm no good at social media stuff like Chris. I unwind my scarf and unbutton my coat, checking to make sure my hat is still in my pocket. My Instagram account is mostly posts of drinks I've mixed. I hate posting pictures of myself, and one can post only so many tanning on the beach photos. I don't have anyone to take impressive action shots of beach volleyball sessions—the only exercise I get these days. Bartending has supported me well enough, but I can't keep serving others. I need to serve myself—find something that makes me happy. I scoot the chair closer to the table. Something other than screenwriting if that doesn't pan out.

Maybe I can fuel my passion for writing into something else. I glance at Chris's poster. I could try writing copy for social media. Or blogs. Or ghostwriting a book. Not as much fun as bringing my characters to life on film, but at least I'd still be writing. I tap my knee so fast the basket of sugar packets wobbles. I slide it toward me and organize them by color. I'll have to see what courses I can take when I get back to LA. Or search YouTube for some free lessons. Yeah, that would be better. Anything to have a plan rather than admitting defeat and crawling back to Toronto, my tail between my legs, and working at the bakery. The reorganized basket—a rainbow array of sweet, sweeter, and sweetest—does nothing to calm my nerves.

"Here you go." A croissant and a mug of hot chocolate slide my way. The letters on the dark brown ceramic spell Morkes. Where do I know that name from?

"Thanks." I smile at the girl dropping off my food. "I like your earrings, by the way." The red hearts have a glitter-encrusted cupid's bow through them. Very on point for the day.

Like this place, she's cute. I tuck a strand of hair behind my ear and give the place another onceover. I could see myself hanging out here. And good taste in music. With a bite of my croissant, I bounce along to a song with lyrics about riding in a car. Shawn's driver's license is in my pocket. A thrill shoots through me. My toes are as jittery as my knees. All of me is. I set the hot cocoa down before my trembling hand leaves most of it on the floor and splay both palms against the cool metal surface of the table. My heart joins the anxious dance. I might see him today.

Will he take me in those sturdy arms of his, bend down, and kiss me right away? I squeeze my eyes. Geez, Sarah, this isn't that scene from *To All The Boys I've Loved Before*. Need to scale back my expectations here. First, he has to be home. I wrap both arms around myself and squeeze my heart into submission.

Please, let him be home.

This is what I want. I breathe in. I want him. I hold my breath and count to three. I want us. So bad. I breathe out as I count to five. My eyelids lift and let the memory play out, grasping for what I hope we can recapture. Like that night two months ago. He not only awoke something inside of me—he took part of me with him when he left. The butterflies in my stomach kick into high gear, heat rising on my cheeks. I have to get a grip here. Just a little longer, Sarah. It'll be worth it.

Please, let this be real.

Mémère, help me here.

Croissant gone, I drain the last of my hot chocolate. I put my coat and scarf back on. No more sitting. I can't wait. I return my cup to the counter, thank the barista, and drop some cash into the tip jar. I don't have a lot on me, but I know how much these things mean. She smiles at me; her heart earrings flash red against her neck.

"Happy Valentine's Day." The wish comes off her matching pink lips with sincerity, like she believes it's a possibility.

I hope so. The pompom of Mémère's hat feels soft under my fingers as I rub it for good luck. Look at me having hope. Who'd have thought?

Big fat flakes fall in slow spirals when I step outside. Everything appears quiet and calm. The world has shrunk to this one street, these houses that have stood here for a hundred years. I press my palms together and bring them to my lips. Shawn's world. The tingles that travel from my hands into my chest might be from the cold air, but I doubt it.

A woman and her daughter make room for me as I pass by, checking each house for a plaque with the address number. The area reminds me of the street Mémère lived on when I was a child, each house the same but with its own unique qualities. A red door here, green siding on this one, and a big bay window over there . . .

This is it. My pulse picks up as I step to the side and double-check the address on my phone. His house. It looks . . . ordinary.

I eye the welcome mat and repeat Mémère's words: "Take risks." I steady my shaky legs. I've come this far. This is the right thing to do. He needs his ID back. I should be nervous, but I'm not. What gives?

The snow crunches under my feet on the stairs. One, two, three. I make my way to the covered porch, raise my hand to ring the doorbell, and catch my reflection in the glass of the door. I whip off my hat, stuffing it into my coat pocket. I fluff my hair and try to make it look like it did that night, so Shawn will recognize me.

This is it.

Heart in my throat, I press the little button and hear the ding-dong of the doorbell.

Sixteen

NICK

I close the door to the bathroom when the doorbell rings.

"Should I get it?" I shout down the hall. Mackenzie is putting the breakfast plates into the dishwasher in the kitchen, and I'm only steps from the entryway.

"I got it. Probably Clark," Mackenzie hollers. "Dad's waiting for you." She brushes past me, her hand grazes my forearm, and her eyes catch mine. That used to spark my desire, if not my interest. Now that I know what kissing Sarah feels like, I don't get how I was ever attracted to Mackenzie. She presses her fingers into my biceps, but I shrug them off, enter Mr. Tucker's office, and close the door behind me.

Mr. Tucker is sitting at his massive wooden desk, reading something on his laptop, and doesn't look up. I clear my throat and put the cup with the flat white beside him. "Morning."

He raises his head. "Hey, Nick. How was LA?"

"Good." The exhilaration of getting accepted wins over the disappointment of not finding Sarah. My heart beats in my throat and reverberates in my ears. Even though I left my parka hanging on the hook by the door, I feel like I'm still wearing the heavy coat. I wipe my burning forehead. "Great actually."

Sharp gray eyes find mine, and he smiles but doesn't press. I like this about him. He never needles at me, not like Mike or Mom.

"Glad to hear it." He takes a sip of the coffee. "Thanks for this. What did you want to talk to me about?"

"My shifts." It comes out as a croak. I clear my throat and speak up. "My shifts. I won't be able to work for you in the summer, like we discussed." I rock on the balls of my feet.

Mr. Tucker lowers the coffee cup and purses his lips. "No? How come?"

"Uh." I rub my chin. A confetti of hope, pride, and anxiety sprinkles over my back. I don't want it to come off like I'm bragging. "I got into the program in LA, so I'll be moving earlier." I wince and look away. Here it comes, the I'm-letting-you-down-but-still-need-your-help bit. "But I still need the money. I was hoping I could pick up some more shifts while I'm here or see if you had any other work I could do for you."

Mackenzie's voice carries through the closed door. She sounds angry. Is she fighting with Clark again? That relationship isn't good for either of them. I cringe. At least she didn't scream at *me* when we were together.

"Congratulations," says Mr. Tucker. "I knew you had talent." The words take a minute to sink in. It's not condemnation, disappointment. It's . . . he's happy for me. I breathe easier. He thinks I have talent. I stand taller. Why can't he be my dad?

Mr. Tucker places a piece of paper in front of him and starts writing. "I'll talk to my clients who're looking to shoot commercials and see if there's any interest in hiring you."

"Thanks, I appreciate it." Warmth crawls up my neck and threatens to break out as a grin. I shove my hands into my jean pockets. "I really do."

Mackenzie's voice gets louder, and I look behind me through the stained design in the glass door of the office. I can't make out what she's saying, but I can tell it's a woman she's talking to.

"I'm calling the police," Mackenzie blasts.

Is someone threatening her? I jet to the door and jerk the handle toward me. She may not be my girl anymore, but no one is going to hurt her. My teeth lock together. I rush into the hall to find her, back against the closed front door, staring down at something in her hand, her long brown hair shielding her face.

"Are you okay?" I ask.

Mackenzie startles and drops the thing she was holding. The hairs on the back of my neck rise. We both dive for it, but my arms are longer, so I get there first. I pick up a piece of plastic.

I look at a grainy black-and-white image. A photo of me. My heart stumbles. Time slows down.

Tick.

The first blow slams into my ribs. Big bold letters beside my face spell out Shawn Rosstav.

Tock.

Blood pumps in my ears. This is *my* fake ID.

Tick.

A million what-ifs flash in my mind. The ID I left in my jacket pocket.

Tock.

The jacket I last saw around Sarah's shoulders on Christmas Eve. Panicked beats reverberate in my chest. A cavalcade of possibilities stampedes through me.

Tick.

Sarah had my ID.

Everything rushes into fast forward. Mackenzie is saying something, but I don't hear her. I shove my feet into my boots by the door and tell her to get out of the way. My heartbeat moves from my throat into my ears. The woosh deafens me to whatever comes out of Mackenzie's lips.

Sarah is here.

I rush past Mackenzie and tug the door. It's locked. The muscles in my forearm tense. I twist the doorknob, turn it one way, but the damned thing doesn't move. The brass knob creaks under the pressure of my fingers. I try the other way, pulling at the door to get out. I punch and kick the wood blocking my exit.

"Give way," I yell.

"The deadbolt, dummy," Mackenzie says behind me.

I flip the steel latch and with a final yank, the door flies open. I charge and run into a broad chest.

"Shit, man," says Clark. "Watch where you're going."

Mackenzie's hand clutches at my arm. "Nick, stop."

Over Clark's shoulder I spot a petite blond running down the sidewalk toward the main road.

Sarah? Can it be? My breath accelerates.

"Let go of me." My feet carry me over the threshold. I rip Mackenzie's fingers off my shirt and throw her hand away from me, turning sideways to pass by Clark. He grabs my sleeve and pushes me back.

"You can't treat her like that. Apologize." He blocks the doorway.

Worst timing ever for him to pretend to be a good boyfriend. He's not going to stop me. Sarah's here. I haven't spent years in hockey for nothing. I tighten my core and Kronwall him with a shoulder to the chest maneuver, and he tumbles backwards down the stairs, slamming against the railing.

I follow his trajectory, taking the stairs two at a time.

"What th—" He tries to grab at me as I fly by him.

"Sarah?" I shout down the street, but my voice is hoarse. The burning in my throat matches the anguish inside. "Sarah!" I cough her name.

A hand on my ankle tugs me down. I trip and fall into the snowbank, my face landing on something that's not snow. A small piece of paper scratches my cheek. I snatch it. It's part of a boarding pass. Yesterday's date, Flight 337, Seat 32B, Toronto to LA.

LA. I must be hallucinating. I'm still asleep, still dreaming. I blink. But I haven't been in a dream where my throat itches and my head hurts.

Clark's off his back and is pulling me by my leg. What's he doing that for?

"Get off me." I kick Clark's arm away. He lets go and scrambles up the stairs.

I'm on all fours, about to get on my feet, when my eye catches a patch of blue. I reach for it, turn it over, and can't believe my eyes. It's a Toronto Maple Leafs hat. I rub the snow off my face. The cold crystals melt and remind me I *am* conscious. This is Sarah's favorite team. I'm not hallucinating. My hands tremble as I unfold the precious object. There's a label inside. *Property of the Leafs #1 fan: Sarah Côté.*

Pieces of a puzzle click together in my mind. The conversation I overheard at the airport yesterday. The emergency landing of the flight from Toronto. The blur of the blue hat. This hat I have in my hand. The croissants churn in my gut. Sarah was on that flight.

I scramble to my feet, stick both items into my pockets, and look in the direction the girl of my dreams ran.

Where is she? My stomach launches into my throat. I search the sidewalk, the street. There she is—all the way at the end of the block, dragging a red-spotted suitcase.

I can still catch up with her. I'm fast. I take off running and watch her climb into the back of a yellow cab.

"Sarah, wait." I try to yell, but my hoarse voice doesn't carry as the taxi moves away from the curb. My heart follows. I know she can't hear me, but I can't help it. Maybe she can feel my desperation and sense I'm here, trying to get to her. "Sarah. Sarah." Cold air burns my throat, and I cough some more.

The taxi gains speed, and so do I.

The stoplight at the end of the street turns red. Maybe that's the lucky break I need. The taxi stops, and I force my legs to move double speed. If it stays there thirty seconds longer, I'll catch up. My chest burns as my feet try to find purchase, and I gulp the icy air. I'm glad I'm not wearing my parka. It would've slowed me down. I stumble over the icy patches covered with fresh powder, bracing myself against the wind. The snow is falling harder now, and I have to wipe large flakes out of my eyes with my frozen hands.

The light turns green when I'm ten feet away.

"Sarah, I'm here," I shout as loud as I can, ignoring the raw feeling in my throat. I should be close enough for her to hear me.

The cab rolls forward. "No, Sarah, wait!" What I want to scream comes out as a broken whisper.

It's no use. The car roars off, speeding through the intersection, and veers onto the ramp to the highway.

No. I shake my head. This can't be happening. I run into the intersection. A horn blares. I don't care. Hope jerks me forward.

All my attention is on the yellow shape growing smaller and smaller as it speeds away from me. I keep on and cross the rest of the road, ducking between the oncoming traffic. More horns blare, and I reach the bottom of the onramp. The taxi merges onto the highway and disappears from view.

A car tries to enter the onramp and blocks my way. The driver rolls down the window. "Are you fucking *trying* to kill yourself? Get the fuck off the road, you dimwit."

Why is he blocking me? Why is everyone in my way? All hope evaporates like the snow on the hot metal of the car. I slam my fist on the hood, and the pain from my knuckles radiates into my chest.

"Cut it out, or I'm calling the police."

"Fuck you." I try to walk around when he moves the car to block me again. That was a hundred percent deliberate. He could've run me over. Flames run up my spine, and I see red. I pound the hood then kick a tire. My eyes burn. I failed. She was here. Hot angry tears stain my cheeks. I hit the car again. I should've caught up with her. My lips part in a silent scream. Another hit.

A siren blares in the distance, and flashing lights stop near us.

"Step away from the car." A metallic speakerphone voice cuts through the rage in my head. "Put your hands in the air and step away from the car, or we will have to use a Taser." That gets to me. I jerk my chin up. Tase me? What's going on? My brain synapses fire. I look around and begin to actually comprehend the scene around me.

Up and down, cars crowd the road, unable to move because of me. The hood of the silver sedan I've been hitting is covered in red blotchy snow. My breathing is ragged, my throat seared by the cold air, the cough, and the shouting. I look down at my knuckles. They are a bloody mess. What happened here? A hand shoves me to the side, away from the car.

"I'm sorry, sir." I don't recognize my voice. I rub my neck to soothe the stinging.

"Keep your hands where I can see them," says the officer behind me.

My head swims. "I just lost it."

"I'm gonna put you in the back of the car while I talk to this gentleman here. Are you drunk?"

"No, not at all." I want to turn and look at him and explain, but I know better. I've been through this before.

"I'll have to cuff you now."

"Yes, sir." I keep my hands up.

He takes my wrist, and a cold metal circle closes around it. He repeats it with the other one.

"I'm going to double cuff you now. Stay still."

I do. I've never been double-cuffed before. Panic replaces the rage. I shiver. Two more clicks.

"Turn to your right."

I follow his instructions.

He guides me toward the police car, and I lower my head to avoid hitting it on the doorframe. He closes the door and walks back to the driver of the silver car; a white curtain of snow falls between them and me. I hit my head on the headrest. The pain in my throat is nothing next to the fire and brimstones I'll have to face at home. Mike's going to rip me a new one. Whatever. He'll have to come pick me up; I'm not calling Mom.

I close my eyes and recall the blond hair in the back of the cab. I squeeze my eyelids until it hurts. Sarah was here. In Chicago. Looking for me. My nose tingles. I'm not alone in this. Despite this fucked-up situation, a flicker of hope ignites inside me. Sarah cares. A tear escapes the prison of my eyes. Her hat is tucked into my back pocket, but where it sticks out, I can feel the itch of the wool. Fate left me a clue—her name. Sarah Côté. As soon as I get out of these cuffs, I'm Googling it. I lean forward to get a better hold on her hat. Sarah felt it too. I welcome the pang in my heart. She came to find me. I have her name. Maybe I can find her phone number.

What we had—no, have—is real.

Seventeen

Sarah

Everything was a lie.

The fare on the taxi's meter keeps climbing. The traffic is the opposite of what it was on the way here. If we don't move soon, I won't be able to pay. My pitiful finances are almost a big enough distraction to keep me from thinking about what just happened. I hold the tears at bay. The snow's coming down harder now, and the road ahead is a blurry image of crawling red taillights. If this were a movie, it'd be romantic. But it's real life. My life. And my life isn't that sweet. Or fair. My tongue pushes against the back of my teeth as I clench my jaw. No, my life turns idyllic snow into a major irritant that threatens to make me miss my flight.

What was I thinking? Believing in fate and hope. Stupid, Sarah, real stupid. My temples throb. I created a whole love story around some random guy who was probably lonely on Christmas Eve and used me as a substitute for his girlfriend.

This lunacy of a plan was never a good idea. The chances of it working out and Shawn even remembering me were zero from the start. I clamp my arms around my middle. My heart took over my brain again. Stupid heart.

"Argh," I cry out. The taxi driver catches my eye in the rearview mirror and turns up the volume on the radio. "And now a different kind of love song. Here's Cheap Trick with *I Want You to Want Me.*"

Cheap trick indeed. I bark out a laugh. Keep it together, Sarah. You're scaring the guy. You need him to get you to the airport. I switch my scowl into a smile. This is not the end of the world. I shouldn't have believed the whole 'it's a sign' bullshit. The tears press against the back of my eyes. Romance exists in the stories I make up, not for me.

Where is my gate? I shove my way through droves of people. Where is everyone going on Valentine's Day? Bags, legs, children are everywhere: in my way, blocking me from getting out of here. I pull at the collar of my sweater. Breathe, Sarah. Find something to focus on. I start counting red suitcases. One . . . Two . . . that one is closer to purple, but I add it to the list.

What is wrong with me? Why can't things work out for me for once?

I tap my sock-clad foot on the well-worn carpet. The black conveyer belt inches the plastic bin with my stuff toward me. Is the universe conspiring to slow everything down? To keep me in this place? I lean my head back and hiss into the ceiling. My punishment for trying. I have five minutes to make it to the gate, and the belt is taking half of them. I reach over two other travelers waiting for their trays, snatch my stuff from the container, and dash down the hallway.

My boots are under my armpit, so is my scarf. A fist takes hold of my windpipe. Where's my hat?

No. No. This is not happening.

I look around and run back, scanning the gray squares of the carpet for the bright blue dot of my hat. My lungs seize. It's nowhere to be seen. I rummage through the bins. I mutter curses I can no longer suppress. It has to be here. Passengers eyeball me like I'm about to explode. They might not be wrong. The pressure inside my head reaches its limit.

The bins are empty.

"Last call for passenger Sarah Connor. Please, report to gate forty immediately for boarding. Passenger Sarah Connor, your plane is about to depart."

Damn it. I sprint to the gate. Every smack of my heel on the floor pounds in my skull. When was the last time I saw the hat? Losing it in Chicago—where I'll never get it back—that's so like me. I can't . . . it's all I have of Pops . . . of Mémère. My inheritance. Blood pulses in my ears. Alain and Sarah Côté. The couple I've always measured my relationships against. I clutch at my throat. The hat was Pop's last gift to his wife, her last gift to me. Pops had the message inside embroidered for his dear Sarah, my namesake. Their inside joke and a profession of love, written only for the wearer to see.

Yep. Loser. The ache snaps me in two. I've lost everything.

"Ms. Connor?" The middle-aged woman at the gate seizes my ticket and glares at me before she sends me down the ramp to the plane. An irritated woman in a starched uniform greets me and closes the door behind my barely-in-the-plane butt. Everyone is seated but me and a man rifling through his bag in the middle of the aisle.

"Sir, you have to store this before we can take off." The flight attendant is breathing down his neck.

"There's no room above, and I need it here." He tries to stuff the oversized bag under his seat.

Can't he just shut up and sit down? My chest roils. I want to go home.

But which one is home? LA or Toronto? The fumes of anger and despair rise. I'm not sure anymore.

I left Toronto to escape my fate. If I'd stayed, I would have inherited Mémère's and Mom's life: up before the sun to get the bread ready for the first rise, endless hours in the bakery, raising three kids in between croissants and chocolate éclairs. Mom loves the place, but I don't know how she does it. I hop on one leg and pull on my boots. To me, she was permanently too exhausted at night to have any fun.

We've always been opposites. A pang of guilt hammers the point home. My night owl to her early riser. I'm getting home just before the sun rises, falling into bed after a night of bartending, reveling with the partygoers and soaking up their exuberance, feeding off it. I get up with the lunch crowd. Writing in the afternoons before my shifts. Still, even I know I can't do it forever. I fist the sleeve of my coat. I need to find some stability.

Why am I fighting fate? I've tried it my way. My track record in LA is nothing if not consistent—mistake after mistake. I suck air through my teeth. Shawn wasn't waiting for me, pining away after our night together like I was. Nothing to hold on to there. From the moment that twig of a brunette opened the door, doubt crept in.

"You're not Clark." Her voice rang in my head.

"Clark? No, I'm looking for Shawn," I said, hoping against hope she's his . . . sister? Not that they looked anything alike.

"Who?"

"Shawn Rosstav."

"There's no Shawn here."

I held up Shawn's ID like a calling card in some Victorian novel. She snatched it out of my hand, and I didn't do a thing.

"What the—" Her eyebrows crawled up her forehead, deep brown eyes glaring at me. "Where did you get this?

"I . . . he . . ." I whispered as my heart deflates, the cold reality sinking in.

"Is this a joke?" Her voice was so loud.

I shook my head. "No . . . He's not here, is he?"

"What do you want with him?" The snark in her voice cut any threads of hope I had left of my fantasy coming true.

I opened my mouth to say something, but what was there to say. "Give me Shawn's ID back?" What would be the point? He was not waiting for me to find him. More likely, he was out buying roses for this chick. He wasn't mine to have.

"Well? Don't just stand there. Explain this or I'm calling the police."

But I didn't.

I ran.

The ache in my chest swells, and I battle the rising emotions, trying to gain control. Keep calm, Sarah. Hold on a little longer. You've made it this far without crying.

I buckle my seatbelt, nothing but the dead screen on the headrest in front of me. Nothing to distract me from feeling it.

All of it.

The betrayal. The lies. Her death.

I suck in a deep breath and let it out slowly. My eyes burn. My nose tingles. I dig my nails into the armrest. Somewhere behind me, a child starts wailing, the first few tentative cries foretelling the upcoming onslaught of a tantrum. I want to scream with the toddler. Have my own meltdown, let out the black bile I've been carrying around since I got the call about Mémère. Mom sobbing on the other end of the line. The sense of dread. Dad taking over the phone, "Muffin, it's your grandmother . . ."

They lied. Mom kept it from me. How could she do it? She said Mémère wanted it that way. Didn't want me distracted. I hear their calm words, their reassurances. Everyone thought she had more time. More memories roll in. No one expected her heart to give out, just stop beating in the middle of the day. The futility flattens me. Chemo got to her before cancer did. It was her time.

But what about me? No one asked me what I wanted. I chew on my trembling lip. I missed my chance to say . . . anything. To tell her . . . I don't know what I would have said, but I should have been given the chance to try. I press my palm to my sternum. There's a hole in my heart. I can feel the gaping wound. Bleeding. How do I make it stop?

Shawn. Mom. Mémère. A sob claws to the surface. Why didn't I see the truth?

"Ladies and Gentlemen, this is your captain speaking. We trust you enjoyed your stay in the windy city. We're experiencing a short delay due to a communication issue with the tower, but we'll get it sorted. Hope to be pulling away from the gate soon."

I chuckle. The irony of another communication issue isn't lost on me. Chicago is trying hard to ruin my life. I choke on my cackle. Is the captain in on it as well?

Breathing slowly isn't helping anymore. I bite the inside of my cheek, trying to focus on the pain there instead of the internal injuries inflicted upon my heart. The hole grows, and I don't know how much of the blood-pumping muscle is left. It feels like chunks of it have been torn off. Part of it with Mémère, part of it with Shawn. Never to be seen again.

Sarah, you can do this. You've survived worse.

Have I?

Can I?

I scramble to unwind my earbuds, but my hands are shaking. Lizzo will keep me distracted. The screen of my phone blurs. I wipe my eyes, and my hand comes away wet. No, Sarah. You are not doing this here.

But I am. I can't stop it. A drop hits my boarding pass, smudging my name. Then another. Obliterating the words, the paper.

I cry for what was, what could have been, what I hoped for. It's all lost now.

My phone vibrates in my hand—a reminder I haven't put it on airplane mode. I better get to it before the Wicked-Witch-of-the-West flight attendant turns her wrath on me again. I go to press the button when I see the notification.

An email from the Starlight Foundation. I wipe my face while hiding the screen from the eagle eye of the airline personnel as I open the message.

Congratulations.

My thoughts about leaving LA fly away with one word. The veil of darkness weakens. I read through the rest of the paragraph. I'm on the short list for the screenwriting program, with its cash grand prize and chance to work with industry experts. A breath rattles my sore ribcage. A legitimate opportunity. I double-checked before I sent in my entry. They'd like to interview me this week.

Maybe it wasn't all for nothing. I wipe the wetness on my cheeks. Maybe I've been looking at this wrong. Mémère did do this for a reason. But the reason wasn't Shawn. The reason was me, my future. The blinking lights of the runway speed up through the window. I used the kiss with Shawn as my inspiration for my entry into this program. That's why Mémère did it. I lean my cheek against the headrest. She always encouraged me to follow my dreams to be a writer.

Getting into this program is the break I've been waiting for. I won't waste it, Mémère. I'm not going to let anything get in my way. A small flame of not hope, but excitement maybe, ignites inside me.

The plane takes off. I'm not going to resist fate. She keeps sending me losers, and I've finally got the message. I'm done with men.

Eighteen

Sarah

I tap the ball and it soars over the net straight at the tall, skinny girl with chestnut hair. My skin prickles with dislike. She reminds me of—

Nope. Not going there. Today is my day off. Off work after two weeks of double shifts. Off pinching pennies and stockpiling my tips. Off thinking.

Sun, sand, and sangrias are planned for today. My roomie, whose fair Irish skin burns to a crisp under any amount of sun, had other plans. Siobhan's been *talking* to a trio since we got here and bullied me into giving up my horizontal position of lying on the sand for a vertical one that involves running on it in a game of volleyball.

This attempt at setting me up with one of the guys is so blatant, I'm sure the dude thinks I'm incapable of finding my own dates. Siobhan's eye is on the muscular blond in Hawaiian-print board shorts that match my roomie's hot pink romper and teal hair. They'll look good on Instagram: California beach babes. I wipe the smirk off my face before anyone notices. Siobhan wants me to get back into the game. It's not volleyball she's talking about. She keeps waxing on about our nights full of trolling the bars together as wingwomen and refuses to board the new Sarah train. It's been half a year since I've had a date or even a hook up. Siobhan thinks that's a sin.

But she doesn't get it, doesn't understand the significance of what's happening. With the Starlight Foundation's Future Filmmakers competition, I'm not going to have time to pull more than the minimum workweek The Diamond Club requires, never mind deal with a boyfriend. Or a hookup. I dig my toes in the sand. This is my chance, and I'm determined not to waste it.

I nailed my interview, knew it as soon as I walked out. Not gonna lie, it felt good to have my gut feeling confirmed with the official 'you're in' email. The warmth of Mémère's phantom hand settles on my shoulder. I lift my face to the sky and mouth, "Thank you." My future as a screenwriter in Tinseltown might not be a pipedream after all.

The sun casts long shadows across the hot sand, hinting at the California summer in full swing. The light makes the brunette's tanned skin glimmer like gold as she hits the ball back to our side. I move toward the ball's potential destination, but blond #2—he's taller than Siobhan's crush, and I can't remember either of their names—gets there first, swatting like his life depends on it. I can't help admiring how the muscles on his tall frame ripple with the motion.

It reminds me of *him*. Shawn. His shirt riding up and exposing the little trail on the square of his abs. My cheeks heat. I bat the thought away, but it's not as easy as batting a volleyball. My overactive imagination has been making my life hell. I swear I saw Shawn driving away as I parked at my favorite taco truck yesterday, but it was just an echo of a memory. One I fail to erase. My heart won't let me. Stupid heart. It betrays me at night, sends me dreams about him, reliving our Christmas kiss, creating new fantasies. My lips tingle.

Beach-beauty hits the ball again, this time right at me. Nice try, missy. I don't need to beat her or show off the skills I gained playing volleyball for four years in high school, but I want to. She reminds me why I'm not with Shawn, the cheating liar. I wipe at my mouth with my wrist. I remember Coach Jackson's words and spike the white ball. It sails over the net and scores the winning point.

My teammates hoot, and blond #2 pounds his chest like a caveman, picks me up, and twirls me around. I struggle for him to put him down but pause when I catch the view from up here. I can see across the beach, over the heads of everyone else, right to the boardwalk, where a tall man with honey brown hair is staring at me.

My breath hitches. Is that Shawn?

Blond #2 plops me back onto the soft sand. "Sorry, got carried away." His broad shoulders are blocking my view. I sidestep and look back at the boardwalk. It's teeming with people like ants on a half-eaten apple by a garbage can, but no Shawn. Just my mind playing tricks on me. Again.

Shawn's not here.

He's in Chicago.

With his girlfriend.

"No worries." I offer my hand up top in a congratulatory high five. "Nice game."

"Yeah." He rubs the back of his neck with his hand. "You're good at"—he points to the net—"this."

"Thanks. Played a bit back in the day."

"Shows. Um . . . maybe we could play again sometime?"

Oh, buddy, hate to piss in your cornflakes, but it ain't gonna happen. I give him my signature thanks-but-no-thanks smile that I've perfected over years of being hit on as a bartender. "Pretty busy these days. Speaking of, gotta go check on work."

I walk away, shouting "Ar aghaidh linn" at Siobhan, who's busy talking up blond #1 and his dar-haired friend. It's a Gaelic phrase basically meaning "time to go," and we use it as our "let's bail" signal. Siobhan's been teaching me her native language in exchange for my extremely limited French. To complete our multilingual household, Claudia has been giving us all Spanish lessons. I have to say, hers actually comes in handy here in LA.

Our towels lie on the white sand. I stretch out on my stomach, my back to the volleyball crowd, re-tie the straps of my string bikini, and fish my phone out of my bag. In case blond #2 decides to follow and continue our exchange, I make a show of checking my texts. There's a thread in the Canuck group chat about upcoming Canada Day celebrations. My heart pinches. Part of me feels the nostalgic draw of home. The other part knows I'm where I'm meant to be.

My new life starts tomorrow. Goodbye, Sarah the-girl-who-likes-to-write. Hello, Sarah the screenwriter. I pull up my email and open a new one from the Starlight Foundation. My heart moves into my throat. I absorb its contents, starving for any additional information about our first day.

"Hey, watcha doing?" Siobhan's sweaty skin brushes against mine as she lies beside me.

"Got some info from Starlight."

"What's it say?"

"There's a meet-and-greet tomorrow morning. Plus, they've given us all email addresses. I'm SConnor@starlight.com. And they set up a Discord channel, dividing us into teams. I'm supposed to introduce myself."

"Oh, let me see." Siobhan is addicted to chat room apps.

I tilt my phone her way and click on the link. My familiarity with Discord extends to chatting with a group of writers I met at last year's NaNoWriMo meetup at the library. The Starlight Channel pops up, an image of a star with a trail of stardust hangs in the corner. I draw in a breath of delight as if I'm a Disney princess greeted by a circle of woodland creatures.

"I'm on the blue team." I claim the role by clicking on the indigo heart representing the color.

There are already several messages.

BSato: Guess I'm first here. Excited to meet you all. I'm 18, they/them, and costume design is my jam. Lived in California all my life.

RDehwar: I'm 18, he/him. Cinematography and set design. @BSato where's the best coffee on campus?

BSato: @RDehwar I'll DM you about coffee and some local eats you can't miss.

"How many people are on your team?" asks Siobhan.

"Not sure." I shrug the shoulder she's not hanging over. "Besides me, and the two on the server, I think there's at least a director and a sound person."

Siobhan snatches my phone. "And how are we going to introduce ourselves?"

I take the device back. "It's not a dating app. Plain and simple, just like me." We sit up and I start typing.

SConnor: As your scriptwriter, I feel I should have something witty to say here, but I'll save it for our winning film. I'm 22, she/her, and I've been living in LA for almost two years. @BSato I'd love to get in on those recommendations. Can't wait to get started.

Siobhan reads my words and nods in approval. I echo her and hit send.

I hold the camera up to the rolling ocean and snap a pic, half aquamarine waves that match Siobhan's latest hair color, half white sandy beach. As I upload the photo for my profile pic, three little dots appear beside BSato and then the words "I'm making a list for us" pop up.

Siobhan links her arm in mine and rocks me to her off-key rendition of BTS's *Dynamite*, singing the opening line about stars, and then rests her head on my shoulder. "Promise I'll be your date to the Oscars."

Her enthusiasm is contagious and colors my anticipation of the first day of the competition in sunny hues. I put my arm around my roommate and grin at her. "It's a deal." The weight and stress of the last two years rise and disappear like the champagne bubbles in a flute.

"I hope Timothée Chalamet gets nominated for something that year. I think we'd be good together." Siobhan's hands press over her heart.

"Ah, that's why you want to learn French."

"Oui oui, bien sûr, it can't hurt." Her deep laugh resonates through our linked bodies, and I join her.

"And I thought you were into the tan surfer types," I say.

"Mmmm, need something to hold me over until Timothée falls for me across the red carpet." She winks. "Speaking of, there are a couple of blonds saving us a seat at The Tiki Bar. I told them we'd stop by for a drink."

"You're nothing if not persistent." I roll my eyes. "But I can't afford the distraction."

"I don't know how you live without the 'distraction.'" Siobhan air quotes the last word. "Just one drink. It's your day off. Please." She lifts her head off my shoulder and furrows her pale eyebrows, her blue-green eyes pleading with me to reconsider.

How am I supposed to resist? "Guess I can play your wing-woman for one drink."

"Yes!" My roommate punches the air. "I'm gonna get so distracted tonight."

I'm about to put my phone into my bag when another message chirps. I tap to open.

NStavros: Your director has arrived. Literally. Got off the plane yesterday, checking out the beach right now. I'm 19, he/him. Used to live in LA as a kid. Have a great taco truck I stopped by yesterday to add to the list @BSato

Bet mine's better. I DM BSato with the name and address of the place near Griffith Park. Despite its association with Shawn, I can't resist the delicious food.

"Did you sign up for a babysitting gig? They're all fresh out of high school." Siobhan takes my phone and scrolls up to the top of the thread. "Eighteen, eighteen, nineteen. No partying at the club with these underaged kids. You'll be the team mom."

Two years ago, I was a kid, too, with starry eyes, dreams of instant fame and world domination. So much has happened to me in those years, but I regret none of it. "More like an older sister." I pluck my phone from her hand. "We won't have time to hit any bars. Eyes on the prize. But that's tomorrow. Right now, I'm thirsty. Let's go find some distractions for you and a sangria for me."

With our first round, I forget about the tall liar and his skinny brunette as we toast new beginnings.

PART 3

JULY 4TH

Nineteen

NICK

THE FUTURE I'VE BEEN fighting for is finally here. A fresh start, clean slate.

There are more people on the UCLA campus in July than I imagined: students litter the grass like weeds, soaking up the early morning warmth before the heat spikes. Everyone's in shorts, showing off bare arms, flashing tan midriffs, and running in flip flops. I might regret my long-sleeved shirt later in the day, but I'm still in Chicago mode and haven't adjusted to the new reality yet.

Air conditioning blasts my skin as I enter the arts building, and a heady spike of adrenaline mixed with excitement quickens my pulse. This is happening.

The lecture hall the Starlight Foundation's email directs me to for our orientation session is easy to find. The space is a bright square room. The lectern at the front and stadium-style seats covered in a burnt orange material give the auditorium a retro vibe. I could add a sepia filter and film a scene from the fifties here. Half of the chairs are occupied, and more students file in behind me.

Who in this class is competition? Who's on my team? Some of these people will help me find out if I have what it takes to be a director, a filmmaker—a success.

No one believed my dreams could come true. Yet here I am, determined to prove them wrong.

Mom thought my photography and videography was a hobby, a passing fancy on my way to finding a serious career, something stable and safe. My big bro, Mike, was up in arms at my unreasonable idea to move back to LA and live with our father, who he blames for breaking up our family. Neither of them thought my silly, yes, silly *Schools in Chicago* documentary would catch the interest of the bigwigs in Hollywood. And these are the two people who supposedly love me the most.

What could I expect from my former hockey teammates? They think I'll have fun at the beach and drag my ass back to the Midwest soon enough. The only person who didn't laugh at my dream of becoming a movie director was my Christmas crush, Sarah Côté. She felt so real, much more real than any girl I liked before. The only girl I let see the Nick I am inside. She gave me hope on Valentine's Day, then disappeared. How hard can it be to find someone in LA?

Since arriving two days ago I've been in stalker mode: I went to the taco stand she took me to, the resort club I met her at, even at the local beaches we talked about. I inspect every short blond, and that's a lot of women. Blond seems to be the prevalent hair color in California. I've never noticed so many shades of it before.

At the beach yesterday I was positive I saw her for a moment, in the arms of another man, but the vision was only my mind playing tricks on me. I see her everywhere, yet the illusion always fails, and she's never actually here. The logical option would be to accept defeat, yet my brain can't give in to that logic. My heart won't let me. The three blonds already in the room are nothing like my Sarah: they don't have blue eyes or are the wrong height.

I choose the best place to sit in the lecture hall. Not too close to the front, not in the back with the cool kids. This is serious. A conscious decision.

A blond girl wearing jeans and a white T-shirt with a design on the front that I can't quite make out from this distance runs up the other set of stairs. I watch her stop at the back row. She points to the empty seat beside a girl with thick, white-rimmed sunglasses nestled in her dark curly hair. The blond's the right height: a Thumbelina, as Sarah called herself. Adrenaline surges again. My soul wanting, willing this girl to be her. My heart rate increases, hope pumping through my veins. The blond girl nods and breaks into a smile.

I can't breathe. My vision blurs, but I'd recognize her smile anywhere. I've watched it over and over in the short clip I recorded on our one night together. Sarah.

My eyes strain to confirm what my brain is telling me. I don't dare blink in case she disappears on me again, afraid she's a figment of my imagination. Six months since I've seen her face. Four since she ran away from me in Chicago. My chest pinches with awe. The video from our time together at Christmas is nothing compared to the real thing. To her.

Because this is Sarah. Here. In the last place I expected to see her. In a way, this makes perfect sense: we talked about her screenplay. Why wouldn't she be here? She's brilliant, and her winning a spot in the competition is less of a stretch than me getting in.

She takes the seat, and I start to get up to go sit next to her, but a short man in a mustard button-down flashes the lights on and off, introduces himself as Mr. Takamado, and asks everyone to quiet down.

He talks about the schedule for the day and I try to concentrate. This is important information that I need to know, but my gaze keeps going back to where Sarah sits, her laptop open, typing away. My pulse hammers against my ears. Months of dreaming about her, about being with her again, and she's right there. I still can't get to her. She tucks a strand of hair behind her ear, and I must groan audibly, because the girl next to me shifts her tablet away.

Over the past four months while I lay in bed in Chicago, a million versions of what I'd say to her churned in my head. No matter the words I imagined using, the point was to tell her the truth. Instead of paying attention to the presentation by Mr. Takamado, I'm masterminding how to approach Sarah. In his ninety-minute speech that teaches me what agony means,

Mr. Takamado covers not only the timing of the competition, but the rules, emphasizing the regulations around plagiarism, intellectual property, and using any professionals outside of our team to create our movie.

"We'll spend the last hour in your assigned groups for ice-breakers, and then you're free to mingle afterward or be done for the day." Mr. Takamado switches off the screen.

At last.

I stuff my things into my pack and prepare to run, jump, fly to get to Sarah. The lights go on, but Mr. Takamado is still talking. "At this point, I'd like to introduce our team leads. Can I have all the directors come down to the front?"

What? No, no, no. This can't happen. Sarah still thinks I'm Shawn Rosstav. She doesn't know my real name. I need to explain to her. The hairs on the back of my neck rise. She can't find out like this.

What can I do? Six other people are already making their way to the front of the room. My heart pounds. I try to catch her eye, but she's paying attention to what's happening on the stage.

I throw my backpack over my shoulder and descend the steps, my shoes like concrete around my feet. Mr. Takamado introduces team colors and the corresponding director. I hit the floor as he's presenting the Green Team, and I try again to catch Sarah's attention before he gets to me.

"Ah, and here we have the director for the Blue Team. Would you please introduce yourself?"

For a moment, a blissful moment, I see the vision I've been dreaming of for months. Sarah's brilliant blue eyes widen, and her face breaks into a smile. There's the feeling again, inside my chest, like everything is right in the world.

"Hi." I raise my hand in an almost wave, watching her and only her. I don't want to say it, but the room is waiting. "I'm Nick." Why am I whispering?

"Speak up." A yell comes from the rows in front of me.

I concentrate on Sarah, relying on our connection. "I'm Nick Stavros."

I bask in the glory of her smile for another second, and my heart sputters when her expression crashes. She blinks, her brows fly up, and she breaks our eye contact to glare at her laptop. The light around me dims. This is not how I planned to undo my lie from Christmas Eve.

"Thank you, Nick." Mr. Takamado pats me on the back. "It's a wrap for this part of the day. Ten-minute break begins now. Your rooms are on the Discord 'Things to know' channel. I'll stop by to see how you're doing."

Everyone starts moving. I take two steps at a time to catch Sarah, but she's faster in joining the swarm of other students flowing out the door at the top of the auditorium in search of the right rooms. My palms sweat. I scurry after her and elbow my way through the bodies between us. This isn't happening. I'm not letting her out of my sight this time.

"Sarah, " I shout.

Her head twists then straightens as she speeds up and enters the second door on the left. I jog to it and rush through. The small classroom has six gray plastic student desks arranged in a semi-circle in front of a whiteboard.

Three of them are occupied. A guy my age with a nose piercing, straight black hair hanging over one eye, and the rest of his head hidden under a gray hoodie sprawls at the first desk. His thumbs type away on the screen of his phone. Sarah settles in the middle spot, half-turned to another girl, whose warm skin pops against her hot pink sundress.

"... and B stands for Brigitte. It's with 'g' in the middle, no 'd', two 't's, and an 'e' at the end. Brigitte Sato." They pronounce it with an accent on the second syllable and the practiced mannerisms of someone who's had their name misspelled and mispronounced more than a handful of times. "But I go by Bri."

"Nice to meet you, Bri," says Sarah. "I'm Sarah. Sarah Connor."

Bri's mouth opens, and we say at the same time, "Connor?"

Sarah throws a sharp glance my way and returns to Bri, who follows up with, "Like in the *Terminator* movie?"

Why did Sarah say Connor and not Côté?

"Yup, just like that. Except I'm named after my grandmother, not John Connor's mother. "

"Are you in or out?" A voice behind asks me. "You're blocking the hall."

I stumble in and over to Sarah's desk. My tongue stills. My pre-planned speeches didn't account for an audience of strangers. "Can we talk?" I sound pathetic, even to myself.

"You two know each other?" asks Bri.

"No," says Sarah as I say, "Yes."

"I thought we were here to get away from high school drama." The guy on the other side of Sarah huffs and removes his hoodie.

"Please, Sarah."

"Not now, Nick." Her lips pucker as if she had a shot of vinegar before saying my name, and she addresses Bri. "No drama. I know nothing about Nick Stavros."

A lie. No one knows me like Sarah. Her denial sinks a knife into my heart. I need to fix this. Now. "A minute. Can you give me that?"

"Never fear, your sound editor is here." We pivot to behold the grinning fool standing in the doorway, arms spread wide. His black T-shirt reads, "I may be old, but I got to see all the cool bands," though he can't be older than me. "This is the Blue Team, right? Can someone show me how to use Discord? It's bloody confusing."

We stare at him.

"You're Nick, our great and powerful leader?" He points at me. I glance back at Sarah, but she's purposely not looking anywhere near me. Why does hearing my name around Sarah sting? Like it's a slap. Like I'm hurting her.

"I'm Wil." His palm juts my way.

"Yeah, Nick." I wanted everyone to call me Nick. I dreamed of using this version of my name, instead of the baby Nicky, but now I'd rather be nameless. At least until I get Sarah to stop flinching every time she hears it.

Wil scans the room and when he notices Bri, his eyes widen. "And who are you?"

"Bri, and this is Sarah."

"Ladies, pleasure to meet you." He angles closer to Bri and Sarah. "I like this team already."

There's a pause as we all inspect the guy in the hoodie. Without taking his eyes off his screen he mumbles, "Riyaz."

"Nice to meet you, mate." Wil's British accent makes the simple phrase sound fancy. He drops his bag by the seat next to Riyaz, leaving the last seat on the end for me.

"Shall we get started?" asks Sarah, refusing to meet my eye, drilling holes through my chest instead. I get the hint. Loud and clear. My explanation will have to wait.

Everyone stares at me. "Yeah." I clear my throat. "Let's go."

Twenty

NICK

The icebreaker exercise Mr. Takamado instructed team leaders to do works better than expected. It allows me to get the first feel for my teammates. Riyaz doesn't have any social media accounts, but he shares a website with his portfolio. Bri is huge on Instagram, has their own fashion blog, and is a nonbinary youth advocate. Using "they" when addressing Bri was an effort at first, but by the third round of questions everyone said they or them when talking to or about Bri.

Although Wil is German, he sounds British because he spent every summer in Sussex with his cousins. This is his first time in the US, he's a DJ, and has SoundCloud, YouTube, TikTok, and Instagram accounts as DJStoneHelm. Sarah uses Facebook to keep her family updated, and her Instagram is private, but she accepted our requests to follow. My IG account has four more followers now.

Sarah still won't look me in the eye.

I read off the next prompt. "Have you worked on a movie before?"

They glance at each other, but no one says anything. I don't want to play favorites, so I make an effort not to start with Sarah.

"Wil?" He seems the easiest one to ask to get the ball rolling.

"A short student film as part of my last semester's project." He scans the room like he's most comfortable being the center of attention.

"Bri?"

"Depends on how you count it. I mean, I've styled friends for their YouTube videos, assisted styled that is. Then the wardrobes for our school theater plays were under my direct supervision, plus I led my theater summer camps five summers straight. We mostly made our own costumes there, and my sewing skills got a workout. I can baste, gather, and hem but can't do any of the fancy stitches without a machine. I left mine at home." Are they going to breathe? "I have experience, and me being here should already tell you I'm the crème de la crème."

Sounds like a no to me, but a very long one. "Riyaz?"

"Three."

We watch him, waiting for more details. None are forthcoming.

"Student films like Wil? High school stuff, like Bri?" I ask.

"Interned on three studio films."

That was what, five additional words?

"Sarah?" I expect my voice to break, but I sound normal.

"I came to LA last year to get a screenwriting certificate." Sadness crosses her face. "Since then, I've penned a full screenplay but never worked with a team like this or had my words made into a film."

Her reply is the best. Answered the question and gave a bit of color to her background. She makes so much sense. My chest swells with pride for her. It sounds like Wesley and Holly's story is done. I'd love to read the full version of the screenplay we bonded over. Did the scene in the restaurant I came up with make it into the final? Probably not. I got too excited when she listened, cared about what my imagination conjured for her characters. I search Sarah's profile as she refuses to shift my way, keeping her gaze on anyone but me.

"Nick?" Bri's voice rings in my ears.

Right, my turn.

"Several documentaries." Now my voice shakes, as do my hands. I seem woefully unqualified for this role, and they'll see my inexperience soon. The trembling reaches my knees. I need to make this sound better somehow. "Music videos in high school, and a local commercial." Is this impressive enough?

Wil leans forward. "Can we see the music videos?"

"If you want. I'll post some links on Discord." The team members give encouraging nods, and I continue through the questions.

An hour later we've worked out what everyone's role on the project will be, what are our team and individual schedules, who's living on campus and who's not, and even touched on what they plan to do after the competition. Everyone has school except Sarah. The others were impressed when she mentioned working at The Diamond Club, but I was confused. I tried to find her at the swanky resort. Twice. Maybe she's no longer a bartender? Maybe there's another location?

Sarah glances at her watch and makes a face. I check my phone.

"Let's call it a day." We went fifteen minutes over the scheduled length of this session. "Meet back here tomorrow at 10:00 a.m. and we can start brainstorming ideas."

Mr. Takamado pops his head in. "How's it going in here?" He steps into the room and studies me. "Everything under control?"

Most definitely not. Bri likes to make her opinion known, Riyaz is a mystery, Wil's cracking wiseass jokes like we're at a club, and Sarah is addressing everyone but me. "Yep. We're all set. Got a great team."

"Good. Already had one person ask for a transfer. Creative differences. They didn't even try." He chuckles. "This classroom is reserved for you on Mondays and Tuesdays. You can book other spaces like the editing room as you need them."

"Is there a sound studio?" Wil asked this twice in the last hour.

"Sure. Over at the music school. Tell the front desk you're with the Starlight Foundation and they'll find you one to use."

Wil beams like he hit the jackpot.

"On Wednesdays you'll meet outside of your teams with your fellow directors, set designers, costume designers, sound engineers, and script writers." Mr. Takamado turns to me. "Did I hear you're done for the day?"

I nod.

"I need to talk to you before you leave."

The room fills with rustling noises as the group packs up. Mr. Takamado stops in front of my desk. "Here are the papers you need to fill out. You can submit the hard copy, but we prefer everything online. I've printed out the timeline for when we expect different parts of the project to be completed." He leans back on one of the desks and crosses his arms. "Your budget is there, and you're not allowed to pay anyone from your personal funds. You'll have to submit every receipt. The point of this exercise is to be creative. Scrappy. Think strategically."

"Can people volunteer to help us?" I ask.

"Within limits. And no professionals. If in doubt, you probably should not be doing it." Mr. Takamado gives me a plastic card with my legal name, Nicholas Stavros, in capital letters. "You're by default the treasurer of your team, but you can delegate the role if there's a better candidate."

I take the papers and the credit card. "Anything else?"

"There'll be more emails. Keep on top of them. You'll need to provide weekly status reports, including the financials. Like the others, you'll have meetings with your fellow directors, but there will be more." He holds up a finger. "We'll need to meet at least bi-weekly." Another finger. "Plus, there are sessions with the judges to pitch your story, etc." The third finger shoots up, and my head swims with details. This is far more complicated than I imagined. "Lastly, you'll have to show dailies to the review committee." The fingers stop flying, but he's not done. "Make sure your team attends their sessions as well. Got it?"

I don't, but I nod anyhow.

"My email and phone number are on the business card inside the packet. There's also a team lead on Discord for FAQs. Reach out. Don't wait until you're in a bigger mess than you can handle." He heads to the door. "Break a leg," he shouts at me over his shoulder.

"Thanks." I scan the papers in front of me. The rules and regulations are at the top of a large stack. So many forms. My eyes glaze over. This is going to be the worst part about the competition. I'm not good at this paperwork shit. Mom always took care of everything: my hockey forms, doctor's appointments, college application. If Mom didn't like being a hair stylist so much, she would've made a great project manager. She has a knack for keeping everything organized, and I didn't inherit the skill.

I glance up. Wil's in the doorway talking to a guy who's not part of our team. Bri's snapping selfies against the banner with the image of a star—the trophy the winners get at the end of the competition—and Starlight Future Filmmakers in gold letters. Riyaz continues typing on his phone.

Wait . . . where is Sarah? My heart sinks. Her seat is empty. I scan the room. Nothing. My skin prickles at the lack of her. I shove the tome of papers into my backpack and jet.

"Let me through." I squeeze past Wil and his friend.

"Hey," my teammate shouts at me, but I don't care. I run down the hallway to the exit, swiveling my head around, pausing on anyone who looks remotely like her. But none of them do. I swallow the rising panic. The parking lot attached to the building is the next place I search. A vintage blue Beamer Sarah named Betty sits two rows in. I recognize the hood Sarah and I sat on at Griffith Observatory, then Sarah's sunlit head behind the wheel.

Chasing a car to catch Sarah isn't new. I burst into a sprint, my backpack bouncing on my back, and I'm at the trunk in seconds. A wasted effort since the car hasn't moved. She's just sitting in the driver's seat. I crunch the polyester strap of my backpack in my palm. My tap on her window makes her jump. I half expect her to start the ignition and drive away, but instead she opens the door and gets out.

"Sarah—"

She holds up a hand. "Don't start. I gotta get to work."

"I only need five minutes."

She blinks at me and walks toward the road.

I follow. "Where are you going?"

"Some of us have to work for a living." She stops at the curb. The cars whizzing by create a kaleidoscope of red, black, silver, and white. Her stillness is prominent against the frenzy behind her, and I want to capture the scene on film. The wind ripples her long hair as she studies her phone. Warmth blankets my chest. I'm reminded of that night, the video I've watched a million times, and I want to tuck a tendril behind her ear.

But I don't. I point back to where her Beamer sits instead. "What about your car?"

"Won't start."

"What's wrong with it?"

The eyes I've dreamed about for so many nights meet mine for the first time. A different kind of fire burns behind them. "Was anything from that night real?"

My ribs hurt as if I got slammed into a goalpost. How can she ask such a question? She has to know, has to have felt what I did on Christmas Eve. What I have ever since. My chest contracts. "I didn't mean to lie, Sarah. Please."

Her mouth presses into a hard, thin line at my last word.

I change tactics. "Our night together was special."

I lose her gaze, eyes falling back to the phone. How do I fix this? I inch closer.

"I'd never used the ID before. I didn't expect to meet you. I wanted to tell you, give you my real name, but there wasn't enough time."

A black Toyota pulls up beside her. "There never is." She opens the car door, slips into the back seat, and the sedan drives her away.

Twenty-One

Sarah

I TEXT SIOBHAN AS I sprint out the staff-only exit of the Diamond Club.

Me: Borrowed your shirt. Might need to borrow money. Betty needs a tow.

I shove the phone into my back pocket and yank the knot I tied on the white shirt with the double diamond logo of the Club. The top fits my roommate but is a size too big on me. The V-neck slips lower as I round the bar. I tug the material up.

"Dude." Ryan circles his finger in the direction of my torso, which is currently showing more skin than a Kardashian at an awards show. "I know it's gonna be slow tonight, but there has to be a better way to rake in the tips."

"It's Siobhan's. Housekeeping lost mine." I clench my teeth. Can this day get any worse? "I'm going for natural air conditioning. Need it in this heat."

"Problems you won't have to worry about after winning this competition thingy and becoming a famous screenwriter living in your private Malibu mansion." His eyes narrow at the grimace I make at his words. "Oh no. Don't give me the face. What happened?"

"He was there. But it wasn't him. Well, it was but it's not his name. Everything was a lie." The word vomit starts, and I can't stop. "He's three years younger than me. Not old enough to drink. How could I not get it? Is there something wrong with me? He's a baby—"

"Whoa, whoa," Ryan says. "Who's he?"

"Nick."

Ryan scrunches up his nose. "Who's Nick?"

"Shawn."

The wrinkles relax, and understanding spreads across his face. "Let me get this straight. Shawn Rostov is Nick?"

I squirm. "Nick Stavros."

"And he's part of the Starlight program as well?" Ryan has this uncanny ability to understand my ramblings, even when I don't understand them myself.

"Worse. He's the director of the film, leader of my team." I cross my arms as if I can shield myself from the reality. My cheeks heat. "I have to work with him for the next three months."

Ryan lets out a low whistle. "Ouch." He throws an arm around my shoulders and squeezes. "Makes sense now. Why we couldn't find him."

I lean into my friend, needing the side hug more than I want to admit.

"What did Shawn, I mean, Nick, say?"

I roll my eyes. "Soon as he recognized me, he tried to backpedal. Probably thought I'd be a problem, and he could fix the situation with a generic apology."

"Hmmm." Ryan rubs his chin on the top of my head and murmurs in my hair. "He remembered you, huh?"

I ease out of his arms. "As the sucker who let him drink at a bar with his fake ID." My shoulders tighten at the memory.

Ryan picks up his tablet and starts today's inventory. "What are you gonna do?"

What am I going to do? I press my palms against my eyelids. "I don't know."

"Well, when you do, let me in on the plan. I'm ride or die." I can count on Ryan. Strangely he's one of the most reliable people in my life. Not like . . .

Nope, keep busy, Sarah. Don't think about this morning.

I grab the cart of freshly washed glasses and stack them behind the bar as I take in the two customers lounging about. The woman is a regular I've seen at the resort this week. The older gentleman in a suit that's weird for the outside bar in this humidity, I don't recognize.

"We're low on the Aviation American Gin. I'll get some." Ryan disappears to the stock room. I bet he'll be on his phone gathering intel on Nick. He loves a good puzzle. Ryan and I spent countless hours scouring the internet for Shawn Rostov and found nothing. Now we understand why.

Another customer enters the patio. Tall. Beach blond hair. Bottle-green eyes. "Sam." I come around the bar and right into his open arms. Sam was my partner-in-crime at the bar last summer. I take in his warmth and hold on to him a little longer than I should. As usual, he seems to sense what I need and squeezes me back. "What are you doing here?"

"Ali had some family stuff." Ali to him and Ms. Stinson to me. Soon to be Mrs. Samuel Harrington. "Heard from the boss you were in today." He takes a seat at the bar as I grab a glass and pour him a beer. "How's the competition going?"

"Today was the first day. Met my team, and now I get to make a movie."

"Awesome. You're going to do great." Sam's always supportive. Everyone at the resort was surprised last year when he revealed he was hiding his identity: the son of some rich tycoon in New York. Bet Shawn's not . . . shit, it's Nick, not Shawn. I bite my lip.

"A question?" I pick up a towel and wipe down the bar.

Sam sets down his beer. "Sure."

"When you first came here, you lied about your name. Why?"

Sam steeples his fingers. He's been here five minutes, and I'm grilling him. I open my mouth to apologize.

"Well, the Harrington name came with certain expectations." He beats me to it. "I . . . I wanted people to see me, the real me, without all the baggage of my past. A fresh start."

Sounds fair, but I need more. "Did you feel bad lying to your friends?"

"Still do." He dips his head down to catch my eye. "I wanted to tell some people, wanted to tell Ali most of all, especially when I knew I was falling for her, but it got harder and harder. I didn't want to disappoint them."

I shiver at the thought. It would suck to be caught in a lie, especially if you had a decent reason for the deception.

"I'm sorry if I hurt you," Sam says.

"Hurt her how?" A gruff voice cuts through the air. What's he doing here? My heart sends dashes and dots to my brain, but Nick's face is a mask of something I don't recognize. Different from this morning when he appeared as if he had a broken limb. Is this anger? Pointed at Sam?

"Why are you here?" I ask. His brown eyes meet mine, and I can't take the stare. The heat travels from my cheeks to my neck. I glance away and focus on wiping down the counter I've already wiped down. "I can't serve you."

"I understand." Shawn, no, Nick rubs his chin before his fingers drop. "Can . . . I . . . Please, give me a chance to explain."

"Everything okay, Sarah?" Sam stands and creates a barrier between us.

"Yup. Sam, this is Shawn. Or is it Nick this afternoon? I get confused." I can't keep the bitterness out of my voice. Not that I want to. He shouldn't be here.

Sam holds out a hand. "I'm Sam. Used to work with Sarah."

I can feel Nick's eyes on me, but I ignore him. "I'm Nick."

"Today," spills from me.

Nick plops onto a barstool, his shoulders slumped, long arms loose on the bar, his stupid honey-brown hair flopping over his eyes. "Sarah, please."

"I'm sensing there's a story here." Sam always did play peacemaker.

"Nope. Just another LA liar." I spin away from both men and sort wine bottles leftover from the lunch crowd. My chest is on fire. I can't look at him. I just can't.

"I'm sorry," says Nick. I can't stop my ears from listening to his words. Hearing the pain in them. "But not about what happened. Using the ID is the reason I met you. And I'll never be sorry for that."

Twenty-Two

Sarah

IF ONLY I COULD believe those words. Hot coals churn in my gut. I want to. Months spent searching for him, then more trying to forget him. Both unsuccessful. I swore off men. No one compared to the perfect memory of what it felt like being attracted to a person not only on a physical level, but emotionally and mentally. I press my hand to my stomach. I crave the connection we had, because nothing triggers my heart into a frenzy of longing, security, and excitement at the same time as he did.

Last night Siobhan had us partying at a bar with two guys we met at the beach. One of them was sweet as pie and offered to do anything I wanted. Old Sarah would've taken him up on his offer, but I couldn't. The illusion of Shawn haunted me like the ghost of Christmas past.

"Hello, Sarah." Sam's fiancée is smashing in head-to-toe white, not a crease or smudge on the silk of her dress.

"Ms. Stinson." I tug on my borrowed top, covering wine stains that don't exist. "Nice to see you again." I was shocked but happy when these two got together. Somehow, they make sense. "Can I get you anything?"

"Thanks, but I'll pass. I'm going to steal Sam away, if that's all right with you."

I nod. "He's all yours."

"Keep posting your updates. I can't wait to see what you do next." Sam's belief in me reminds me why he's such a good friend. Before he leaves, Sam addresses Nick. "Don't give up. She's worth it."

"I agree," Nick says.

Goosebumps spread across my skin. The notion Nick would fight for me despite the obvious leave-me-alone vibes I'm sending make him either a sappy romantic or a barbaric stalker. I'm hoping for the former. A smile tugs on my lips. Wait, is that what I want? I'm not in the right mental state to answer the question. I need space.

I round the bar and head for the guy in the suit. "Afternoon."

The suit takes his time to rake his eyes over my breasts, and I bite the inside of my cheek to not clock him with my tray. They get to stare—one of the downsides of the job.

"'Bout time." His condescending tone matches his leer. I tug the hem of Siobhan's shirt. I've just about had enough of this shit. I have to win the Starlight competition and get out of this life. "A glass of the house red."

To delay my return to the bar and *him*, I check on the other customer nursing an iced tea. No refill needed. Back at the bar Ryan and Nick are talking.

". . . staying with my father for now," I hear Nick say. "But I want to get my own place before the fall semester starts."

So, Shawn/Nick has enough money to afford to live on his own. Must be nice. I have two roommates and we barely manage to make rent each month. My blood boils.

My hand wobbles a little as I pour the red wine, and a few drops dribble down the side of the glass. I rub my forehead, find a new glass, and start again. There's no way this guy isn't going to complain if his glass is sticky. I roll my eyes. I recognize his type—expensive jerk on the outside, cheap bastard on the inside. The instructor at the screenwriting retreat I got suckered into when I first came to LA was the same. This town is full of them.

I'd normally take one of the bowls of pretzels we keep at the bar over with the wine but can't find the heart to care today. With the glass centered on the tray, I pretend I don't see Nick and Ryan and head back to my waiting customer, the Suit.

He ignores my presence and flips through his phone. I lift the glass off the tray like I've done a million times, but this once the drink slips from my grip, plops onto the table, and the red wine sloshes over the side.

"Watch it, you stupid bitch." The Suit bolts out of his seat to avoid the river of red running toward him. My body jolts. I pull a towel from my apron and mop up the spill, an apology on my lips. The customers are always right. Even if they're jackasses.

"Don't speak to her that way."

I turn to see Nick blocking out the sun, towering over the Suit. This is not happening. Like today isn't bad enough.

My customer yanks the lapels of his jacket, puffs out his torso. "Who the hell are you?"

"I'm the guy who's going to teach you some manners." Nick inches closer to the Suit, lips pressed together, face rigid, his normally melted-chocolate eyes dark and turbulent. It's the expression he gave Sam, only worse.

Fear breaches my long-established defenses. My heart jumps to my throat. I've ejected many an angry or drunk customer out of my bar over the years, but Nick is bigger than most. I might need Ryan's help here.

I place a hand on the center of Nick's chest. His heart slams against my palm under the fine cotton of his shirt. The anger is like a prickly crust around him. Nick's eyes transform into pools of lava when they meet mine. The mask of rage washes away, replaced by the man I know as his shoulders fall and his stance slackens.

"Sarah?" My name reverberates through his chest against my palm. He raises a hand and places it over mine. His skin is hot and damp, and my body reacts to his touch. The fear leeches away, replaced by a sense of calm—no, rightness. His tender gaze sees me, and the bar fades: it's just the two of us, breathing in sync.

In and out.

The thump, thump, thump of our hearts beating as one.

"Your boyfriend needs to keep his mouth shut. A cute ass isn't going to make up for his insults." Asshole Suit kicks his chair, and the bubble bursts. The splashes from the pool nearby, a horn honking—the noises of the resort rush back in. I blink to clear my mind. Reality returns. The reality where Nick needs to leave before this situation goes even further south.

I wrench my fingers from his grip. "You need to go."

"He can't talk to you like that." Now there's caring in Nick's voice, and I relax. Whatever erupted a moment ago inside Nick has passed, and isn't coming back, I hope.

"Customer's always right." The customer service motto tastes like bile on my lips. Over Nick's shoulder I see Ryan walking toward us. Bless him. "Get Nick out of here."

"Sarah." Nick's plea grates against my skin. I give him my back and focus on the Suit who I catch studying Nick and me, smirking. Shit. I need to fix this before he asks for the manager.

"Sorry, sir." It's the wrong way around: he should be apologizing to me. "Let me replace this. Would you like something else? On the house?"

Jackpot. His eyes light up at the offer.

Ryan says something to Nick, but I don't hear the words. The sun comes out again as Nick steps away from me, the air warms.

"I'll have Johnny Walker Blue. Bring the bottle." This guy is such a prick. I'll have to buy the bottle and not let my boss, Mrs.

Marino, find out. I give the Suit my fakest smile and hightail back to the bar.

Damnit Shawn—no, Nick. My fingers dig into the tray. Damn him for putting me in this situation. I slam the cheap plastic onto the bar. Damn him for making me feel. I focus on my breathing, trying to get the fury in my body to quiet. With a tall square bottle full of amber liquid and a tumbler glass containing a large round ball of ice on my tray, I put on my game face and deliver the goods to my least favorite customer. He grins like the Cheshire Cat, and I swallow my pride. Even if I have to work side by side with Nick, I'll win this competition.

Twenty-Three

NICK

"Dude, trust me." The laid-back bartender grins at me.

I don't know this "dude," but he better get his hand off my arm before he loses it.

"Push Sarah now, and you'll never kiss her again."

How the fuck is this guy aware of our kiss? I tear my eyes from Sarah apologizing to the creep and meet my chaperone's stare. His sharp blue eyes remind me of Sarah's. The surfer vibes I got from him at the bar are gone, replaced by a serious face, lips pressed, jaw set. I glance over at Sarah, whose back is to me. On purpose, I'm sure.

If Sarah told this Ryan guy about our kiss, he might be important to her, like the blond at the bar who apologized for hurting Sarah. I take a deep breath. If I have any hopes of getting her back, I can't piss off her friends. I raise my hands in defeat and let Ryan lead me out of the bar area.

We pass a manicured hedge, head down a path, and into the parking lot with rows upon rows of high-end cars. He pats me on the back. "Good boy."

Not a dog. My muscles tense. I pry his grasp off. "The kiss. How?"

"Dude." He keeps walking, studying the loafers he's wearing without socks. "The bar gets slow. We talk. Sarah talked a lot about you."

"She did?" Sarah spoke about me. A bubble of hope forms behind my breastbone. She didn't forget, didn't think our evening together was inconsequential.

"Constantly. We spent hours googling your name. The fake name, that is. Then some church choir or something you filmed?"

"The a cappella group." More hope bubbles up. I wish she were the one telling me about the hunt for Shawn. She truly listened, remembered.

"Sure." Ryan rubs his tan forehead. "Then she came back from her grandmother's funeral." He tugs on the medallion that hangs over his T-shirt. "And the fun stopped."

"Her grandmother died?" I stumble and stop. Ryan does too. "When?"

"Yeah, back in February." Ryan follows my gaze, and both of us stare at the entrance to the club.

"Must have been such a blow." The only time I saw my dad cry was when my grandfather died. My dad never displays emotion. I was too young to understand, but the memory stuck with me. I swallow and glance back at the bar, battling the urge to march back in and hold Sarah.

"When she came back, she was a mess," says Ryan. "I thought her sorrow was solely about the funeral. Thought resuming our hunt for you would cheer her up. Quite the opposite. She got all pissy. Said she already found you. And your girlfriend."

My fake ID. Her knocking on Mackenzie's door. My vision narrows. Sarah's been living with this assumption? "No, that's wrong."

"What?" Ryan's eyebrows knit.

"The girl she saw, she wasn't my girlfriend." I shake my head. "I mean, we went out, but we broke up months before I met Sarah. I worked for her dad."

"Hmmm, that's good."

"Good?"

"Listen." Ryan twists one of the thick silver rings on his fingers. "I've seen her burn through a string of, um, guys in the last year. Not once did she light up as much as she did after your little Christmas canoodle." He shifts to another ring. "Couldn't get her out of that jacket of yours either."

The bubbles fill my body. Sarah still has my jacket. Does she keep it close, like I do with her hat? I slept with the thing. Held on to the knitted beanie instead of her. The heat of irrational optimism burns in my chest, the pain of losing her replaced with faith. We're not done. Not yet.

"After Valentine's Day"—Ryan stops playing with his rings—"the light and the jacket were gone."

The fire in my heart sputters. I grab Ryan's shoulder, like he can rewind and say other words, ones that don't take my hope away.

"Don't panic, yet." He pats my back, and this time I let him. "Way I see it—you still have a shot."

I shove my fist in front of my mouth and bite on the skin to drown the advancing pain, covering up the belief that I have a chance to win Sarah back.

"You've got two things going for you." Ryan lifts one finger up. "One, she hasn't dated in months. Like not one flirt."

"Really?" The despair and hope inside me stare at each other like I'm staring at Ryan.

"And our girl is a flirt."

"Cut the crap." He may be helping me here, but he can't talk about my girl like that.

"Sorry." Ryan raises both hands in the air above his head. "Facts are facts."

"Don't care. Not interested in her past, only her future." I take a step closer to him. "What's the second thing?"

"Huh?"

"You said I have two things going for me."

"Oh, right." His face breaks into a grin, like he's a kid with a secret. "The jacket."

"What about it?"

Ryan leans in. "She still wears the thing sometimes." His voice is low, and his head moves with exaggerated slowness, eyes wide.

I mimic him. I get it. "The jacket." If she'd given up on me, she wouldn't wear anything of mine. She'd burn my coat.

"So, you see, you've got a chance. But you can't push." Ryan wags his finger in front of my face. "Never push, dude. Give her space."

After six months apart, space is the last thing I want to give Sarah. My fingers flex. My sole wish is to hold her close, see her every day, every hour, every second, kiss her, tell her how much I miss her. Space sounds like torture. Some cruel punishment for my crimes. For the lies. Space will be my equivalent of the prayer of forgiveness.

"Space, huh." I touch the spot on my chest where I can still feel the imprint of Sarah's fingers.

"My advice, dude." Ryan resumes patting my back. Every hit, a nail in the coffin of my dream of going back to Sarah this second.

Space. If space is what she needs, I can give her space. I'd give her anything.

"Okay, then. Space it is." I point to her car. "A favor?"

"Don't ask me to talk to her on your beha—"

"No, I'd rather you not talk to Sarah about our . . . chat. Could you tell her I brought Betty here?" The distance between us and the car is the same as between us and the entrance to the bar.

"Her car?" Ryan's face twists. "What's the story?"

"No story. Betty's battery was dead, but I jumped it. Gave the car a good run so it should be charged. Might need a new one though."

"Keys?" Ryan takes his hand off my back and turns his palm up, expecting me to produce the keys I do not have.

I wrinkle my forehead. "No keys." My tongue is heavy as I imagine what Sarah will think of how I got her car here.

Ryan eyes the car then me. "No story, you say. And no keys. Which is the lie?"

Twenty-Four

NICK

LIES. I CAN'T SEEM to live without them. They come out like second nature. I promised to stop. I will stop. For Sarah. With Ryan. "Skills learned on the streets of Chicago. Let's just say Betty isn't the first car I had to hot-wire."

"Are you some kind of criminal?" Ryan's eyes narrow.

"No." Crap, that's almost a lie. "Got caught once but the charges were dropped. My record is clean." Not lying is harder than I imagined. Ryan sizes me up, and no matter how much I want for this conversation to be over, it's not. No lying means no omissions either. "I got in some trouble in middle school. Got hauled into the precinct a couple of times. Stupid stuff. It's all in the past."

"In the past, yet you hot-wired the car of a girl who told you to fuck off. Like that's not giving me any creepy vibes." Ryan crosses his arms. He's not as tall as me, but he's got muscles.

From surfing or tending bar, I'm not sure. Any friendliness I sensed from him evaporates.

"It's not like that. She needs her car. I took a chance that the problem might be something simple like her battery, and I was right. I wanted to help."

Ryan taps his shoe on the pavement. "Could've called a tow. Paid for a mechanic to deal with it."

"Who has money for that?" I mimic Ryan again and cross my arms. "I saw a way to help her. I had to try. I was only thinking of her."

"Sure." He doesn't sound convinced.

"I don't hot-wire cars anymore, but it's not something you forget, even though it's been a while." I rub the back of my neck. "Convertibles are easy to get into, and Beamers even easier to hot-wire. Not like I damaged anything. Her console doesn't show a trace I was there."

"Except when I tell her. No more lies, right?"

"Yeah." I meet Ryan's gaze. "From this moment on. I promise."

"Thanks, but it's her"—he points with his head in the direction of the bar—"you need to make the promise to."

"I will, if she ever talks to me again."

"She's not gonna like you messing with Betty." He inspects the BMW. "Car's her baby."

"I'll go tell her everything right now." I start walking backward.

"Whoa, whoa." Ryan catches my shoulder. "Let me break the good news. Space, remember?"

"Right." I crane my neck at the path leading back to Sarah. "You'll watch out for her?"

"Sarah may look helpless, but she is far from a lost little girl. The woman can handle herself. I've seen her take down men twice her size." I open my mouth to protest and complain about the creep, but Ryan holds up his palms to stop me. "She's my friend. I've got her back. Always." His expression is hard, determined. I get the message. He's being nice to me, but if I cross the line, it's her side he'll be on. Her he'll protect.

I let out a puff of air and extend my hand. "Thanks."

Ryan takes my offering, and his body transforms, softening into the stoner surfer dude persona from before. "Hey man, been there, lost the prize."

My jaw drops. "You and . . ." I don't want to complete the sentence. My heart skydives. I was beginning to like him.

He runs his fingers through too-long sun-bleached hair. "Ancient history. I screwed up, but she let me back in as a friend." It's his turn to contemplate the bar. "We work better this way."

Ryan leaves me with a final pat on the back. He needs to lay off this patting thing. Tension freezes my spine.

I walk over into the shade of one of the palm trees lining the entrance to The Diamond Club. I love the heat of LA, but with the furnace still burning behind my breastbone, I appreciate the couple-degree temperature drop.

I check for any messages or calls from Dad. He grumbled about the change of location when I asked him to pick me up from here instead of the UCLA campus building the Starlight Foundation is using to run classes for the competition.

Me: ETA?

The phone rings with Dad's name on display. "How far are you?"

His voice echoes, meaning he's in the car. "I'm parking."

I search for his silver Toyota. "Where?"

"Diamond Club VIP parking lot."

There's a VIP parking lot? I step back and find a sign. Sure enough, there's one for a VIP lot. I walk around and enter the cordoned area, where the high-end vehicles are, including a ruby red McLaren Spyder. And my dad's Toyota. I open the door and wedge myself into the front seat.

"What were you doing here?" He backs out of the spot before I lock my seatbelt into place.

"Helping a friend."

"Don't use my tab here. I'm not going to sponsor you. You freeloading at my place is already a strain on my budget." His crisp white shirt with silver film reel cufflinks and a day-old haircut don't scream struggling artist to me.

"You were renting the couch to someone else before?" The heat must be getting to me. I shouldn't wisecrack.

"Funny guy. The electricity, the water, the food. It adds up." The car jerks as we roll over a speed bump. "Planning on reimbursing me for any of those items?"

"I thought you said you'd wait until I found a job." I chew on the inside of my cheek. Starlight pays for the international students' rooms on campus and offers us all a small stipend, but not enough to live on.

"I did. But it's been three days." Dad adjusts his wire-frame sunglasses. "I need two hundred a week from you. Or a hundred and you don't eat any of my stuff."

"Didn't realize cheerios and frozen pizza cost so much."

"You should go grocery shopping around here."

I study the palm trees whizzing by. "A hundred and I get my own food."

"Starting next week. Figure it out. McDonalds around the corner is always hiring."

"Next week. A hundred. Got it." I slam my teeth together. Thanks, Dad, for taking care of me. Father of the Year Award, coming up.

"Nick."

"Yes, Dad."

"No more rides either. There's rideshare. Taxi. The bus. Or get your own car."

The seatbelt creaks under the stress of my grip. My own car was the plan, but with pneumonia after my race in the snow without a coat on Valentine's Day, I didn't get anywhere near the number of extra shifts at the camera shop or side gigs as I planned. I'm still a thousand short from even the cheapest clunker on the lot. Before I left, Dad made all these promises if I abandoned Chicago and came to LA. Less than a week of living with him, and his story keeps changing. No longer a free stay, no more promises to show me around the city, no more dinners out at the fancy restaurants he took Mom and me to during Christmas.

Dull, industrial concrete of the highway replaces the greenery. I wanna love the man. But.

Maybe Mom is right. Maybe this is his way to make sure I learn to take care of myself, but Dad's push for me to be independent feels more like shoves out of his apartment. His verbal jabs hurt more than a body check by the opposition's defense. Not having a son for ten years and then having a nineteen-year-old version living with him in a one-bedroom East LA apartment might be too much for Daddy-o.

Still, he tries. I let go of the seat belt and lean on the headrest. Dad's the only one who didn't laugh at my career choice. Following in his footsteps. Entering the movie business. I'll make him proud. I'll make them all proud when we win the Starlight competition.

Twenty-Five

Sarah

It's ages until Ryan returns, strolling back into the bar as if he doesn't have a care in the world. How does he do that? I'm sweating, literally, and he's cool as a cucumber. "Is he gone?"

Ryan leans against the side of the bar and puts his hands on his hips. "I've got good news and bad news."

"Give me the good."

"Betty might only need a new battery."

"What?" My breath catches. I didn't get to the part about my baby dying on me in the Starlight parking lot. "How do you—"

"Your new man, he's quite, well, let's say, ingenious. Hot-wired Betty and drove the car here to charge the battery."

I make for the parking lot. "If he hurt her, I'll chop his balls off." Or sear them off with how hot my fingers are. The Beamer is the only thing I have left of Mémère after losing her hat in Chicago.

Ryan grabs me by the elbow and stops my charge. "Tsk, tsk. Such language from a lady." I swat at his hold on me. "Your car is fine. Couldn't even tell Nick was in there."

The pounding in my ears recedes. "I don't understand."

"Not sure I do." Ryan lets go of me. "Yet."

I kick his shin. "You promise she's okay?"

Ryan holds his knuckles over his breastbone. "Cross my heart. Would I lie to you?"

I groan.

Ryan grins. "Too early?"

"Way." I catch a glimpse of the Suit, who's yammering away on his phone, and focus on Ryan. "And the bad news?"

Ryan breaks out his full-on one-hundred-watt smile. "I like him."

My fear that Betty won't start at the end of my shift doesn't materialize. She purrs her usual calming sound. The flashlight I carry on my keychain, thanks to Dad's insistence, reveals no scratches or damage on her console. Nick/Shawn is mistaken if he thinks hot-wiring my car can restore my trust.

I walk through the dark living room. The hairs on my skin hurt. No light comes from under any doors down the hall where my roommates probably went to bed hours ago. Claudia's shift at the TV station begins at five. Siobhan started a new class last week and gets up at a decent time for once. My feet are heavy, but I watch my step, trying not to disturb them.

Ready to fall onto the couch, I blink as sleep calls to me. Lead fills my eyelids. However, not showering off this long day that covered me in wine, sweat, pool water, and the stares of one too many creeps is not an option. The hot water and my favorite strawberry body wash help with the outside but do nothing to wash away the angry thoughts circling in my head.

I wrap a towel around my hair and put on Siobhan's soft kimono-style robe with bright peacock feathers splattered in gold. Not my style, but it's comforting to wrap the smooth material around me in lieu of her hug. I need a hug and a voice not inside my head to tell me I'm not irrational. What Nick did is not okay. Not something people do. The weight of the day remains on my shoulders. I sink into the sofa, tuck my feet under me, and put my churning thoughts into words. The only way to scrub my mind clean of them.

Me: You stole my car?

It's 11:45pm, and I'm certain he'll be asleep in his comfy bed and won't see my message over Discord.

NStavros: Think of it as valet service.

Never used one. His answer is cute though. I wipe the miniature smile off my face. It's arrogant, not cute. Nick is not cute.

NStavros: You needed Betty. How else would you have gotten home?

The beat in my temples accelerates. He remembered her name. No. I tighten my lips. Can't be. Ryan must've told him. How dare he pretend he fixed my car out of the goodness of his heart and not a scheme to make me swoon over his gestures? I'm not some damsel in distress, needing a prince to save the day, thank you very much. My back straighter, I shift upright on the couch.

Of course, he's trying to suck up so I don't cause a disturbance in the force and lose the competition we both need to win. My huff rolls through the quiet apartment. I need honesty, not pretense. Liars who say they have my best interests at heart but are really using me as their stepping stone so they can get ahead don't get my time. I did that once. I paid a lot of money for my mistake. No one else gets to bamboozle me with pretend concern. The towel holding my wet hair slips, and I throw the damp cloth on the floor.

Me: I can take care of myself.

Several seconds pass as I stare at the moving green dots under his name. I tap my nails against my teeth. Is he writing an essay? What does he think he can say to make this better?

NStavros: I'm sorry.

Well, shit, what am I supposed to do now? My anger ebbs and then flows again. I don't hear his voice or see his face, but the two words on the screen have a sincerity to them I can almost taste. The ragged edge of my cuticle is rough against my tongue. He didn't make excuses. Just a simple apology. It's ridiculous. I'm not supposed to read more into them than they mean. He was wrong. I tear the annoying piece of skin. Hot-wiring my car was wrong.

NStavros: Can we talk?

No. I twist my hair into a knot. If the words on the screen are swaying me, his voice will do real damage. A yawn reminds me of the time, and I lie on my side, holding the phone. The brightness from the screen is the only source of light. Talking is out of the question.

If I have to be on the team with him, I'll deal. The competition is what matters here. I must break into the industry, leave the resort and the greasy stares peppered with ass slaps. The wail of a car alarm outside yanks me out of my self-pity. Nick's my team lead. I don't need to talk to him at this hour of the night. Teammates. This is what we are. This teammate needs to sleep.

Me: It's midnight. Everyone's asleep. I should be too.

NStavros: OK

That was easy. My grasp on my phone relaxes. Not sure I could've said no if he insisted.

NStavros: Tomorrow? Before class? I'll buy breakfast.

Here it is. My breath hastens. I can't say no. But I can stall.

Me: Busy before class

NStavros: After?

Me: Fine.

NStavros: Sweet dreams.

His words seem genuine. No. I shake my head. Words on the screen of an app cannot look like anything more than words.

I set the alarm for six hours from now. I should get up and walk the ten feet to my bed, but it might as well be ten miles. I put the phone to my chest and hug it. Why couldn't he be the twenty-one-year-old Shawn? Without a girlfriend. Shawn Rosstav who made my stomach flip, whose arms on mine brought security I haven't experienced in years, whose imagination played along with mine, who gave me his jacket to protect me from the cold. Warmth sprints from my hand and into my heart.

I miss Shawn.

With my eyelids shut tight, I mourn the guy of my dreams who's just that: a dream. A dream I don't get to live.

A slam of the front door wakes me up. The apartment is no longer pitch black. A gray light seeps in through the living room window. Dawn.

Panic licks at my throat. Did my alarm not go off? I search for my phone under my pillow, find it in the fold of cushions behind my back. Five-fifty in the morning. Ten minutes to spare. I open Discord and read through my midnight exchange with Nick, proving the apology wasn't a dream.

"So, you did steal my robe." Siobhan strolls out of the bathroom, wearing a matching teal thong and bralette ensemble. The lingerie's new.

"Yeah." I stretch, my neck protesting from sleeping against the couch arm all night. "Where'd you get the outfit from?"

"Remember Volleyball Pierce?" She twirls around and points to her undergarments.

"He got you this?"

"Said with my teal hair, I needed the proper lingerie."

"You like him?"

"I like parts of him. One part especially." She winks at me in a totally unnecessary gesture. Siobhan and I have a similar approach to men. Well, at least we used to. "I'm off to visit him before I go to my figure drawing class. Gives me a legitimate excuse to leave after I'm satisfied. No cuddles. Wham-bam, thank you, sir. Off to start the day."

"So, no. You don't like Pierce?"

"Not having this conversation again. You have no time for chitchat anyhow. You need to drop Betty off at the mechanic's in an hour and make your way across town by eight. We still live in LA. No one cancelled the traffic."

Twenty-Six

Sarah

I'M LATE. I FLY through the double doors into the arts building and pick up the pace. Day two and I'm late again. Two for two. Not the first impression I hoped to make, but today will be my day. Figuring out the story for our movie project is my jam. I can't wait to share the pitches I came up with. One of them has to get the team's interest.

The class is full of chatter when I enter the same classroom as yesterday. Well, Bri and Wil make the noise. Riyaz remains silent, reclined in his chair, his dark hoodie hiding his eyes, which probably stare at his phone. I shove my phone into my bag and fight with the zipper. Nick isn't here.

"You have to see the new shoes I got yesterday at a second-hand store." Bri stretches powder pink leather pumps with a pointy toe my way. "Vintage Chanel. People have no clue what treasures they are getting rid of. These babies cost a couple hundred on TheRealReal."

"Coffee anyone?" Nick stands in the doorway, a tray with four coffees in one hand and a fifth in the other.

The room fills with the smell of freshly made brew. The one mug I had at the apartment doesn't seem enough anymore. One day I'll get to a point when I can wake up and not think about needing a couple or five more hours of sleep to feel rested. Winning this competition will get me there.

"I don't drink caffeine," Bri announces when Nick puts the tray of takeout cups on the table. "I like ginger tea, but only if it's organic. Too many fillers in the generic stuff. Might as well boil water and add sawdust. It would be healthier. If you can't get any, peppermint will do." Their hands fly as they speak. Nick doesn't roll his eyes or appear bored. "No milk. And no fake sweeteners, raw sugar only. Or honey. Honey is best."

Riyaz stretches, walks over to pluck a coffee out of Nick's tray, tosses the lid on the table, and returns to his seat. No cream, no sugar, no thank you.

"D'you drink coffee?" Bri points toward Nick and forces me to acknowledge his handsome face.

I want the coffee, but I don't want him to think the gesture means anything. After all, he didn't bring the drinks just for me. I play with a loose thread on my jeans. He's the director, he needs to get into all our good graces.

Shoulders back, I kick my confidence into gear and employ the strut I use to keep drunks at the bar in line. I'm not afraid to come near him. The brew smells good. I reach for the closest cup.

"There's cream and sugar." Nick holds out the bag. I take it out of his grip, making sure our hands don't touch, and select one of each.

"Thank you." I'm not Riyaz. A tight grin is not too much. I have manners, but that is all this is. Thanking him for coffee. Nothing more.

"Brilliant." Wil's by my side. "I'll take Bri's too." He breaks the tension gathering between Nick and me. I just might like Wil. He seems to find a way to be in the right place at the right time. Maybe his luck'll rub off on me. "Any croissants?" Wil takes the bag from me and snoops inside.

"Not in the budget," says Nick.

Is he spending the team's money on this stuff? I doubt that's allowed.

Nick sets his cup on the desk next to Wil, puts his blue backpack on the floor, and takes out a stack of papers. He places several on each of our desks.

"Today's goal is to decide on the movie theme and see if we can all agree on what the general direction will be. The papers in front of you outline the parameters for the competition, including at least one original song, at least three different locations used, at least two actors but no more than ten, and there are bonus points if we can include the things you see on the list there." He walks to the whiteboard and picks up a marker. "Let's start by brainstorming genres we feel comfortable with."

That's not right. The coffee burns a hole in my gut. I was supposed to come up with pitches. All screenwriters got the assignment.

"Nick?" His real name sounds wrong in my mouth.

Nick pauses. The hand with the marker drops to his side, and he regards me with what I can only describe as hope in his eyes. My stomach revolts. I'm shutting this down. "You're wrong." The softness in his eyes washes off. "All screenwriters had to write a pitch and present it to the group. I have mine."

I replace Nick at the center of our semi-circle as he sits and shuffles through loose pages scattered over his desk, seemingly avoiding my gaze. Bri smiles, Wil leans back as if waiting for a talent show, and Riyaz shifts in his seat. For a moment I think he's going to put down his phone, but he settles in the chair and continues scrolling.

I clear my throat. "A British student, whose parents immigrated from Zimbabwe to work in London, is in Canada for an exchange semester at the University of Toronto, where he spends mornings at a bookstore called Indigo." I've spent so much time writing loglines, summaries, potential plotlines, character descriptions, and backgrounds for this project, I can spew my pitch if woken at 2:00 a.m. "He reads books, drinks coffee, and pines for the barista, Isabel Archer, who makes the best coffee in his world, ignores his stares, despite his generous tips, until Rudo—that's our hero's name—starts leaving her notes with quotes from 'The Portrait of the Lady' by Henry James, whose heroine's name she has—"

"Can it take place in the eighties?" Bri's interruption sends my thoughts scrambling.

"There are some great backbeats in those famous eighties songs like *Take On Me* by Aha," Wil adds. "My mum loves that shit."

"Imagine the hairstyles." Bri leans toward Wil.

"Oh, Depeche Mode," says Wil. "We *have* to use one of their songs."

Wil and Bri are squirming in their seats.

"Did they have coffee shops in bookstores in the eighties?" Nick asks me, as if I came up with the idea.

"Mid-to-late nineties." Riyaz takes a sip of his coffee. "Nineties will be a better option."

"If Sarah wants the eighties . . ." Nick rubs his chin and eyes me.

I'm not the director. I'm not the one who suggested eighties. Shouldn't he be voicing his opinion?

"Late nineties will work." I didn't give the era of the movie a thought before Bri's suggestion. "Indigo is a bookstore in Canada. So, when I was assigned to Team Blue, my imagination kicked in—"

"Late nineties. We gotta have Cher's sneakers from Clueless. I-co-nic." Bri picks up their phone and starts typing and scrolling. "I'm thinking slip dresses. I could make them."

"Nineties music. Much more my jam. The club still goes wild for *the old stuff*. I can work with those types of tunes." Wil beams at me. "Do we need music from Zimbabwe? Not sure I've ever listened to any."

"I guess we can hear what you find." I want to tell Wil "I'm not your director." I want to ask Nick "What are your thoughts on this?" But looking at Nick means entering the danger zone.

"LA's a nineties architecture wonderland." Riyaz speaks, and we all stare at him. I forgot he was even here. He doesn't acknowledge us. Guess that's the end of his contributions to this brainstorming session.

"He's right." Bri's face lights up. As if it wasn't incandescent already. "So many classic movies were filmed around here. A Buffy the Vampire tour is a must. My friend told me about it the other day." They're bouncing again. "Let's binge the first season. Buffy had the best wardrobe. Oh, and her sidekick had those cute hats. I think I saw a store in Venice Beach with some just like what she wore." I love Bri's enthusiasm but . . .

I fill the team in on the rest of the story, and everyone chimes in with questions and suggestions. Even Riyaz peers up from his phone to inform us we need permits to film at any public location. Everyone, except for Nick. Nausea rolls through.

"This is good," Nick says words not related to me for the first time in two hours. "You all have your individual sessions for the rest of the week. Everyone sure of where they're going?"

We give him thumbs-ups like dutiful kindergarteners.

"Great," says Nick. "Maybe we should meet again, say, this weekend, to hammer out a timeline for the story, run through a high-level outline?"

"But it's, like, July Fourth this weekend. You want us to what, work on the weekend?" Bri turns their nose up at the idea.

"Just this once. You want to win this competition, right?" Nick is saying what I'm thinking. "Then we gotta do what it takes. This isn't a game."

I think I hear Riyaz snort but ignore him.

"Good." Nick meets everyone's eyes. Bri last. "Suggestions for a time and place on Discord."

Riyaz stands, stretches, and makes his way out the door.

The room empties, and Wil's the last to throw a glance at us before leaving Nick and me alone.

My mouth is dry. The acidic tang remaining from the coffee is causing havoc. Why is there no air in this room? I unzip my bag and search for my phone. My skin prickles at Nick's closeness as he hovers by my desk, not saying anything, but making it clear he won't let me slip through the door.

Twenty-Seven

"Talk fast. I have to pick up Betty." I need to get there before 3:00 pm to make it to my shift on time. Siobhan's words this morning ring in my head. I don't want to give him any ideas.

Nick pinches the bridge of his nose. "I'm sorry I didn't tell you my real name at Christmas."

Starting with an apology. Smooth.

"We spent hours together." I lean back and cross my arms. "You could've said something at any point if you wanted. You didn't want to. Hiding behind the fake name, protecting yourself from your girlfriend finding out."

"Mackenzie isn't my girlfriend." His stare is intense, and I choose to focus on the white ceiling tiles over his shoulder.

"I seriously don't care who you date. What's your point?"

"That night, that Christmas Eve mattered." He inches closer, and I sit up straight, ready to bolt if I need to. I won't, not one to shy away. Nick's voice is low but clear. "I couldn't stop thinking about you."

I roll my eyes. "Stop. It was a blip on the radar. Fun dinner with a stranger. Meant nothing."

"Nothing?" He puts his hands on my desk. He squeezes the corners of the flimsy thing so hard the fake wood creaks. "Now who's lying? You came to Chicago for me."

"What?" My heart thuds against my ribcage. How would he know about Valentine's Day? Did Ryan tell him? Time to have a little chat with my friend and make sure he stops spilling my secrets. I thought Ryan was on my side.

Nick releases my desk. Walks back to dig into his backpack. "I was there at Mackenzie's house." I open my mouth to ask why her address was on his driver's license if she wasn't his girlfriend, but he cuts me off. "I worked for her father. I was there to ask him for extra shifts. Needed to make more money to buy a car, like you suggested."

He took my advice? The base of my throat itches. I remember the conversation about not being able to live in LA without a car the night we drove up to Griffith Park—him squished into the front seat of Betty. His knees hit the glovebox as we plotted the fight scene from my opus. The image of him leaning against the hood as we took in the views of LA at night. The feel of his arm pressed against mine, his hand, his—

Nope, Sarah, not helping. I roll my lips between my teeth. Don't think about the kiss. Mad, remember? Upset at the liar with the girlfriend. Focus on the goal. Win the competition. Make a movie. Set Nick straight.

Nick finds whatever he was rummaging for in the backpack. "I chased your cab down the street. Called for you, but I guess you didn't hear me." He pulls out a toque.

Not just anyone. My eyes snap to the hat. Blue and white. With an unmistakable white maple leaf emblem.

My toque. The pounding in my ears is louder than the bar on a Saturday night. My mémère and grandpa's special token. No. This can't be.

"Where?" My voice cracks.

"I found it on Mackenzie's porch after you returned my," he grinds his teeth, "fake ID. You must have dropped the hat when you . . . left. I kept it safe for you. Hoping to get a chance to give it back."

Everything he says sounds fantastical. Unreal. Like something out of a movie. This must be another lie. My hand flies to the V of my T-shirt to calm the needling pain.

I take the beanie from his hands, not letting myself believe it's true. Maybe he got one from eBay. I tried to find one myself but gave up because it wouldn't be the same. My hat is special, the symbol of two soulmates who loved each other for a lifetime. And beyond.

My fingers recognize the old wool, and my heart tells me this is my hat. There's an easy way to be sure. I peel back the hem and search for the familiar shapes. Relief and gratitude rush through my veins. There, tucked on the inside of the hem, are the stitched letters spelling out the name of the person I'll never see again. Sarah Côté. I close my eyelids. Heat prickles behind them. I'm not going to cry.

Thank you, Mémère, for bringing this, you, back to me. Something I've been holding onto for months, guilt for losing this precious item, misplacing this testimonial to my grandparents' relationship, shifts inside me and floats away. The worn fibers offer a comfort, making this day the best one in a while.

"I texted, called, emailed every Sarah Côté I could find in LA and Toronto, but none of them were you."

"She was my grandmother." The word hurts.

"Oh." He sits down in the chair beside me, and I can't stop myself from matching his posture, angling toward him.

"I'm named after her. She is my favorite person in the world. Was." I still can't get used to the concept that she's not here, not a phone call away.

"Ryan told me you went to Toronto in February for the funeral."

The memories flood back in. The bitter cold, the empty chair in the living room. The pain won't let go. "On my way back to LA, my plane made an emergency landing in Chicago. I was wearing your leather jacket, and I found your ID. The fake. I saw the address and thought it was some sort of a sign."

"Maybe it—"

"A sign for me to get over you. And I did."

Nick blinks at my words. My heart lurches at the sight. Stupid me, I want to comfort him. What's wrong with me? I sling my purse over my shoulder. "And I don't want to talk about this anymore."

We're teammates. This is all I can do. My fingers trace Mémère's name. I draw strength from the raised stitches and look Nick square in the face. He's rubbing his chin, and the sorrow in his eyes leads me to doubt my decision.

I say, "Let's just be friends."

This is more than I wanted, but I need to see the sparkle back in his eyes. I wait for the light to appear. It doesn't. He searches every part of my face with his dark stormy glare and gives me the barest of nods.

Friends it is. I raise my chin. Steel sinks into my spine. I can be friends with Nick Stavros.

Twenty-Eight

NICK

Blend is exactly what I expect a coffee house on a university campus in California to be. Light floods in from the window, and everything appears shiny and new. White metal chairs sit tucked under long beechwood tables standing on the wood wide-plank floors. A large display case contains a cornucopia of treats, and my stomach growls.

"You've never worked in the hospitality industry?" Harold, the manager, squishes his wiry gray eyebrows together. I didn't expect to be interviewed by someone my dad's age.

"My mom runs a hair salon. I helped out after school and on weekends. The ladies loved my cappuccinos." I offer him a smile. "Can even make the hearts in the foam."

The manager's head perks up. "Oh, good." There's a loud crash from behind the counter, and Harold jumps out of his seat. "Felicia, I told you not to stack the takeout boxes so high. Get a garbage bag and throw these out. They're unusable now."

Harold returns to our table. "When can you start?"

I retrieve my phone to check my calendar. "When do you need me?"

"I have a four-hour shift my now-fired barista showed up high to. If you start now, I'll pay you for the full four hours."

I smile. That was too easy. I expected more questions, a background check, a request to make the cappuccino I bragged about. "I'll have to make a call, and I'm all yours."

"Excellent. I'll get the hiring paperwork started, and you can fill it out during your fifteen-minute break. You get one every two hours."

Sounds fair. Harold leaves to take over the register where three customers are waiting. I dial Dad. When he doesn't pick up, I text him that I won't be home until after 8:00 pm, and he doesn't have to count me in for dinner. I don't wait for his reply. Instead, I text Mom: *Mission accomplished.*

Maybe my luck is turning, because when my shift at Blend is over, even though Dad didn't reply to my message, I see a string of activity on Discord. I didn't have high hopes that any of my team members would take my suggestion of an extra session seriously. Leading a team of fourteen hormonal boys on skates to shove a puck along the ice into a four-foot-wide net is easier than getting the *Indigo* movie crew to choose a time and a place to get together for our review session.

BSato: I have tickets to the concert in the Bowl. I need to leave by 7.

WPeters: If there's beer I can come anytime.

SConnor: How about my apartment? My roommates are having a party on Saturday, but it's on the roof, so we'll have the place to ourselves. You're all welcome to stay to watch the fireworks.

SConnor: But no alcohol for those under 21.

I huff as I stare at Sarah's pointed barb at my age. Friends, she said. The same thing she offered Ryan. He never got out of the friend zone. My jaw stiffens. I can't be like Ryan.

My tongue stings from where I bit down to stop myself from arguing with her, when she asked to be friends. If friends is what she needs, I can do friends.

Thing is, friends don't look at friends that way. I'm not delusional, even though my head stops working when I'm around her. She thinks I don't notice her watching me. But because she refuses to interact with me directly, every glance she does throw my way is like a snowball, and they hit hard. Doesn't matter that she pretends the stare never happened. Those hurt, but I can take anything she tosses my way. To me, the jabs mean she's here. She's nearby, and I know how she's doing, hear her voice, learn about her, see her. Hope she sees me. I stare at my reflection in the coffee shop window. I can do friends.

For now.

Me: The apartment then. Thx. Everyone be there at 3.

Me: What can we bring?

Mom's smiling face replaces the Discord screen. My forehead relaxes. Mom's been calling every day, texting . . . every hour, feels like. She's the only one who comments on my every IG post—my love letters to LA. She's equally enthralled with the dirty alleys, hidden corners of the campus, and ocean.

"Nicky?" Mom sounds tired. "Why work at a coffee shop?"

I need the money? It's close to the Starlight Foundation Building? Better than flipping burgers? Dad is charging me rent to sleep on his couch? Somehow, I don't think any of these honest answers will make Mom worry less.

"Lets me work around my classes. I can do early and late shifts. Without a car, I can save on commuting: both time and money in my pocket." It's true. "And I'm a fan of their signature blend." Also true. The coffees I picked up from Blend the day Sarah asked me to be friends were good. Damn expensive, but good.

Mom's short laugh drains some of the tension the money conversation dredged up. "Don't tell me you're living on caffeine. Should I start sending care packages to LA? Not sure my chicken souvlaki would make the trip, but I could send granola bars. They're healthy."

"Blend has these mango scones I'm addicted to. They might be healthy. Everything in this town is." Healthy or decadent. No in-between. Like friends, not lovers.

The door swings open and a gaggle of girls rush in with laughter on their heels. Harold shoos the server behind the counter to take their orders. The smell of coffee intensifies. This isn't a bad place to earn some cash.

"Don't work too much," says Mom.

"No worries. Mike's been texting me new workout routines on the daily." Big bro's been spamming me with new sets for the gym and explicitly not asking about Dad. I'm not giving him any info. So what if he might have been right about our father? The thought jabs at my heart. I'm not ready to admit anything yet.

"I'm good. Really. You saw—enjoying the sun and living the California dream." Doesn't matter how many images fight for space in my overcrowded head. Competition. Money. Sarah. Dad. Loneliness, even though I'm rarely alone. Time. Sarah.

"It's temporary, though. Right?" I can hear banging cabinet doors as she cleans her hair salon and gets the place ready for the next morning. "At least you have your dad to watch out for you."

Yeah. Dad, who I rarely see, who puts his name on the food in the fridge so I don't eat it. "I miss you."

"Miss you too, baby boy." Her voice mellows. "There's a conference in September in LA. If I can find the money, I could visit before your classes start."

September is eons away. I've barely survived a week.

Twenty-Nine

NICK

Sarah's apartment is on the top floor of an off-white four-story building that hasn't been painted since before I was born. The bus that dropped me off five blocks from here ends its route at Venice Beach. I can't see the sand or the ocean, but it can't be far away.

Timing the long-ass ride was next to impossible. Better early than late. Should I sit on the curb and wait the extra half hour? It's sweltering out here. Fuck it. I text Sarah.

Me: I'm in front of your building. Too early to come in?

I billow my T-shirt, trying to keep the cotton from sticking, and sniff to make sure my deodorant is holding.

A ding.

SConnor: Come up.

A guy in way-too-tight bicycle shorts and a green helmet holds the door open. Great security in this building. Is Sarah safe living here? There's no elevator, and I take the stairs two at a time; my long legs have their advantages.

The number four on the wall next to her apartment is silver while the zero and two are a tarnished gold. I steady myself and knock. The door swings open, and instead of the tiny blond I expected, a tall girl with shocking teal hair stands before me, her tank top revealing an arm full of intricate colorful tattoos.

"What?" she says.

"Sarah here?"

"Nope. No one here by that name." I always considered the Irish accent cool, but when paired with a sneer, it bites.

"Let him in." Sarah's voice filters out from the depths of the apartment.

"Your lucky day, boyo." She steps aside, and I duck into the open concept space: living room with a brown couch and glass coffee table on my right, kitchen on my left. Squished into the corner is a walnut table. Sarah sits on a chair with one leg tucked under the other and a silver laptop on her knees.

"Hi." I wave in her direction. "Happy Independence Day." Her hair is twisted up on her head in some kind of a knot and dark rimmed glasses frame her eyes, giving her a hot librarian look. My mouth goes dry. I can't blame the heat this time. "Didn't know you wear glasses."

"You don't know much," the other woman mutters as she walks over to the cupboard and pulls out a large plastic bowl with watermelons printed on the outside.

Sarah takes off the glasses. "I don't, really. These have blue light lenses; they help protect against eye strain when I work on the computer."

"Oh, smart," I say.

"Our Sarah is the genius in the family." The teal-haired girl dumps a bag of generic brand chips into the bowl. "Except when it comes to men."

Sarah folds the frames and sets them on the table beside her laptop. She pads over to the kitchen, plucks a chip out of the bowl, and waves it at her roommate. "What happened to the Irish hospitality your folk are supposed to be famous for?"

The girl with the tattoos gives her the finger. "Left it at home with me pot o' gold."

"You'll have to excuse Siobhan." Sarah wraps an arm around the other woman's waist. "My friend here woke up on the wrong side of the bed this morning."

"More like the wrong bed." Siobhan's shoulders sag. Sarah squeezes her, and her friend regards me. "Can I get you something to drink?"

I hold up the bag with the bottles I took out of Dad's pantry. They've been there since I arrived. I scratch the stubble on my cheeks and hope he won't miss the Coke until I replace them after I get my first paycheck. "I brought soda."

Siobhan snatches the bag and inspects one of the two-liter bottles. "Brand name. Fancy. Thanks."

"I'd love some water." My bottles disappear into the fridge in place of a case of beer. Siobhan tucks the bowl with the chips under one arm, picks up the beer, and brushes past me. "I'll be upstairs with the others. Join us when you're done."

Somehow, I don't think the invite includes me.

Sarah fills a tall glass from the tap and hands it to me, making an obvious effort to keep her fingers from touching mine. The tendons in my wrist go taut. Her attempt to keep me at a distance doesn't seem to be going anywhere.

"Thanks." I drain half of the water in one go and glance down to find Sarah staring at me with an odd pout on her face. "It's hot."

"Sure is." She blinks and spins away.

I put my half-empty glass on the table. It could be so easy to close the gap between us, cross this room, take her in my arms, and feel her pressed against me. The water helped with my parched mouth but did not dampen my thirst for her skin. I lick my lips, pick up my drink, and drain it, trying to drown the desire surging through my veins.

Should I ask about her car? I would love her to tell me if Betty is back in working order, but I don't want to open old wounds. My fingers tighten around the glass. I didn't give what I was doing a thought when I tried to fix her car, went straight to *do something* mode. Now I overthink everything, afraid to disagree or upset her. I stop squeezing before I go too far and break the glass.

There's a crinkling noise as Sarah rips open another bag.

"Does your roommate who was teaching you Spanish still live here?" I ask. If this isn't a safe topic, I can't imagine what is. I'm talking to the back of her head as she pours more chips into a metal bowl.

"Claudia? Sí."

I find myself standing beside her at the counter. I could swear I teleported here with the sheer power of my mind. The apartment isn't big, but there's plenty of space in the living room for me not to hover inches away from her. A whiff of strawberry hits me and I inhale, soaking in the long-lost scent of Sarah, and the nerves in my gut disappear. My arm brushes hers, her skin warm, causing the hairs on mine to stand up. Her palms are flat against the beige Formica countertop. With no effort I could put my hand on hers, entwine our fingers. Man, how I want to hold her hand.

A sharp buzz makes us both jump. Sarah springs away, and I hate the person who's at the door. She presses a button and croaks, "Hello."

"Let me in before I fry out here." Wil's distorted voice squeaks through the speaker.

"C'mon up."

Sarah opens the door and steps into the hall, like she can't stand to be alone with me any longer.

Thirty

Sarah

I PLACE A BOWL of corn chips on the coffee table and take my place in the circle of Team Blue, specifically selected to be as far away from Nick as possible in our tiny apartment. Even with the windows open and the two fans cranked on high, it's hot in here.

"Ralph has to—"

"It's Rudo." Riyaz says his first words of the afternoon. I almost forgot he was here.

"Right." Bri lets out an exaggerated breath. "I'm so bad with names. Rudo has to woo Isabel."

Wil snickers. "Fuck that slow burn stuff. They should hook up, and he can win her over with his abilities." Wil points at the door to the nearest bedroom and raises an eyebrow. "You get my drift."

I glare at him. "Or she could wow him with her abilities."

"Hold on, hold on." Nick runs both of his hands down his face. "Before the hookup, let's talk atmosphere. That'll give us an idea of what locations we need to stake out."

"A coffee shop. Obvi," says Bri.

"I have a lead on that." Nick rubs his hands together as if he has a brilliant idea. "I landed a job at Blend, the place I got the coffees from. I'll ask if we can shoot before the morning shift."

"Great. And it's on campus." Wil's smile fades. He leans closer to Nick. "Are they still hiring?" Look at that, Mr. Happy-Go-Lucky has a serious side.

"I can put in a word." Nick pops a few chips in his mouth and crunches. "What else?"

"They need to go on dates. A restaurant?" Bri says.

"Will The Diamond Club work? I don't think Mrs. Marino will let us film inside, but the pool doesn't open until eight. We can shoot something there." I glance at Nick and press my thighs together. "Pools are romantic."

Nick's right eyebrow rises. "Morning light looks great on camera."

"We'll only get one take. Once they get wet," says Riyaz. We all turn to him.

"I'm sure we can get an actress who'll look good in a bikini, but has anyone had their first date at a pool? Not me." Wil looks at us one by one. Everyone shakes their heads. "Exactly. A bold move for a bookworm like Rudo."

I manage to control my face and not become the lion that roars at the beginning of MGM movies. "Just because he likes books doesn't mean he lives in a library." The quiver in my voice unravels my mask. I'm not defending Rudo, but my father, who I based Rudo on. My dad still plays hockey. He was in great shape in his twenties. I drum my fingers on the armrest. "He can be athletic."

Wil scrunches his nose and opens his mouth to say something when Bri cuts in. "Too bad there aren't beaches in Canada. I love a beach scene, sun, sand, waves, blue skies. Always so romantic. Walking off into the sunset together."

"Sunset plus beach equals cinematic gold." Riyaz speaks again, and I'm so stunned I almost forget to object. Almost.

"I'll have you know there are plenty of beautiful beaches in Toronto alone." I jut out my chin to punctuate every syllable. "I bet half the scenes you've seen in movies have been shot on Woodbine Beach back home. Toronto is the Hollywood of the North."

"Hollywood of the North. Never heard of that." Bri tilts their head. "Is it even warm enough to go swimming?"

"Our summers are as warm as California's." My hands shoot up and point outside. How many times do I need to explain to people in this town that Canada isn't a winter wasteland and we don't all live in igloos? "Sometimes warmer." I collapse onto the back of my chair. "It often hits 95 degrees."

Nick stands and stalks to the kitchen area. "I like this idea. A sunset can be our backdrop, like Riyaz says. Saves on budget." He makes a circle around our circle. "How do we go about finding a beach in the area to film at?" he asks from behind me.

Every inch of my body registers his position and the distance between us. Or lack thereof. How did he manage to end up as close to me as possible, when I was clear about putting space between us?

"Shouldn't be a problem." Unable to escape to the other side of the room this time, I start a text to Ryan. "My friend is a surfer. He knows every beach up and down the coast. He'll be at the party tonight. I'll make sure he gives us the scoop."

The fan rotates and blows Nick's fresh soap scent right at me. I spell baetch instead of beach, my brain scrambled. Nick peers at my text over my shoulder. "Ryan, right?" The air from his lips heats the nape of my neck. I force my attention to the phone, hit backspace, and try again. If only we could afford air conditioning.

"Good thinking." Nick's voice brightens as if I've made the best suggestion. A corner of my lips tugs up at his praise. My pulse races. I curse my body's betrayal and lean forward to create distance between us. He arches over me. "We'll need summer styles for a beach scene."

"Sundress shopping. My favorite." Bri giggles and their eyes light up. I suspect all shopping is Bri's favorite.

"Need to see the mics they have. I could try to capture some natural sound." Wil stretches his long legs under the coffee table and puts both his hands behind his head. "Worst case scenario, we can buy a pre-recorded track."

Nick leaves his position behind my chair, and the fan blasts a gust of Nick-free air but offers no relief to my heated skin. "Only if we absolutely have to. Our budget is negligible, so the more freebies we get, the better."

No one replies.

"Can I get some nods? Thumbs up?" Nick asks the silent room.

"Free cheese is only in a mouse trap." Bri slams their phone on the coffee table, and I'm afraid for the device's safety. "I can't sew a full wardrobe out of thin air. Costume budget must be a priority. None of you really need things. I'm the one who has to get the movie to look like it's in the nineties."

"I'll need props," Riyaz rumbles from under his hoody.

"If they give me the equipment, I'll still need to buy tracks, but most likely we'll need to rent extra stuff." Wil scans the faces of each team member and lands on mine. "At least we're in the clear for the script. No expenses there." He lifts his chin in a silent challenge. "Right?"

A simmer of not-quite-anger bubbles in my stomach. I walk over to the fridge and extract the last can of ginger ale. My part might not cost us anything, but they're not going to exclude me right off the bat. The tab snaps as the liquid fizzes. "Maybe so, but I want full transparency." I shift my eyes to Nick. "Are you going to keep track of the expenses? Do you even have experience with it?"

"Not in the least. You can take that on if you want." Nick pulls a stack of papers out of the binder he brought. "These are the docs and the explanations on what you have to submit."

"I didn't say I want to do it." I drain the can in one long swallow. Just because I'm the oldest in the group doesn't mean I want to play mom.

"Weren't you just questioning my ability to do the task? That's not the kind of teamwork I'm looking for. If you can help, I want to know about it. I'm technically the one who's in charge of every aspect of this production."

I crush the can in my palm. "First we're a team, and now you're in charge?"

"I don't need a fight before our first week of competition is over. This is nothing personal, Sarah." He emphasizes personal in a way I hate. The simmer turns into a rolling boil, and I imagine steam coming out of my ears. This sure feels personal.

I need to gain control, as I sense everyone's eyes on me, gauging my response. No chance I'll give them fuel for any rumors. I don't want to be known for having a relationship with my boss on my first serious project. Reputation is a fragile thing, and no matter how much I want to get into it with him, I'm too close to getting what I want to jeopardize it over this.

"Nothing personal on my end either. Good luck with that budget." I pretend Nick is one of the annoying customers at the bar and offer my cajoling bartender voice. "I'm all set with the screenplay. You don't have to worry about me."

His gaze drops to the floor, and his shoulders rise and fall once in a deep breath. "Right."

Nick shoves the binder back in his bag and returns to his seat across the room. "Let's look at the latest updates Sarah sent and add the locations wherever we can. Bri, you start a list of wardrobe needs for each scene. Riyaz, you do the same for props. Wil, for music."

Nick's knee bounces. His fingers open and close a few times. My breath matches his rhythm. The oppressive heat in this apartment isn't helping my rising anxiety. One week into the competition and this looks impossible. Pressure builds in my stomach. I shouldn't have chugged that ginger ale. We sort of have a plan, but with seven weeks to find actors, for them to learn lines, for us to shoot and edit—time isn't on our side. Nick has a lot resting on those broad shoulders.

THIRTY-ONE

Sarah

THE TRAY IN MY hand wobbles as I climb the metal mesh stairs to the rooftop patio. Between my years at Mémère's bakery and the bar, my wrist should be as solid as marble. The tremor that reaches my heart or comes from there continues. I stop and steady the plate.

Nick's chest grazes my shoulder. "I can take those."

"I do this all day. I've got it." Why does his offer irk me? He's just being nice.

Nick and Wil were supposed to leave with Bri and Riyaz, but the Canadian in me couldn't say no to their request to watch the fireworks. The guys staying for a bit isn't that big of a deal. There're plenty of people at this party for us to not even talk for the rest of the evening.

"I bet the view is to die for," Wil pipes in.

"It is," I say.

Nick clears his throat. I resume the ascent before his closeness raises my temperature to fever levels. To dampen the heat pooling in my stomach I watch the pizza bites in my hands I so-called cooked and imagine Mémère rolling in her grave.

The thump-thump of the bass reverberates through the door. I shove my shoulder against the beat-up metal. Nick's long arm extends over my head and pushes it open. Is this his way to get into my good graces: killing me with attention and kindness?

I duck under his toned bicep. "Thanks."

Red, white, and blue patio lanterns brighten the industrial-looking space, which is more a rooftop than a patio. I head over to the folding table Siobhan and I dragged up here earlier, drop the platter beside the laundry basket filled with ice we use to keep beer cold, and dust myself off. The twenty or so guests put a dent in our drinks stash. Empty cans sit around the perimeter but everyone seems to be holding something in their hands. Everyone except Nick, who's in the middle of a bro handshake with Ryan. Nick's face splits in the first genuine smile I've seen today.

"Dude." Ryan is a man of many words. Or, should I say, one word, many times. He spots me, comes over, and scoops me up in his arms. "Saaarah." Oh, boy. When I get extra As in my name, I know Ryan's had a few.

I untangle myself from his embrace. "How was work?"

"Shitshow without you or Siobhan. New kid, Layden, didn't seal off the CO_2 line on a keg and we almost had our own fireworks display. Technically not how fireworks work." He pushes his hair behind his ears. "Last year I made a batch. Used a mixture of potassium nitrate, charcoal, and sulfur in a 75 to 15 to 10 ratio by weight for the black powder and for the flash powder some potassium chlorate, sulfur, and—"

"Egit," Siobhan chimes in. Her eyes are unfocused, and the Irish accent is thick, so she's half in the bag as well. Six months ago, I would've been right there with her. I swallow and set my palm on her elbow. Seems I have some catching up to do.

Wil breaks our contact and steps between us. "Hi." He extends his hand toward Siobhan. "I'm Wil."

"Oy." Siobhan drags her big—I think they're blue tonight—eyes down and back up Wil's body, shaking her head in approval. Wil's thick eyebrows inch toward his black hair. He grins. "Care for a beer?"

"No," Nick and I say in unison. I roll my eyes as Nick shoves a digit in Wil's direction. "Nineteen."

The smile slips a bit on Wil's face. "I've been drinking beer, legally, since I was sixteen back home. One pint won't hurt anyone."

"Had to wait till eighteen in Ireland, then came here and had to wait till twenty-one. The backwards progress wasn't fun." She winks at Wil, but her eyes are too slow, and the move is more like an uncoordinated blink. "Such a shame."

Siobhan twists away, wading into the crowd of our friends, hips swaying seductively. Wil scowls at me like I told him he wasn't tall enough to ride the rollercoaster at Disneyland.

Ryan slaps Wil on the back. "Don't fret, little dude. There's plenty of fish in the sea." Ryan takes a swig of his beer. "In fact, there are five hundred and nineteen species of fish in the Mediterranean Sea, of which seventy-three are sharks." Ryan's definitely reached his walking Wikipedia stage of intoxication. "But no fish in the Dead Sea, of course."

"Of course." Skepticism is written all over Wil's face. "But here, at this party. Any fish?"

Ryan presses his lips together like he just realized he was babbling, and his eyes do the hooded thing he likes to use when he's impersonating a stoner. "Totally. Let me introduce you to a few." He drags Wil away, and once again I'm left standing beside Nick. Alone.

The ice stings my skin as I fish a bottle out of the laundry basket. I don't have to talk if I'm drinking.

Nick shuffles his feet. "How's Betty?"

I shrug and take a sip. The bitter almost-cold amber liquid fills my mouth.

"You said you took her to a mechanic. Was it the alternator?"

So, Mr. Old Fashioned wants to go there, does he? Breathe, Sarah, breathe. "Yup. Another chunk on my credit card."

Nick whistles. "Sucks. My credit card blew its limit two days after landing in this town. I'm living off day-old mango scones and quiche from Blend."

"What about your dad?" He lives with the man, doesn't he?

A pained expression darkens Nick's face. "Yeah, he . . . we . . . I'm crashing on his couch for the summer. Hoping to find somewhere else to stay."

This is news. Wasn't he close to his dad? They spent Christmas together after all. I angle toward him. "And your mom?"

"She's back in Chicago with my brother, Mike. Neither of them really liked the idea of me coming out here."

Laughter bubbles up in my throat. "Must be a mom thing."

"Yeah?"

"My mom was against my whole LA-slash-screenwriting plan. She figured I should stay in Toronto and take over the family business. We own a bakery there."

"Côté Fraise?" Recognition dawns in his eyes. "I found it when I was searching for you."

He really did try to find me. My heart flutters. "Means strawberry coast in French." My gaze travels up his torso to his face. Heat pools in places it should not. Shit, he's tall. I like tall. Evens out my short. I stand on my tiptoes, raise my chin, and whisper, "She loved it almost as much as she did my grandpa." Nick's eyes peer into mine. The eyes from his driver's license. The fake one. I slam my heels into the springy surface of the rooftop and move my gaze to the lantern above his head. "Can't trust my brothers with the place."

Nick moves his head down to maintain our closeness. "Sounds like your brothers should meet mine." His voice is a low rumble.

I take another swig of my beer. There's zero reason for me to meet his family. "Oh, your brother's reckless and irresponsible?"

His eyebrows knit. "Quite the opposite. Mike'd kill to take on the project of straightening them out. It'd give me a break."

"Mom would love that." My arms want to hug away the sadness in his gaze. I clutch the beer bottle to keep my fingers from straying where they don't belong. "I was supposed to be the non-screwup in the family. Went to college. Got a degree. She was proud. Now I'm a bartender in LA and my brothers are rapidly rising on her scale of favorites." I chew on my lip.

Nick shoves his hands in his pockets. "Not me, I've always been on the bottom. It's not too bad there. The higher you climb, the more is expected from you." He draws his shoulders up to his ears. "This directorship hasn't exactly been a walk in the park, and we're only a week in."

"I can help." My body sways to his. "I've been running the bar at The Diamond Club for almost two years. If you need me to whip Riyaz into shape, just say so." Why am I offering to help again? I'm supposed to be staying away from him, not finding excuses to hang around.

A flicker of something lighter flashes in his irises. "Might take you up on your offer."

This beer must not be very strong, because I finish the bottle and don't feel any effect. I take another colder one from the laundry basket. The damn cap won't budge. My hand trembles again.

"It's not a twist off." Nick pulls the bottle from me and pops the cap off on the edge of the table. "Here."

Our skin touches, and for the span of an eyeblink we stand frozen.

I yank the beer away. "Looks like you've had practice." I take a long drag to douse the raging fire in my core.

"Yeah. The upside of being on a hockey team offseason. Lots of cheap beer and—" Nick stops speaking and irons the wrinkles between his eyebrows.

"Girls?" I guzzle more beer, hoping the alcohol kills the effect of whatever Nick's trying to seduce me into.

"Sure." He tries to give me a charged look but breaks into soft laughter. "If you're into that."

"I'm not." I finish the bottle, yet my mouth remains parched. "I'm into tall guys."

Nick pries the empty out of my grasp. "Good to know." He draws his hand back slowly enough for the pads of his fingers to skim my knuckles.

A burst of white dots shimmers in the darkening sky and falls in an urgent waterfall, followed by a loud boom. Red sparkles expanding into a ball of light follow.

Out over the city, the fireworks pop, fizz, and scream. The party slides sideways, like the rooftop is a Tilt-a-Whirl where everyone crushes against the wall of the patio facing downtown. I join them, but as usual, my Thumbelina size works against me. I rise on my toes but even with the extra inches, all I can see are bits and pieces of light in-between the gaps of the less-vertically challenged around me.

A tap on my shoulder. "Wanna lift?"

Nick's words don't make sense. I'm not leaving the party. "Sorry?"

His face dips, and I stare down to see Nick on one knee like he's proposing. I clutch the S pendant below my throat. What the hell? I have not had that much to drink.

He jabs a thumb at his back. "Climb on."

I squeeze the necklace hard enough for the silver to dig into my palm. The first night I met Shawn, now Nick, I dreamed of surveying the world perched atop his broad shoulders. Now, he's offering the view to me. What do I do?

As if the answer is outside of me, I search the backs of my friends. My eyes meet Siobhan's and I silently ask her what she thinks. She winks and returns to the fireworks. I'm on my own.

"The view's great from up here. I promise." Nick's face is barely readable away from the patio lanterns.

"Are you sure?" I release my hold on my necklace, the imprint of the S visible on my skin.

"Absolutely. You don't want to miss this."

His words prick me, like the cactus my mother tried to keep alive when she won the tiny plant at the Ex—the Canadian National Exhibition. I shift my weight to my other foot. He's trying to be nice, Sarah. What's the harm?

The harm is I can barely stand being around him without my insides melting. My lips tingle yearning to kiss him. Taste him. Touch him. Remind myself of the texture of his hair. The strength of his arms wrapped around me. I stretch my fingers to his shoulders and jerk them back. I can't climb on. Can't have him hold me. Can't touch him.

Can I?

I step closer. Electricity hums in my veins. "Okay." I'm doing this.

He hoists me up like the effort is nothing, his hands clasping the back of my knees. My arms are around his neck, a reverse of the night we kissed. His skin sears me through his T-shirt. With a bounce, he shifts me into a more comfortable position, and it's oddly not odd at all. I feel safe, at ease. The jitters itching at my skin since I woke disappear as I drink in his musky scent. I only had one night to overdose on the heavenly aroma, but this feels familiar. Right.

The ocean breeze whips my hair into my eyes. My lungs overinflate. The sensation of being high in the air is euphoric. I hold Nick's shoulders and throw back my head. The night sky shimmers with glittering gold and sizzling reds. Bombs bursting in air indeed. In his arms, I have an unobstructed view. I grin widely. My heart bursts as well. The world is different from up here.

Nick's hands tighten on my shins. I tear my eyes from the light show and study the guy I avoided looking at since the first day of the competition. Really look at him. Light stubble covers half his face like it did the night we met. I search for the little scar from where the hockey puck hit him. That's too close. Dangerous territory, Sarah, look away.

My gaze flicks to the glowing sky but like a stretched rubber band snaps to the shadows Nick's eyelashes cast on his cheeks. The blue-and-white of the fireworks colors his skin, highlighting the smile lines in the corners of his eyes. A pulsing vein in his neck matches the meter that pounds where my chest presses against his back.

The ends of his curls tickle my cheek as he twists his head, and I quickly glance up, ignoring the pounding of my own heart. I close my eyes. When I think I can form words without my voice shaking, I whisper into his hair, "Thank you."

"That's what friends are for."

My stomach plummets. Right. Friends.

THIRTY-TWO

Sarah

AFTER OUR . . . whatever it was on the rooftop, at every team meeting I remember how easily Nick agreed to the friends deal. I should be happy. That's what I wanted. I cross my ankles. My reputation is important to me. He's technically my boss, and my dreams about what he looks like with his shirt off every night this week are completely inappropriate.

Also completely inappropriate is staring at his completely kissable lips. Not in my dreams and a hundred percent not in the middle of our third round of casting calls. I move my gaze from Nick's face to the actors in front of our small circle.

"You're the only one for me. Ask me to stay, and I will." Tristan, who the team agreed aced his first performance, is perfect for Rudo. The male lead spews my lines like he's Sir Patrick Stewart in Shakespeare's *Macbeth*. His lack of experience with a British accent is the only flaw.

Ruth, the brunette we're seeing for the second time at Nick's insistence and my dismay, is good. I roll my eyes. She isn't who I imagined Isabel. My mom is who I imagined for Isabel: blond, blue eyes, petite—a classical beauty. Ruth is short, but her olive skin and darker locks are the exact opposite of the features I saw when these words poured out of me onto the page.

"Okay, let's stop here. Tristan, that was great." Nick gets up and ushers them out of the room. He pauses in the doorway and says something to Ruth. Something that's not loud enough for me to hear but manages to make her blush. I bite the inside of my cheek to stop from shouting, "Get a room." The acrid disappointment singes my chest.

If the reason Nick's insisting on her for this role is to get in her pants, I'm not gonna let it happen. We may be friends, and I have no claim on him, but she will be his subordinate just like me. I tighten my lips. I'm not losing our chance at winning so Nick can find someone else to boost on his shoulders.

Mackenzie was a brunette, too. Maybe he has a type? I tap my pen on Ruth's headshot in the folder before me. This girl and Nick would look cute together.

"She's perfect, right?" He closes the door, and his eyes are burning brightly. I remember the night when I was the reason for this look. I clench my teeth and take a deep breath through my nose. We are not going to agree. I have to leave in thirty minutes, or I'll be late for my evening shift.

"Their chemistry is off the charts," Nick addresses Bri, Wil, and Riyaz this time. "The way the air shimmers between them when their eyes meet?" He glances my way, but I move my gaze to my notes.

"I think we've got our Isabel," Nick says as if it's a done deal.

"I disagree." I slam my notebook on the table. I'm not blinded by whatever confused plans Nick has for Ruth. Is she the leading lady in his dreams as well? I have a list of valid reasons for opposing her as our lead. "First, she's never done anything on film before. All her credits are for plays she did in high school. Second, she's eighteen. Isabel is at least twenty-one. We can find somebody more mature and with some semblance of experience. Three"—my most important reason, but I'm not going to put it front and center, I know how this works—"she's neither blond nor has blue eyes. Don't even know how she got to audition. We advertised for a very different look."

"She's doing this for free because she needs screen credits." Wil folds his arms and leans back in his chair. "The pool of actors we can get for free on short notice in the middle of summer even in LA is not that large."

Bri nods in agreement. "Her high school theater background is great. I've done costumes for so many plays at mine. Theater people know their lines. We won't have to do a massive number of takes because she can't memorize the dialogue. She'll understand stage direction, so that'll save time, too."

"They have chemistry." Riyaz yawns.

"We have our Isabel." Nick heads back to the door. "I'll let her know, and we can schedule our first rehearsal."

"I don't think we should rush. Let's get more candidates." The knot in my stomach tightens. I can't let this happen. She's not right for Nick. I mean for Isabel. "One more round?"

"We're out of time." Nick shakes his head. "Ruth is the one. Four against one. She's got the part."

I cross my arms. "So now this is a democracy?"

"No. I . . ." His long fingers dive into his brown locks, and the pads of my fingers tingle at the memory of the silky strands. His gaze scans the others as if for help. "I . . . want everyone's input on the actors, but we have to keep moving, and Ruth is the best we've seen."

I want to stomp my disagreement. "There's better out there."

"Maybe, but Ruth is here now." Nick locks eyes with me.

I glare back at him. "I want to continue looking."

"I just said we don't have time." He steps toward me, jamming his hand in the pocket of his jeans. "Actors are the least of my worries. There's a lot more to making a movie than writing some lines of dialogue and finding someone to say them. I have to get permits to shoot our beach scene and figure out how the dailies work."

My back stiffens. "It means using the first girl you see?" The truth of what I actually mean almost slips out. I backtrack. "I'd be more discerning if I were a director."

"But you aren't." Nick's words sting, and I'm not sure why. It's like I forgot we aren't partners here. This isn't last Christmas Eve, and we're not discussing Holly and Wesley's screenplay. This is different. Everything is different. And I don't like it.

"I need you to finalize the changes in the script we discussed yesterday. Before our first rehearsal." Nick is towering over me, and I stare right at his kissable lips as they form words that slice at me. "Please, be nice to Ruth. We need her more than she needs us. Don't make this about you. We're a team."

We were a team. I huff and glare at the spot Ruth occupied. Right now, I feel very much alone.

THIRTY-THREE

Sarah

READING EVERY BOOK ON screenwriting I could get my hands on at the library, watching YouTube videos, taking online classes—every bit of advice helped. But sitting in a room, where the word *beats* reflects story structure and not music, with six others who have the same dreams as I do, who don't think MC is a guy in charge of a wedding reception, whose eyes light up at the mention of the Dark Night of the Soul beat—this blows the other stuff away.

We speak the same language, sniff the vapors of the same dreams, and think being a screenwriter is a profession—not a passing fancy. I take a deep breath. With everyone there for themselves, wanting to win, and not sharing, I thought I'd feel alienated. It's the opposite. The camaraderie I have with these kids is exactly what I've been longing for. I shift on the burnt orange cloth of the auditorium seat and on a long breath out, let go of my fears.

Our third session together, and the scripts are mostly done. Filming begins next week, and to say I'm not having panicky moments from time to time would be a lie. I shake my pen. Actors will be saying my lines. The words will no longer reside on my computer but materialize and live in another dimension. My heart rises into my throat. Committed to film. Unchangeable. Final. Thrilled and terrified are the two states I've been vacillating between. And tired, how could I forget about that one?

"Next week we'll talk about how the shooting is going. What adjustments you've made on the fly, and how the dailies are shaping up." Ms. Monroe, or Teddy, as she insists we call her, the screenwriter with ten years of experience, who seemed like a god to me when I first met her, gets up first. Our small circle comes alive, and I pack up my laptop.

"Well, that was interesting." Outside the main building, Karina, the screenwriter for the yellow team, pulls her thick, white-rimmed sunglasses out of her short black curls and pushes them on her nose. I take out mine and raise my chin to the sun. Another bright, beautiful California day, and a good one because I don't have to deal with Nick.

"I think I have too much dialogue in my script." Today's session was called "You Can Fix It," and I had no idea there were so many pitfalls professionals will dismiss your screenplay over. I knew the first scene, the first act is, as Billy Wilder said, the "Grab 'em by the throat and never let go" attitude, but overused dialogue? Never thought that was possible for a screenplay. Yet this is why we're here. To learn the new stuff.

"You've done a read-through already?" Karina tilts her head and grimaces at me over the top of her sunglasses. "We haven't even agreed we'll do one. This is the theme with them. My team can't seem to do anything until it's down to the last minute."

Well, I give Nick credit for at least this one thing: the extra sessions he insists on every weekend really put us ahead of the game. Sounds like the yellow team might be in trouble. My gut is calm at the knowledge we're not in the worst shape. Nick's constant reminders to work together are paying off. Shit, now I'm thinking of Nick again. Stop it, Sarah. This is supposed to be your Nick-free day.

"We were lucky. Aside from our set designer who refuses to speak in general, the rest of the team were game. I suggest you don't do the read in the middle of a coffee shop though. So many stares. But worth the effort. It revealed some stumbling spots I was able to fix in the moment."

Karina shifts her knitted macrame bag hiding her laptop to her other shoulder. "We're waiting till we have the actors join us next week. Have you met yours yet?"

"The leads only. Tristan goes to UCLA, he's playing Rudo. Having a little trouble with the British accent though. Keeps trying to sound like a Duke in 1890, not a college student in 1990." The guy is trying a little too hard. "Wil, our sound engineer, is giving him lessons."

I have to say, I misjudged Wil. He's surprised me these past few weeks. There's more to him than meets the eye. He and Nick are getting quite buddy-buddy. I jab at the crosswalk button. I'm not thinking about Nick.

"And Ruth is playing Isabel. The script called for a blue-eyed blond, but when she read with Tristan their chemistry was off the charts. So now our character Isabel has brown eyes"—I still nurse the wound of letting go of the perfect image of Isabel—"but Ruth agreed to put highlights in her hair. She's so invested." Ruth fought for the role, and I don't know, I just gotta respect someone who fights for what they want.

"You guys are way ahead," says Karina as we cross the road. "We're auditioning Monday and Tuesday and will do the read-throughs on Wednesday. Maybe. I gave up. I never wanted to do a sci-fi thriller. I mean, *Star Wars* is great and all, but maybe we could not try to copy George Lucas with the low-budget effects." She laughs at herself, and I join her.

Man, it's so good to laugh. Things have been too stressful lately, with no time to sleep or even think. Siobhan's in a funk after Mr. Volleyball asked her to "go steady," and she told him she never does. My roommate prefers rollercoasters. Claudia dropped the bomb that she's moving out mid-August. At least she's paying for a full month. Finding a good roommate is third on my list, right after the competition and work. I kick a pebble out of my way. If we don't find someone, our already tight budget for things like rent and food will be in jeopardy. I can't pick up extra shifts at The Diamond Club to cover the gap until the competition is over.

Then there's avoiding Nick. That little game is exhausting. "I could do a read-through with you, if you'd like."

Karina stops in her tracks and stares at me. "You aren't from around here, are you?"

I laugh. I get this a lot. "You found me out." I lean in and whisper, "Canadian. Born and bred."

"Explains a lot." She hip-checks me. "I'm surprised this town hasn't eaten you up and spit you out yet."

"Oh, it tried. And failed."

Karina takes both my shoulders. "Wanna grab a coffee and you can weave me the tale?" Her tone is serious. "Might put my current woes in perspective?"

"I can definitely help." The bitterness is back in my voice. Will I ever get over what happened? "Coffee sounds good."

"Great. There's this cute place, Blend, with—"

"No." Nick-less day means not seeing him at his place of work. "The weather is so nice. How about the Farmers' Market? I hear they also have a spot with awesome baked goods. I need some carbs to tell this story."

"Farmers' Market it is."

The market is a cornucopia of sights, sounds, and smells. My blood buzzes. I relax my jaw. Even though I've lived in LA for over a year I can't get used to the abundance of fruit and vegetables available in California. Back home we get strawberries, good strawberries, for about a month. Anytime I need my strawberry fix now, I head out to a market like this and indulge in a pint of the plump sweet fruit. I pick up a small basket.

Two coffees and one gigantic cream cheese Danish split in half later, Karina and I people watch from a bench in the shade. Or, as I like to call it, working on character building.

"What's the story?" Karina regards me with the calm curiosity of a fellow storyteller.

This isn't something I talk about. Siobhan's in on the details: I moved in with her when I started working at The Diamond Club and had no money to pay first and last month's rent until my first paycheck showed up. Mémère knew. Mom and Dad got the gist, not the specifics.

"Well, if you and I were to write this as an opening scene"—shit, I'm stalling—"Teddy would tell us to try something a little more original."

Karina chuckles.

"But truth being stranger than fiction and all." Out with it, Sarah. I take a deep breath and dive in.

"Like most transplants, I came to LA to chase a dream. Since I can remember, I wanted to write. Working as a screenwriter appealed to me, so I decided the best way to achieve my goal was to commit to the idea. Go all in. Move to Hollywood. Learn from the professionals. But I wasn't silly enough to come here without a plan. I had stars in my eyes but still used my brain." The sights and sounds of the market dim. "Or so I thought."

I nibble on the corner of my Danish, not tasting the carbs I craved. "I enrolled in a 'program'"—I air quote the word—

"that offered a six-month certificate and guaranteed real film experience. I'm not a fool. I did my research. They had credentials, testimonials from film industry executives I read about on IMDb—everything seemed legit.

"An amazing opportunity from everything I could see. I sent my information, the script I was working on, did a video interview with the head of admissions, and got accepted." I remember the feeling of utter elation, screaming and dancing with Mémère in the kitchen of Côté Fraise, imagining myself on the red carpet accepting awards, living in a beachside mansion in LA. "I transferred the enrollment fee, packed my bags, and drove for almost three days straight to get here."

The hot coffee burns my tongue. "When I showed up for my first day, I found the building at the address 'Theo Smithee' provided empty, the numbers disconnected, and the email address undeliverable." My brother Grayson threatened to find Theo Smithee and break his legs. But Mr. Smithee disappeared along with my cash. A little too late, I discovered Smithee is a fake name used in Hollywood for ghost writers and films where the studio doesn't want the actual director to get credit for their work.

Fake. I sigh. Story of my life.

Shame floods my veins, and I can't bring myself to glance at Karina. To see her dumbfounded or pitying expression is too painful. Duped, and it was my fault.

"Was the company the Screenwriters Corporation of America?"

I raise my eyes to hers. They're angry. "How did you know?"

"A friend of mine fell for the same scam." Karina lifts her coffee cup to her lips. "He wasn't as resilient as you. Went back to Ohio. I think he's using his bachelor's degree and working as an accountant now."

Images of the ovens at Côté Fraise, Mom covered in flour sitting in the cramped office adding up the day's sales, and Mémère spreading strawberry jam between sheets of pastry rush through my mind. My family and friends were miles away, in a different country. That first week in LA I remember being alone, truly alone, for the first time. Going back was safe. Staying in LA was risky. For an instant or a month, I considered giving up and moving back to Toronto. Mémère insisted I stay.

I pop a strawberry in my mouth and brush away the crumbs from the Danish. "Well, I wouldn't say I've exactly been living the life. For the past year, my nights have consisted of serving over-priced cocktails to over-dressed snobs."

Karina tuts. "You were offered a spot in this competition. You wrote a screenplay. You have a foot in the door of Hollywood. I call that winning."

Girl has a point. I straighten my shoulders. This is where I belong.

THIRTY-FOUR

Sarah

I TURN ON THE blinker and pause by the no stopping sign. Wil ceases the erratic drumming on the back of my headrest and jumps out, his guitar case banging off the side. He sets out at a run toward The Devil's Martini bar and doesn't look back at Nick and me in the car. He's late for something that he won't specify.

"You're welcome." Not that Wil hears me.

I peel away from the red curb, not in the mood for a ticket to follow the disaster of a sunset shoot. They should've listened to me. We should've done the pool. Did we even get anything useful?

With Wil out of the car there should me more room in my convertible, but the cabin shrinks around Nick and me, wrapping us tighter together. His smallest motions send ripples of awareness across my skin. Exactly what I've been avoiding. "To your dad's place?"

"Sure."

The worry over our first shoot draws frown lines on his forehead even the visor on his worn-out Chicago cap can't hide. Nick angles his knees to the door, his shoulders folded in, head bowed. He hides his face in shadows like drunken patrons at last call who know that whatever awaits them at home is bad news.

My stomach rumbles. "I'm starving. Mind if we stop for something to eat first?" My foot pushes on the brakes. Did I ask him out? Betty shudders to a stop inches from the car ahead of us.

Nick's cap lifts, and his gaze catches mine. Dark sparks ignite in his eyes, burning through my defenses. I'm powerless. Looking away is as impossible as not breathing. Nick's throat flexes. He wraps his fingers around the grab handle and straightens. The déjà vu of my offer at Christmas and driving to the taco truck by Griffith Park sends pangs into my gut. My stomach clenches, but not from hunger.

"I could eat." This time, there's an edge of excitement in his words.

My invitation shouldn't affect him so much. This is not a date, just two coworkers getting some sustenance. "Have you been to Heavenly Burgers yet? They have a quick drive-thru."

"Haven't been anywhere," Nick grumbles.

I step on the gas and take a side street shortcut. The pink and green neon sign of Heavenly Burgers comes into view. There are two cars in front of us in the drive-thru. I twist in my seat. "What d'you want?"

"You choose." Nick's gaze flicks to mine and falls on my fingers strangling the gear shifter between us.

I shift into neutral. "Flaming jalapeno burger with extra hot sauce on the side it is then."

"I don't do—"

"Spicey." I suck in my lips. He doesn't get my joke. "I remember."

His eyes find mine again, and this time there's a light in them. The light of hope. My heart thuds against my ribs. This was a bad idea. I grip the steering wheel. Nick sinks back into his seat.

"Welcome to Heavenly's. Can I take your order?" The metallic voice blares from the speaker.

"Two number ones, no pickles. Wait." I turn to Nick. "Would you like pickles?"

Nick clears his throat. "Please."

"Make that one with pickles, one without. Fries. One Coke and a Sprite." I rush the words out like there are ten cars waiting behind us.

"That'll be $14.55," the small box squawks. "Second window." I pull forward.

"Umm." He takes off his cap and sets it on his bouncing knee. "Smells good." Nick licks his lips. "Haven't eaten anything but protein bars this week." He swallows, and I tear my eyes away from his mouth.

My chest heats. The July heat should've cooled by this time of the night. I drag my finger between my skin and the collar of my T-shirt. "Might want to try adding some fruits and veggies into the mix."

Nick gives me the grin that makes my stomach flip. "That's why I got the pickles."

I try not to smile at his joke, yet the corners of my mouth slide up. I shift into gear and roll Betty forward while I search in the backseat for my wallet. He leans to reach into his jean pocket. His hair grazes the exposed skin of my shoulder.

"I got this." Nick has a credit card in his hand. "Payback for the gas to drive us around." He pushes it in front of me, his elbow bumping into mine. "You don't like pickles?"

I shrink into my seat to distance myself from his skin. "Nope. Can't stand them." His arm retreats, and I exhale. "I'd rather drink ginger ale, but not many places in LA carry it. Another thing I miss from home."

"Not much I miss from home. Maybe Mom's cooking."

"At least you have your dad here." Nick shrugs, and I want to ask more but shouldn't pry. "My dad keeps trying to lure me back to Toronto. I told him if we don't win the competition, I'll consider it."

His gaze snaps to mine. "You're leaving?"

"No, I didn't say that." I twist my hair and secure it in a loose bun. A cold shower when I get home should cool the blazing inferno my skin has become. I roll up to the window.

Nick leans across me, handing his card to the cashier. His bicep brushes against my collar bone. He smells better than the best burgers back home. I press against my headrest to resist closing the small space between my lips and his. I want to sample them, see if the sensation I experienced on Christmas Eve still exists, see if he tastes the same.

Greasy bag and a tray with our drinks in hand, he settles back into his side of the car. I pull into a vacant parking spot and we unwrap our food. We chew, swallow, chew some more while *Making the Truth Hurt*—Blatantly Subtle's latest hit—promises that lies don't always come from bad intentions. The aroma of burgers and fries should drown the scent of Nick, pull my attention away from him, but my desire is stronger. No matter how hard I try to avoid him, he's everywhere: in my car, in my competition, in my life.

"Something's not working between Rudo and Isabel." Nick breaks the silence.

"You don't like the script?"

"No, no, I love the script. Nothing's wrong with the words. It's ... I don't know. I can't see it." He scrapes both hands across his face. "I know that makes no sense, but at the beach tonight, even though we were losing the light, they didn't connect. Is it the chemistry? Did I choose the wrong actor? Maybe we should have looked for someone else like you suggested."

"I wasn't a fan of Ruth, that's true, but now I see what you saw in her. She has passion, and there is chemistry between her and Tristan." Something was off tonight. The heat. My inability to concentrate on the actors' dialogue with Nick hovering never less than six feet away. My imagination substituting Tristan and

Ruth's faces for Nick's and mine with every caress, every kiss. "Maybe we're forcing the kiss too early."

"What do you mean?" He squints and focuses on my mouth like he's imagining us kissing as well.

I roll my lips between my teeth. "Well, sunsets are romantic, and everyone rides off into the sunset. But this is not a full-length movie, we have less time to build the emotions. We kinda skipped that part. Turned the story of them falling in love into a montage."

"Right, right." Nick shifts in his seat, knee bumping against the glove box. "We need some small moments, like in the coffee shop. Some almosts." His broad shoulders create a wall between me and the world.

I want to tuck myself in. Feel his muscles under my cheek. "Yeah, create a little tension, so when they finally kiss the audience feels it with them."

"Like him brushing his hand against hers." Nick stretches his hand out. His fingers hover over mine for an instant. I rotate my palm but he jerks back. "Say over the milk. That could work. I could use the milk jug as the focal point, zoom in tight, and just show their hands."

And there he is. The man I fell for on Christmas Eve. Alight with the passion of this project, brimming full of confidence. Not the boy who's been flipping between not listening to me and walking around me on eggshells. Nick holds his fingers up, using my half-empty cup as the milk substitute, describing how he'd shoot the scene, and even I can see it.

We bat around a few more options, how to transition into the sunset scene. He takes out his phone and pulls up a scene from a Spike Lee movie. "See there. We could do something similar."

His long fingers hold the screen between us. I abandon my safety zone and stretch across the console. The line of his bicep sticks to my overheated shoulder. "I mean, Spike is the king, but I don't think he'd mind a little homage to this shot." His head tilts toward mine, so we're ear-to-ear.

"Hmm." I nod. I'm listening, indulging in the warmth of where his arm presses against mine.

"I watched an interview once where he referenced a scene in *Malcom X* he recreated because he loved it in a Martin Scorsese movie," he says. The light of his phone illuminates the side of his face, highlighting the tiny scar he showed me our first night together. My fingers move of their own accord toward his cheek. "Directors do it all the time."

I crowbar myself away from Nick. He's my director. Our team lead. My boss. "We should go." I grip the steering wheel. "Early start for the shoot tomorrow."

THIRTY-FIVE

NICK

"But they're real classic Vans. I need to go *today*, before someone else snaps them up." Bri is babbling in one ear about money to buy checkered print sneakers, and I couldn't give a fuck.

In my other ear, the fluorescent light over the coffee shop's counter flickers and buzzes. I flick the plastic cover and the irregular flash-buzz ceases. Bri's word vomit keeps going. Last time they *had* to have something, they went on a shopping spree, spending over two hundred dollars on used clothing, mostly hats we couldn't, well, use. My temples seize. Three overflowing bags are off to Goodwill. As soon as I find the time.

Wil grumbles as he drags a mop across the floor, a task whoever closed last night did a half-assed job at. The coffee shop is a mess, and we need to clean before we can even begin to shoot. I glance at my watch. The pressure in my head rises. We have two hours before the place opens.

"I'll help in just a sec." I make another promise I'm not sure I can keep. There's still the lighting to set up, the outfits to approve, coffee to make, and seven other things I'm sure I've forgotten. With the side of my key, I scratch a piece of dried-up jam off the table we'll use for the shot. Wil didn't sign up to play janitor, and he's the only one on my side. Or was on my side. Not so sure anymore.

Tristan, the lead who plays Rudo, walks over, script in hand. "Thanks for talking us through the last kiss scene. I think we both got what we need, but can we talk about this dialogue?"

"Sure." My eye twitches. Explaining to Ruth what I wanted her to do with her mouth and articulating what expression I wanted to see on Rudo and Isabel's faces was embarrassing enough. With Sarah two feet away, chiming in beside me, the whole thing was excruciating. She kept taking my mind off the script and onto taking Sarah's face to demonstrate to the actors how it's done. But that would be unprofessional. I bite my lip. I need to stop thinking about Sarah so much.

She's helping Riyaz set up the black screens over the two glass walls of the shop to allow me to control the light inside and make the shop seem like late afternoon when really it's pre-dawn. And to keep the curious and ignorant out of our shots. This scene doesn't call for extras and definitely not noses pressed against the window which I will have to clean. I got permission from the boss to use the coffee shop before the café opens but forgot to get a permit, so if anyone complains, I'm up shit's creek without a paddle. I squeeze the back of my neck in naive hope of not getting a tension headache. Another fail in a long list of fuckups.

"These lines here, after the final kiss"—he points to the part where Rudo tells Isabel he got into the school in England—"they don't flow. We've been rehearsing them, and they need more heart."

Now this. I ball my hands into fists. My palm stings. I spilled coffee all over myself yesterday rushing to fill this big order for the music studio down the road, and I may have a third-degree burn. Least of my problems. "Okay. Give me a minute, and I'll review it."

Tristan's lips do the thing he defaults to when his brain is overthinking—twists to the side in a not grin—and he returns to Ruth, who follows his expression over to me, and then to Sarah.

Yeah, I read you loud and clear. I grind my teeth. Sarah would fix everything right away, but there's only one of me, and I need to set up the camera. I open the box I lugged across campus after signing it out last night and search for the 50mm lens I want to use for the establishing shot. I push the heels of my palms into my eyes. Where's the case?

Fuck. I slap my hand over my forehead. Repeatedly. Can nothing go right today?

The 85mm is here. Maybe I can make that work. My head feels heavy, like I'm wearing my hockey helmet. I'll need the tripod to hold the lens steady. I stand up, searching for it. The stupid contraption better be here.

There's a hand on my arm. "Can I have a minute?"

Her slender fingers send a jolt directly to my heart. The swear word gets stuck in my mouth as I find Sarah watching me. I force myself to relax. "Sure."

I follow her away from the maddening crowd, behind the counter, and into the alcove leading to the storage room. Once we're out of sight of our crew and surrounded by beige boxes that I know contain takeout cups, napkins, and toilet paper, she faces me. Even here, in the most boring hallway in the world, at the crack of dawn, recognizing she worked late last night, she's still stunning. My jaw relaxes. I'd much rather hide out here with her than manage the colossal mess back there.

"Hey." Her voice is quiet, and I step closer to hear her.

"Hey." More bad news? I plant my feet and square my shoulders.

She tilts her head and stares at me. This isn't good. My brain buzzes. I can practically feel Bri's ire burning through the six feet of drywall and air separating us. What am I going to do with them? They are completely uncontrollable. The parade of drums in my chest resumes. Riyaz hasn't secured the locations for tomorrow. I rub the scar on my cheek. What time is sunset? I need to make sure we have at least two hours of light before the golden hour.

I shudder. Everything is falling apart. The twitching in my eye starts again. Why did I think I could do this? I should give up. Sarah could run the show. She always seems to know what she's doing. Maybe I could ask her for help?

Sarah's hands grasp my T-shirt and tug me down to her level. I stumble on the sticky floor with the force of her pull, grabbing onto her shoulders to steady myself. The scent of strawberries surrounds me as her mouth crashes against mine.

Lips. Sarah. Permits. Lines. Budget. Sarah. Coffee. Script.

My brain short circuits.

Hats. Money. Dad. Rent. Sarah. Did I bring the tripod? Sarah. She's kissing me.

Sarah.

Sarah.

The pulsing of my heart stills. Short, ragged breaths catch in my throat. Everything flies out of my brain except the taste of Sarah. In my arms. I wrench her closer, and her warmth seeps into me. The many shouts of my worries, the concerns poisoning my blood, drain. She takes on the heavy, cleanses it, and gives me a fresh, unadulterated version of myself, where the words don't hurt as much, don't strangle me with an ever-tightening circle of "can't," where windows lose their blackout shades and I can see the world around me. My eyes fly open. This world is Sarah. The coil in my chest loosens. Everything is possible again.

We break apart, and every cell in my body screams, missing the connection already. My lips burn and set my face on fire. The electricity between us crackles. Sarah must feel it as well because she presses her forehead against mine. She whispers in my ear, "You can do this."

I open my mouth to beg her to keep touching me, but the warmth of her skin is gone. So is she: out of my arms, leaving me stuck among boxes of to-go cups, napkins, and toilet paper. My world's beige again, but different. I take a deep long breath to fill my lungs. I should feel pain, but I see possibilities. We can stack those boxes and help Riyaz lift the fake bookshelves too short for the frame.

I don't understand what just happened, but it's like she rebooted my brain. Things reorganize inside my skull. No more heavy helmet. "I can do this" flashes across my mind and overlays the doubts trying to fight their way back to the top. Sarah thinks I can. This knowledge gives me enough power to focus on what I can do, what I can solve today.

Before I even make it back to the group, Bri is on me. "Nick, they're the perfect shoes, they'll complete the look for tomorrow's scene, and if I don't get them then Ruth, I mean Isabel, will have to go barefoot. You don't want that, do you?"

I take out my wallet, pull out the credit card, and hand it to them. "Here. The code is 1224." The day I met Sarah. "I want pictures of every item with explanations of how they fit into the script. You only buy what I approve. Nothing more. Got it?"

Bri blinks a few times then agrees. "Got it." Their lips suppress a smile. "Thanks. I won't let you down."

I call Ruth and Tristan over. "Sarah?" I look for her, and she's right there, by my side. "We need some adjustments to the script." I remove the paper from Tristan's hands and point to the lines. "Here and here. Tristan has some ideas. Can you work on this while Wil and I set up the shot?"

"On it," says Sarah.

"Riyaz, the boxes in the back can help with your fake book-shelf stability issue. Grab some later, but first I need the lights with their umbrellas and tents set up here and here." I'm not even asking, just telling. I straighten to my full height. In a shocking turn of events, Riyaz nods, picks up a light stand, and starts assembling it. I pull a table and two chairs to the location I want Tristan and Ruth to occupy during the first shot.

Ten minutes later the scene is set: lights are positioned, the bookshelves don't fall when anybody walks in front of them, boom mics are ready to pick up the dialogue Sarah has fixed, and our actors, hair perfectly coiffed, clothing 90s era appropriate, are ready for their first take. A smile tickles my lips.

I screw the camera into the base of the tripod, secure it, and rub my hands as my smile takes hold. "Okay, everyone. Let's roll."

Thirty-Six

NICK

THE SHOT WE NEEDED? Done. Open Blend by 7 a.m. without the place looking like a set? Done. Some kind of miracle, or maybe this movie thing might work out. And I'm not just saying it. I draw a perfect foam heart on the cappuccino and grin at my handywork. The tension in the scene of Isabel convincing Rudo to leave her for England gave me goosebumps, and Bri's eyes were glistening. The scene is gold. Tiny bubbles of sweet foam might as well be filling my chest. I bob my head to the tune Wil's humming. Would be gold once I figure out the final touch—the music.

Wil and I hear "cuties" and "I'd tap that" and "hot twins" comments all day long while we're burning our hands on hot coffee. I get the first two, but the last one? We don't look anything alike. Besides, nothing ever comes of it—either we scare them off or they aren't single. Maybe that's not a bad thing. Most customers don't even bother to look up from their phones when I call their name. I toss an empty box of almond milk in the recycling. I rarely have time to strike up a conversation. I, being one of the newest employees, am honored with the privilege of scrubbing substances off the bathroom surfaces that nobody should ever have to face.

Three cappuccinos, one espresso, two iced macchiatos, and a lot of pastry round out the orders Wil sent my way in less than five minutes. He should pretend to slow down for my sake. How's he so cheerful? The humming from him is incessant, and his tune is rubbing salt into my open wound of failing to find an original song for our movie *Indigo*.

Our budget is down to crumbs, and the outlandish idea that we'd be able to pay for the copyright to use a track in this crucial scene is exactly that—outlandish. We can use stock tunes for the rest of the film, but this is the big moment. Two cappuccinos done, I call out the customer's name. The music will make or break what Tristan and Ruth have created. The right song will reflect the emotional turmoil of the characters and tear at people's hearts.

Wil's humming picks up in volume. Have I heard that song?

"You're in a good mood." I dump the used coffee grounds into the compost holder.

Wil lifts a box of premade sandwiches and refills the pastry display, preparing for the lunch hour mini-rush. "I'm always in a good mood." He checks his phone. "And in T-minus ten minutes, I'm outta here."

"Another big gig at the Farmers' Market?"

Behind the glass of the display case I can see the ginormous smile spread across Wil's face. Happens every time I mention his busking adventures. Our sound engineer has other talents: he plays guitar. His stories about busking in his hometown of Bremen in Germany are so good, Sarah took notes to add to a future screenplay.

"You have to hear this song El is working on. Such a good beat." Wil slides the glass back in place. "With my help, it's gonna be a hit."

Wish I knew how to play guitar, or anything, really. I wipe off the milk steamer. Making my brother and me do sports was Mom's way to keep us out of trouble. Music and arts were not something she could afford. School offered, but there were kids way better than me who actually practiced. Mom thinks I'm into artsy stuff because of Dad. I'm not sure genetics play that big of a role. I hadn't seen the guy between the ages of nine and nineteen. I set my jaw. My career path is my choice, not something he can take credit for when he wants to.

The café picks up and Wil sneaks out the back as soon as the afternoon shift cashier and barista arrive. I tell them we're sold out of the lemon scones everyone loves, do an inventory of almond milk quarts, and head out.

Leftover pastries and an iced mocha latte in hand, I head over to the Farmers' Market. Time to check on what my buddy is up to there.

The sun beats on my neck, and I cross the street to the shadier side. The colorful tents of the vendors promise fresh, local, organic fruit and vegetables. Watermelons provide a stripy backsplash to the strawberries that dot the stands. The smell of fried dough from the churro cart makes the two stale croissants seem even less appetizing. Wil's not hard to spot. Or rather he is, but the large throng of people gathered around him and the girl he's singing with makes it obvious. She's shorter than Wil but has a bigger presence, her purple wide-brimmed hat and aviator glasses giving her a rockstar glam.

Claps come from around them and some stalls several feet away. I throw the takeout cup into the trash. Good thing I do, or I'd be wearing the coffee. The powerhouse voice belting out the opening line to Queen's *Somebody to Love* knocks me off my feet. Wil's partner can sing. Like, really sing. People are tapping their feet, and the dude beside me is singing along with her. He really shouldn't. Even I can tell he's way off.

The song ends and emptiness fills the air. How's the absence of a song making the bustling market devoid of sound? There must be more songs coming.

"Thanks everyone. That's it for us today, but we'll be back." Wil shouts over the disappointed ahs of the crowd. They feel the loss, too. Their extra claps don't stop Wil and the girl from packing up. The people leave the tight circle one by one, but I stay behind and give the singing duo a slow round of applause.

"I came by to see what all the fuss is about," I say.

The sign at their feet reads "WE! Find us at The Devil's Martini every Saturday at 8 pm." The bar we dropped Wil at the weekend after the particularly disastrous attempt at filming the sunset kiss at the beach scene. Wil behaved like he was late to his own wedding. I point to the sign. "Explains why you made Sarah drive like a maniac on Saturday."

Wil gives me a *shut up* look I completely ignore. "El, this is Nick. He's the director of the movie I was telling you about."

El waves at me. "You're the one obsessed with sunsets."

Oh, this one has a bit of a bite. I try to hide my chuckle by clearing my throat. She's not going to let Wil's attitude slide.

Is Wil's face turning red? "I might've ranted a bit when I nearly missed the start of our gig." This is priceless.

"Oh." I scratch the stubble on my chin and suck in some air. "Had to pull rank. But now that I understand the reason, I'll try to keep Saturday nights free." I cross my arms. Seems my teammate has a secret. He can sing too. "You two are great."

"Thanks," Wil and El answer in sync.

Wil gathers the money they've collected in his guitar case and sorts the coins from the dollar bills. I address El. "Wil tells me you write your own songs."

Wil's eyes go wide. Was I not supposed to mention this?

"Did some humming of my own during my morning shift," says Wil. "Might've bragged to Nick a bit about our writing session."

"You? Bragging? I don't believe it." El's humor is my kind of humor. I wouldn't mind getting to know her better.

A silly smirk makes it to my lips. Sounds like it's Wil's kind of humor as well. His shoulders relax, and the good mood from earlier in the day reappears.

"Oh, man, she knows you well." Not laughing at Wil's expression is harder than I thought. She gets how to poke at Wil better than I do.

Is Wil hiding her from us? From me? Because she's a singer-songwriter? An idea scratches on my brain. She's a singer-songwriter. Hmm. Maybe it's the extra cup of coffee or the power of her voice, or the memory of Sarah's kiss, but I'm more confident than I've been in months. I plaster on my pretty-please mug. "Any chance you'd be interested in writing a song for what could be the next Oscar winner for live action short film?"

Wil stands in front of El like I'd just insulted her. "I think she's too busy, mate."

"Wait." El steps up to Wil's side. "Not so fast. Your friend's asking for help."

Wil ignores me and addresses El. "My friend is over budget and looking for free talent."

"It's not always about the money, Wil. I'll do it, if you do it with me."

"Really?" Can everyone hear the surprise in Wil's voice or just me?

"Yes." Now El has a concerned expression. "Is it too much? Will you have time?"

Wil folds the dollar bills in his hand. "I'll find the time. Helping the movie and writing with you? It'd be fun."

Shots of joy hop from my eyes to my heart, their tiny leaps lighting a road to the perfect backdrop for Rudo and Isabel's parting scene. Done. Maybe I should buy a lottery ticket today. I keep cool and calm, as if my biggest wish for the day, or month, hasn't just been granted. "Perfect. It's settled then. You'll write and record a song for *Indigo*." I lean in toward El. "That's the name of our film."

"Oh, now I'm recording it as well?" El smiles back at me.

"Seems only fair. With a voice like yours, you have to record the song." I rub my chin. My biggest wish of the year is to have Sarah trust me again. My throat constricts. Maybe this could be one more step toward that reality. "Only one caveat."

El's smile fades.

"Sarah needs to be part of the process. She's the screenwriter, and the theme is her idea. She'll want to be included." It's the truth. My toes tap on the hot asphalt. I couldn't brainstorm anything to do with the song without Sarah. Still, how perfect of an excuse is this to hang out with her?

Kisses don't solve anything, and I'm ready for a solution.

"Umm . . . I guess that's okay." El stretches her hand my way. "It's a deal."

"Perfect." I wink at Wil. "I'll see you later. We can tell Sarah and the crew together."

I leave Wil and El to count their money, and I count my blessings. The meeting with Mr. Takamado is next, and I'm excited: he's going to like what I have this time. My feet barely touch the ground as I head back to campus. Another done item for me today. Done. Done. Done. Done. Done. The giant smile on my face must be competing with the sun for brightness. Everything is finally coming together.

THIRTY-SEVEN

NICK

I SIT IN A large recording studio at the music school with Sarah by my side. Opposite us, the foot of air between El and Wil crackles with electricity. If I heard right, if what I think Sarah whispered into my ear about El being Melodie is true, I'd be advising Wil to cut the crap. If he were one of my hockey teammates, I'd think Wil's trying to use her stepfather's connections, but the way they are around each other, how excited they are about this song, Wil might, just might, be genuinely into making music with her.

"No fucking way. Melodie Rockerby? Like Rocker Rockerby? *Born on the Wrong Side* Rocker?" I glance over at El Vella. She was just a girl with a vibe and a voice when I met her at the Farmers' Market. El Vella is Melodie Rockerby. My mind is blown, but I see the resemblance now. In the interviews she wears more makeup, different clothes. None of the glam here. Just a normal teenager.

A smiling Sarah pokes me in the ribs and sings the first line of Bill Rockerby's hit *Born on the Wrong Side*. Mom has a concert T-shirt she bought when she went to see him live, first when she was around my age and then again when Mike and I got her tickets for her fiftieth. She'd freak if she knew I was working with his stepdaughter. I join in with Sarah, and she shimmies alongside, her arm brushing against me for a moment. My skin tingles.

We finish the last line of the chorus, and Sarah regards El. "Have these two idiots even told you what the movie is about?"

"Nope," says El.

Sarah shakes her head. She doesn't say anything, but this is her way of insinuating we're useless.

"Essentially, our hero woos the girl with lines from his favorite books. The girl isn't into nerds, but he wins her over. When he earns a scholarship to study in England, she tells him he can't miss the opportunity." Sarah pauses to make sure I'm following. I wave my hand for her to continue. "Five years later, he's back in Canada on a book tour for his debut novel, the story of their relationship. She surprises him by showing up at the signing, and they reunite. He moves back to Canada to be with her."

"Oh, I like that." El plays with the white strand of hair I should've recognized her by. "And the song?"

"We need something to play over the scene when she tells him to leave. We"—I step closer to Sarah—"were thinking something about letting go of the person you love because it's in the other person's best interest." With her back to me I have the freedom to look at her. Goosebumps prickle on my neck. "Even if the action hurts you."

"Do you have any lyrics yet?" El's gaze finds Wil.

"A few ideas." Wil walks back to where he dropped his messenger bag and digs out one of those black notebooks I always see him scribbling in.

Sarah leans in and whispers in my ear, "I think Wil might be into El."

"Really?" I whisper in hers, maintaining our little bubble. "He's been talking about their music nonstop. More than about our movie."

"That bad?" Sarah's breath tickles my ear, and goosebumps cover my body. We track Wil as he takes a call, gets up, and disappears into the booth out of earshot. I've heard him speak German before, but never with such worry. Sarah's eyes dart between Wil and El, and when she gives me a quizzical glance, I mouth "Together?" Sarah shakes her head and mouths "No," and we return to watching El mesmerized by everything Wil does, staring at him like he's a puzzle she's trying to crack, a mystery she's trying to solve.

"Trust me," I say. This is the closest we've been since the kiss in the back room of Blend. Should I turn my head and touch her lips with mine? No. Not with Wil and El here.

"I do." Those words from her mouth taste better than a kiss.

Wil's back. He picks up his little black book. "We should get back to this." He begins riffling through the pages.

"Here it is." Wil scoots next to El; he extends the black book her way with a page open to a series of words and phrases.

"Would you mind reading them?" asks El.

Wil meets her eyes, shoots a glance at Sarah and me, and taps his nose, as if he's pondering the question. With a grin he bumps El's shoulder with his arm. "Sure thing. I'm thinking 'go away' should be in the chorus, but we need four syllables there."

"Go far away?" El looks up at him.

Wil's index finger points her way. "That'll work."

"Go far away. Forget the past," Wil recites. El mouths the words Wil said.

"Create your life." El trills the next line.

"Can we backtrack?" Sarah whispers in my ear, sending waves of heat across my skin. I'm not sure if she's afraid to interrupt El and Wil or if she's trying on purpose to scramble my brain. I tug on the belt of my jeans. Desire for her clouds the remains of my sound mind, and I can barely keep my body under control.

"What did you miss?" I whisper back.

"The melody."

Right, she hasn't heard the melody Wil hummed all morning at Blend.

"Before we get too far, " I speak up over the tittering of Wil and El's voices. "Could you play the melody for us?" I wag my finger between Sarah and me. "Wil hummed a bit earlier, but Sarah's not heard it before."

El moves away from Wil and dives into her bag. "I have a track on my phone, or I can sing it live."

I glance at Sarah and then back at El. "Live?"

El shrugs, opens her mouth, and notes ripple across the room.

I understand what it feels like when they say someone's jaw dropped. I'm not picking mine off the floor, but my lips find their way into an exaggerated O. I heard El at the Farmers' Market, and she was impressive, but that was a cover of Queen's *Someone to Love.* This song is built for her, her voice rises from her torso and amplifies, stretching out from her body into every crevice of the room. I see the whole scene in front of me: Rudo and Isabel, the angles I'll use on the close-ups of their faces and their contrast against El's melody. A shiver shoots up my spine. I'll make their eyes the focal point, use light and dark to tell the story.

El sings the ta-da-da on the verses and o-o-o-o on the chorus where words are missing. I'm not worried, somehow confident the words will come. Wil picks up the guitar and joins El. On the second chorus, he adds his voice to hers in a counter melody. My stomach flips. I'm not sure if they practiced this before or if they are freestyling, but when they stop singing, I know this is the answer. The perfect song.

We merge and shift ideas back and forth for the next hour until El's phone buzzes. She winces and focuses on Wil. "I have to go."

Sarah stands up from the circle we've been sitting in. "Me too. I have an early shift tomorrow."

I push myself off the floor and stretch my hands above me. When I let them fall, I notice Sarah's lips part before her eyes drop to her sneakers, her hair falling across her face. I check to see if I have crumbs on my chest or something. Nope. All good.

In the lobby, El hangs by my side, and what I see in the way she examines Wil a duplicate of what must be in my eyes when I observe Sarah. El's into Wil. Wil returns the key to the security guard, and he and Sarah chat with Frank for a moment.

"How do they do that?" El asks.

I check out Frank, Sarah, and Wil laughing. "I guess they make friends wherever they go." As if Sarah senses me staring at her, she turns my way, but this time, instead of glancing away, she squares her shoulders and beelines to me.

"Would you like a ride home?"

Am I hearing what I'm hearing? Every muscle in my chest contracts. I throw a glance at Wil, who's already out the door with El, and then back at Sarah's waiting expression. She's offering to spend time with me. Alone.

My heart screams with excitement, but my instinct alerts a potential trap. This is too good to be true. Hope and dread collide in my head—a dangerous mix. This could be the best thing ever, or the end. Any word I choose to say might skew the needle in the wrong direction. No need to tempt fate. I avoid speaking and nod.

Sarah smiles. All the way to her eyes. My heart stops. The panic in my core dissipates. The blood-pumping organ jumps in my throat. Excitement wins. I win.

We walk over to the same parking lot I hot-wired Betty in on the first day of the competition. The roof is up today, and I shove the seat back to fit my legs. The surfaces in the car radiate heat, and I roll the window down on my side. The air outside is still in the nineties, and there is no cool breeze to bring some relief. In this seat, the scenes of our first night together play in my mind. Driving to the taco stand, up to the Griffith Observatory, me filming her, her kissing me. Then. And again last week at the shoot.

"Why did you kiss me?" Not the way to start a conversation, but the answer will tell me what options I have. If I'm misinterpreting the changes in her behavior over the last week, if I'm transferring my ideas onto her. I grip the side of the seat.

Sarah doesn't gasp or demand I leave her car. "I don't know. All the talk with Tristan and Ruth about how the kiss between Rudo and Isabel should go drove me nuts. I"—her hands clutch the steering wheel—"I wanted to see if our kiss would feel the same way it did on Christmas Eve. I've never had a connection like that with anyone."

"Did it?"

"Yes."

Her admission is quiet but like a sonic boom to me. This means more than friends. The whirligig in my head throws me off. This moment is what I was hoping for, feels like what I was hoping for. I want to be 100% certain. I take a fortifying breath and square my shoulders. The next words to come out of my mouth must be perfect. I'm out of chances, and I'm not going to screw this one up. I can't give her any other choice but to be more than friends. Much more. How do I explain this?

Oh, fuck it.

"You changed my life." I go for it. "I'd do anything to have you back. I'll be anything you want me to be."

THIRTY-EIGHT

NICK

SARAH'S GRIP ON THE steering wheel tightens. The band around my chest does too. I don't want my stupid words to be responsible for damage to Betty. "I want you to be you."

Does she mean me, Nick, or me, Shawn, the image of me she built up because I lied?

"The lie, it hurt." Sarah reads my mind, like only she can. Her hands drop to her lap. There are no indents on Betty's leather. The car isn't leaving the parking lot, but my heart is speeding like it's the final lap of a NASCAR race.

"The last thing I intended was to hurt you." Hurting her hurts me. Hot acid bubbles in my stomach. If I could be the one hurt instead, I'd take it, to protect her.

Sarah's eyes meet mine. "I can't deal with lying. Since I moved to LA, there's been too much deception in my life."

"I didn't mean to deceive you. That night I told nothing but the truth. You're the first person I've never lied to."

"Then why did you let me keep calling you Shawn?"

"We ran out of time. You with my real name and me with your number is how the night should've ended. But you saw how my dad is. I panicked." My gut revolts at the memory. I brace against the glove compartment, searching for a sign she understands. "A fake name is just that. A name. I'm the same person."

Sarah closes her eyes and rests her forehead on the steering wheel as if the car can help her decide. If I want Sarah to choose me, I have to tell her all of it, confess everything.

"My friends got me the ID for my birthday. I didn't want one, and I'd never used the stupid thing before. Ridiculous, I know."

Sarah's eyes dart my way. I run my hand through my hair and my elbow bumps Betty's frame. "Believe me. When I met you, I dropped the act. Because, yes, a lot of my life has been an act. I try to fit in, not cause problems, fly under the radar. Nicky, the alter ego, helped me get by."

"Alter ego?" Sarah's nose crinkles in confusion.

"It started with my parents' divorce. I was almost nine when Mom was forced to move Mike and me to Chicago to live with her sister. She got a job at a hair salon, helping with anything they needed while she studied to be a hairstylist herself. My whole world shifted; everything was different. I didn't even understand why my family split up. Mike kept pretending he was my father, and I didn't want him. I wanted my dad, not a stand-in."

Now that I started, I can't stop. My fingers form two hard fists. "I had trouble fitting in and had very little supervision. Alone, I'd watch movies endlessly to fill time. A photography class at school helped me realize I loved viewing the world through the camera lens. The experience added a layer between me and my surroundings, but instead of dulling the emotions I didn't want to feel, the camera allowed me to notice more, see more of life."

I bounce my fists on my knees. "Mackenzie, the girl you met, we got together sophomore year of high school because she wanted to date a hockey player, and I wanted access to her dad's camera equipment." I sound like a complete tool. Like I used her, which I didn't. The job was a side perk, not the main goal of our relationship. A conclusion in retrospect rather than a plan I put into action then.

With a sigh, I move my knees and face the driver's seat. "We lasted less than four months. I'm not sure I got to know her past hooking up. Not in the real way, at least. I've never felt like someone sees the me I want the world to know the way I do with you. I entered the Starlight Competition so I'd have a reason to come to LA early, spend the summer here before I start school in September. Plus, coming back to LA early meant less time until I could find you. I couldn't get you out of my mind. Or my heart."

Sarah's not quite looking at me, but not telling me to stop or accusing me of lying. Listening. She angles her body to mine, and our knees would've touched if not for the gearshift between them.

"I searched for you in February. I was in LA for my Starlight audition and went to The Diamond Club. Some dude told me you didn't work there anymore, and I felt like I'd been kicked in the stomach. When I saw you running away at Mackenzie's the next day, Valentine's Day, I was so happy thinking you were in Chicago searching for me, like I was for you. You didn't hear me, but I called after you as you sped away in the taxi. I tried to chase the car, but you were gone." I dig my shoulder into the back of the car seat and stare at the stereo system. "I . . . I got mad when I couldn't catch you. This car cut me off, and I lost my shit. I was back to the messed up middle schooler whose life was throwing stones at him."

"What'd you mean?" Her voice is low.

I bounce my head off the headrest. "I took my frustration out on the car. Hit the hood, over and over. The owner called the cops."

"You went to jail?" Hearing her say jail hurts more than the puck to the face did. I rub the scar from the hit on my cheek.

"No. The police officer detained me but let me go with a warning." My tongue refuses to cooperate. I swallow but my mouth is so dry there's no saliva left. Nothing to help me stall. I look at the roof of the car. I should just get it over with. Tell her. "But I've spent time in a police station. In middle school. School was a bust for me, I couldn't concentrate, and my grades tanked. Mom tried to help, but she worked long hours. Mike started college, moved to a dorm, and had his own shit to deal with. I started cutting class and got in with the wrong crowd."

I pat the dashboard. "We didn't have a car at the time. They taught me to hot-wire vehicles so we could go joyriding. The freedom was exhilarating. Then things got serious, and Mom found out when she had to pick me up from the precinct." The tips of my ears heat.

The police station was scary for a kid, and I was a lot more of a kid than I wanted to show. I was sure my life was over. I stare at my hands. "I remember her crying the whole bus ride home, insisting my delinquency was her fault. Mom thought she was failing as a parent, while I was the one failing as a child. Her solution was to uproot us and move to the suburbs, enroll me in a new middle school, make me repeat a year. She insisted I join a hockey team, and they even gave me a scholarship because we were so poor. I had no problem qualifying. For the first time, I put a mask on. None of the kids, parents, or trainers knew the troublemaker version of me, so I buried that Nick and became the Nicky people wanted to see on and off the ice." I sink lower in the seat. "I tried to make Mom happy, went with the flow, and everyone started to like me."

"That . . . sounds awful. I can't imagine not being able to be yourself." Sarah and I sit in silence for a moment, my tirade over. The pulse in my temples slows down. Most of the yuckiness out in the open now.

"It's exhausting. I . . . I was convinced there was no way anyone could like me without fake Nicky." I flick my gaze to

Sarah's restless form beside me. "On Christmas Eve the fake ID, the new place where not a soul knew me, they gave me the courage to drop the act, try to see if one person would like the real me."

"I did." Sarah rubs her fingernail along the seam of her jeans.

"And, of course, I screwed it up. Didn't get your number." Her nail stops. "The moment Dad drove off, I made up my mind to come back to LA and find you. In the movie in my head, you were right there at the bar, waiting for me. I sort of shot the whole scene of me carrying you in my arms out into the sunset." I chuckle. "El might be right. I might be a bit obsessed with those. Silly, I know."

"No sillier than me believing you'd be excited for me to show up on your doorstep on Valentine's Day." Her gaze finds mine. The doubt I see in it slices at me.

"It wasn't silly. It was brave." I can't push this, but I inch my hand onto the console separating us. The beats of my heart turn into slow booms. "I would've borrowed the money to fly to LA right then and there, but fate had other plans. I ran after you without a hat or coat and was already not feeling well. When the officer let me go and I finally got home, my body ached, and my brain couldn't cope with not getting to you.

"My bag from the LA trip wasn't even unpacked. Getting the urgency of why I had to go back to LA through my brother's stubborn skull was a harder task. Here I'm free of him sticking his nose into my business, unlike in Chicago, where he insisted on playing not just the big bro but also my father. In February, though, he still thought he knew better." I shake my head.

Her finger trails along the seam of the console between us, inches from my hand, and she leans in like she can't hear me. I clear my throat. "My brother was supposed to leave on a trip, but he stayed and did his bossy thing: made me go to bed, spoon-fed me soup, tried to bring my fever down, and rubbed my chest with some minty goo, as I couldn't do it. Things got worse overnight, and Mike drove me to the emergency room. I had pneumonia in both lungs. I didn't leave my bed until three weeks later. Took me another month until I could even think about working out with Mike at the gym again." My ribs contract. "He still thinks I'm not back to normal. Keeps texting me new workout routines to get my strength back up to his standard."

She's not saying anything, and I can't look directly at her.

I focus on her fingers instead. "I fucked up with you, and it wasn't the first time in my life, but I am not a liar."

The leather of Sarah's seat squeaks. Her tiny body pulls me with inexplicable strength, and we collide like a check against the boards, hands first, lips second. Singularly and all at once my skin absorbs hers. Any place a part of her touches me, I get drunk on. No alcohol required. My awareness of her body is electrifying. Every cell in my body jolts to life. The door to my heart flings open. Doubt, worry, what ifs evaporate. This is where I belong—where we belong.

Everything is supercharged: tasting, touching, taking anything she'll give me. Breathing becomes optional. Same as our first kiss, I'm lost in her. My lungs burn, but I'm never letting go. Sarah breaks the kiss first, gasping for breath.

What is this? I still my hands and my heart. An impulse? Will she regret her actions in a moment? Her lips crash against mine again, and I want to push the feeling away, but this time a little remnant of doubt lingers. This can't be only for tonight. Tears threaten at the corners of my eyes. I need this. I need her. I need us.

Thirty-Nine

Sarah

A PAIR OF COLLEGE-AGED guys bristle when I ask both of them to show me their IDs.

"Really?" One lifts his sunglasses and gives me a charming smile, making sure his taut abs are on full display.

I flex my fingers in the hand-them-over gesture.

The other one puts his palm over his eyebrows and squints at me. "It's all the way in the changing room. Do we have to?"

I nod and stand there, my tray tucked under my arm. Don't care. It's the law.

Tourists overrun LA in August, which means The Diamond Club is at full capacity and all hands are on deck. Missing the meeting with Wil, El, and Nick yesterday to finalize *Our Lines,* the song El and Wil wrote for *Indigo,* was not the plan, but when Mrs. Marino called me in to help with a last-minute event, I couldn't say no. I needed the cash and to stay in her good graces.

"Need a break?" Siobhan points her head toward the stock room, where the walk-in fridge serves as our periodic refuge from the heat.

"In a minute." My wrist hurts from opening too many bottles and carrying too many drink-laden trays. I circle it and massage the sore spot to relieve the tension. I have four custom cocktail orders waiting, and I need to circle around the tables to check no one needs a refill.

"Why didn't you like the last girl we interviewed? She seemed square and works over on Abbot Kinney. We could get a discount on clothes." Siobhan snatches one of my order slips and begins to make the concoction, which is a cross between Sex on the Beach and Miami Vice: grapefruit juice, cranberry juice, coconut cream, and rum. I pucker my lips. Who'd drink something like that?

"She's a Boston Bruins fan." I dip the edge of each glass into a bowl with honey and spin them onto a plate with coconut shavings. The rims now appear as if they are covered in snow.

Siobhan tilts the rum bottle, fills a shot glass, and dumps the amber liquid into the first glass. "I should've never let you include 'What's your favorite hockey team?' on the new roommate questionnaire."

I put four napkins on my tray as Siobhan delivers another shot of alcohol to the second glass. "And have to evict someone when we discover our tastes are incompatible?" I say. "Travesty."

Two more shots, two more glasses. "What's the correct answer then?" she asks.

"Either Maple Leafs or I don't watch hockey."

"I'll add it to our ad." Siobhan picks up a stir stick. "Mustn't be a hockey fan." The cranberry and grapefruit juice mingle with the rum.

"Not a bad idea. Would've saved us loads of time already."

I garnish with a little grated nutmeg and deliver the cocktails with a smile. Still gotta work for the tips.

"I'll do a round of refills, and then I'm disappearing to the fridge for fifteen." I billow my shirt, hoping for some relief from the stifling heat. "Need anything from the stock room?"

Siobhan scans the mini fridges under the bar top. "Get me a case of rosé. The girlies at the table have gone through three bottles already, and I don't think they plan to stop any time soon. And tell Ryan his break is over. He needs to haul his arse back here."

A pitcher of ice water in one hand and an empty tray in the other, I start with the nearest and currently my least favorite table, where a group of wannabe influencers have been snapping selfies for over two hours. I top up six barely sipped on waters. The empty Hartford Court Rosé bottle languishes in the middle of the round marble table.

"Can we have another?" One of the girls points to her wine glass with a long acrylic fingernail decorated with green and yellow crystals. They match her tropics-inspired swimsuit. Ah, to have the money to match my manicure to my outfit. "Can you get rid of these?" Her nail indicates the six plates with leftover appetizers.

"Absolutely." I land the pitcher on the table between two of them, balance the tray in my hand, and pile the china on top. I'd normally carry the load with two hands, but I don't want to come back for the pitcher.

"Let me." Long fingers take the sides of the tray. Nick's fingers. Butterflies flutter in my stomach. They brush against mine and cool the hectic moment. "I've got you." The flutters explode in my chest as well. His eyes smile at me, and I release the tray into his hands.

"Can he be our server now?" The bronze-skinned long-legged goddess-like woman pushes up her sunglasses and gives Nick the once-over. I bite my tongue. I get those once-overs every day, but her leering at him this way irritates me more.

"He's my . . . friend. He doesn't work here." My answer comes out harsher than the way I should speak to customers I expect to tip me. "I'll be right back with your bottle." I grind my teeth so hard they threaten to crack and I give them a wide grin and extra pep in my voice, making every effort not to roll my eyes.

"Can't your *friend* do it?" A third girl in a pink one-piece and matching lipstick whines. Maybe a fourth bottle of rosé for the six of them is too much.

"I—"

"Would be my pleasure, ladies, but I'm underage. Can't be handling the alcohol." He gives them his puppy dog expression, and I see them melt more from a moment with Nick than from the heat they've been sitting in this afternoon. Is no one immune to those baby browns?

Nick trails me as I snake my way around the tables to the bar, where five new cocktail slips line the counter. The skin on my back heats where I imagine his gaze is.

"I should stay and help you make these." I reach for one of the slips.

Siobhan glances at Nick leaning against the bar top, then me. "No need. I've got this. Get some use out of this one." She twirls her finger at Nick as if she has no idea what his name is. "Bring back another grapefruit, and two orange juices as well. Oh, and I'm running low on the large artisan ice spheres."

I capture Nick's hand and drag him away from the bar. We round the hedge separating the outdoor patio from the path leading to the parking lot and approach the servers' oasis, also known as the storage shed.

"Not planning on murdering me, are you?" Nick says.

We stop in front of the door and I poke Nick in the stomach. "Never." After the confession in the car a week ago, and so much kissing my lips were sore for a day, we left friends territory behind. My lips tingle. The way his hands find the best spots on my body, how his mouth fits mine, and how I like being alone with him. The tingling travels down my neck just like his kisses did. I can't kid myself and say we're *just* anything. My fingers find my lips and linger there. The butterflies in my stomach take flight. We're *more*, whatever that is.

I catch his gaze on my finger, or is it my lips. I drop my hand and wait for his move. A relationship status conversation is not in the cards tonight. I lean my back on the shed door and scan his face. Are we a couple? No. Friends? Yes, but there's more. Lovers? Hope to get there, but I've tried to hold back. With Nick being our team leader, I don't want to cross too many lines. Not yet. I release a breath and set the butterflies free. Keeping things PG around the rest of the team is the unspoken agreement we landed on. The competition ends soon, the film is almost finished, and my part's complete.

I grasp the door handle. I'm not interested in defining what's happening. I draw my shoulder blades together. I'm accepting things as they are. Nick is a good guy. The stuff he told me about his mom, the divorce, repeating a year in middle school, and our Valentine's Day misadventure from his perspective. I finally feel like the black goo keeping us apart is gone.

"I need to cool down." I brush my hair out of my face.

Nick's fingers stop midair. "Me, too."

Ryan scrambles off the floor and closes his laptop as we stumble into the cold stockroom. Sometimes I wonder if Ryan is writing a novel or something. He's always tapping away on his laptop like the device holds state secrets. "I need to talk to . . ." He stops speaking and eyes Nick behind me. "Why's he here?"

No "dude." No attempt to go give Nick one of the elaborate handshakes they've been exchanging every time they meet. Nick is now a he. And Ryan is not Ryan. Ice trickles down my spine. Something isn't right.

"I was going to show Sarah the final cut of the scene with our original song. She's been too busy to come to the studio, so I'm hand delivering it. You wanna see?" Nick hasn't picked up on the change in Ryan.

My pulse quickens. I step closer to Nick like he needs my protection, though I have no idea why.

"Couldn't you just have posted it on YouTube as a private video and sent her the link?" says Ryan.

Nick rubs his chin and peers at me. The ice melts under his stare. He's trying not to smile. "Yeah, I could, but I wanted to see her reaction. Can you blame me?"

Ryan does not reply. He shifts his closed laptop from one hand to the other. "Might as well ask you now."

I'm not sure if he's addressing me or Nick. "Can we talk later? Siobhan has a ton of orders, and she gave me a list of things to bring back."

"I have information. I'm not sure what to do. Especially with Nick here." Ryan walks closer to me. "But maybe you already know, so this could be nothing." He flicks his eyes at Nick and then down at his computer.

"A secret?" A ping in my chest sets me on edge. My turn to scrutinize Nick, then Ryan and his computer. "Has Nick spilled something personal, and you're not supposed to tell me?" They've been hanging out, scouting beaches with Riyaz for *Indigo*'s first kiss scene, going to the gym together. Regular bromance.

"I wouldn't do that," comes from Nick, and "No," comes from Ryan.

"Like you didn't blab to Nick about my Mémère"—I tap my foot on the cement floor of the stock room—"or Betty's name or—"

"I did mention the funeral." Ryan tucks his hair behind his ear. "But I didn't realize it was a secret. Nick knew the name of your car. The dude's obsessed with you. He probably has names for all the children you'll have together."

Nick chuckles. "You told me the car's name was Betty our first night together. I remember everything from our night." He comes closer to me, so our arms graze. My cells come alive. There it is again, the thrill that runs through every part of me when Nick touches my skin. This electricity travels up my arm and down my spine.

"Didn't peg you for a matchmaker." I'm talking to Ryan, but my mind only cares about what Nick's doing. The electric hum his presence generates. Should I move my arm away from him or keep it right where it is? "Nick and I are just hanging out."

"And this is why you kissed him? Keep kissing him?" Ryan remains serious. Too serious for my taste.

I purse my lips. I shouldn't have told Ryan about Nick and me. But I tell him almost everything. "It's not a big deal. I kissed you, too, and we never went beyond friends." I look at my shoes. Why are we having this conversation, anyhow? "What's got you all hot and bothered?"

"Did you tell her?" Ryan ignores me and glares at Nick.

Nick straightens. "I said I would."

"Um, hello, right here. What did he tell me?"

"Nick has a record."

Nick's voice is a lovely baritone, but why didn't he say anything when we were recording the song? He did spend a lot of time with Wil and El, and him being a singer would make sense. Why has he never mentioned this to me? I scrunch my nose. The recording of the song he brought, is he singing on it, too? Why would his music be a secret?

"Were you a child star or something?" I ask Nick.

His face lacks the grin from a moment ago. Tightness around his eyes and mouth prompts my heart to skip a beat, and not in a good way.

"Not that kind of record.," says Ryan. "The jail kind. Child criminal."

"Is this all?" I shrug. "Nick told me everything about his hot-wiring skills."

Ryan visibly relaxes. "Good. When I found the arrest records, and you hadn't mentioned them I . . ." His voice trails off, and I follow his line of sight to Nick. His face is getting sallower by the second.

"No, you're wrong. Nick has never been arrested. Just detained. Right?" I search Nick's face for the answer but can't catch his eyes. The familiar ache of betrayal tugs at my heart. Please, tell me I'm right.

Nick doesn't stir, doesn't answer. Ryan does. "Arrested, charged, a misdemeanor. I . . . I mean . . . I . . . my friend tried to find out what for, but the record was sealed when he turned eighteen." Ryan's mysterious friend who's sometimes better than an actual private detective helped Siobhan and me to vet our potential roomies. We've avoided some sketchy characters. His skills are legit.

Ryan's words trickle in. Criminal. Misdemeanor. Record. Sealed.

My turn to avoid eye contact. I step away from Nick. He isn't saying anything. Which says everything.

Another lie. Every breath is harder to take. What else is he concealing? Will the lies ever end? I thought we were done with dishonesty. Why did I think we were done with that? Once a liar, always a liar. I should've known better. I clasp my necklace like it can save me from spiraling into the anger and depression, like it did last time. Deception is an ingrained trait, not something to grow out of like a pair of shoes.

Nick's been doing everything I ask him. Almost too much. Nick and Shawn are not the same person. Nick's proven he's like many other guys who'd rather pretend and use me than tell me the truth, be raw and vulnerable. I abandon the S of the pendant and drop my hand. I was wrong before. I'm wrong again.

"Sarah?" Ryan touches my elbow. "Are you okay?"

My eyes smart with tears. I'm breaking so many rules for Nick. Not crying is one I can keep intact. "Could you take the wine to the front, please?"

"I don't want to leave you alone with him." Ryan stares over my shoulder, where I assume Nick still stands.

"Siobhan needs you. I don't." I cross my arms.

There's pity in Ryan's gaze. *Poor Sarah, duped again.* But he doesn't push the situation. He stores his laptop on the top shelf under a box, grabs a case of wine, and walks to the door. As he passes Nick, I hear him quietly say, "I told you, I always have her back."

Silence fills the room. Aching silence.

The rough wooden shelves behind me creak as I rest my back against them. When someone disappoints me, I tend to get upset and run away from them, crawl under a blanket or into a hug of someone I trust, and not speak to the offender at all or at least for a while, until the disappointment settles into indifference. Until I can deal. Mémère was one of the hugs I used to run to as a child, and she'd tell me forgiving can be a better option. Listening, understanding, and giving the other person a benefit of the doubt.

Today I want to follow her advice. I resist storming out of the stockroom after Ryan. I push harder into the rack and the edges prod through the thin cotton of my uniform. I stand my ground. I wait. Wait for Nick to say something. Something to prove my heart wasn't wrong about him. Prove my overwhelming desire to hug him and hide my face in his chest isn't insanity but a possibility.

But Nick stays mute. Nothing. His silence a twin of the one in my chest. Why isn't he saying anything? Why won't he talk to me? He stares at the wall behind me. "Is it true? What Ryan found out?"

A tiny dip of his head. I want to throw my hands in the air and get him to open up. I want to slap him. Hurt him, like he hurt me.

"What did you do?"

"Stole a car when I was fourteen. Got caught driving it." His voice is soft. The light of the noon sun blasts through the window behind him. "Do you want to know why?"

Do I? "Yes."

"My brother was in his second year of college. I was about to turn fourteen, but with an older brother and being tall for my age, I hung out with an older crowd, the bunch I told you about. They taught me to hot-wire cars for fun. I got caught joyriding with my friends before, but was in the back seat, never driving. This time was different."

"How?" I ask in a low voice.

Nick stuffs his hands into the pockets of his jeans and moves the tip of his shoe in half circles over the scuffed tile. "Mike would kill me if this got out. Not my story, and you can't repeat it to anyone else."

That comment was unnecessary. I shift my weight to my left leg and plant my hands on my hips. "I don't kiss and tell."

"I remember it was a Thursday night because the salon closes at nine those nights, so Mom wasn't home yet. Mike called the landline and was freaking out. Nothing like my usually calm, cool, nothing-bothers-me brother. He was high, or drunk, or probably both, and alone in a rough part of town. Someone beat him up, and he was using a phone at a bar to reach me. They stole his phone and wallet. Left him in an alley."

Nick showed me Mike's picture when he bragged about his big brother's MMA skills. I can't imagine anyone taking down that man.

"Mike begged me not to call Mom, the police, or an ambulance, because if any of it got on his record, he would've lost his scholarship at Northwestern and been forced to drop out. I . . . I had to help him, get to him before something worse happened." Nick squeezes the back of his head. "Thing was, I had no money for a taxi. Checked under the photo of Yiayia, where we kept our emergency stash of cash, but it was empty. I grabbed my coat and headed for the bus stop. I sat there waiting, worried about Mike."

Nick's chest expands and contracts with a deep breath. The room contracts, the already small space closing in and suffocating us. "The next bus wasn't due for another forty minutes, and I sat there freaking out, not knowing if Mike was okay. Having no way to contact him. What if he were more hurt than he let on? There was a Chrysler Sebring parked across from the bus stop. A convertible. Thoughts of getting to Mike consumed me. The car sat there, taunting me. That model is easy to hot-wire. I'd done it before. I could be in and out without any damage, like your Beamer. I would get Mike and be home before anyone was the wiser. Or so I thought."

"You stole a car?" This seems unreal. Beads of sweat form at my hairline. Is this another lie? If it is, he's a better liar than I gave him credit for.

Nick ignores my question. "I found Mike at the bar. When I got there, he was a mess. Kept rambling about getting kicked out of school and telling me he was sorry. There was no way he could drive, and I'd made it that far, so I shoved him into the passenger's seat and drove us home. Except I didn't make it. A patrol car stopped us a couple of miles from our apartment. The owner reported the car stolen, and the officer ran the plates because I was speeding. They hauled us downtown and called Mom, and despite her pleas, the hard-ass working that night decided to teach me a lesson."

Nick picks at the label of an industrial-size can of pineapple juice. "Now, you're the fifth person to know about the record apart from me, Mom, Mike, and, of course, Ryan." His nails catch the corner and peel the edge away. "And I hope the last."

"You didn't think to tell me this the other night?"

"Not my story to tell." His lips press together.

"You're the one with the criminal record." The air conditioner rumbles to life. I wipe the perspiration off my damp temple.

His gaze meets mine. "I don't have a record. It's sealed. Which means the charge no longer exists."

"That's your excuse?"

"Not an excuse. The truth."

I huff. The truth. It's all lies and truth with him. I point to the door. "I think you should leave."

"But . . ." His hand brushes his chin. "I have to show you the scene. With El's song."

"You don't have to show me anything. You're the director. You make the decisions." Like what truths to tell. My pulse pounds in my ears. "You don't need me."

A flash of pain crosses his face.

"Go." I stomp my foot.

He doesn't move.

"I have to get back to work." I shove jugs around on the shelf behind me, searching for orange juice. I expect him to protest, to fight. Instead I hear the creak of the door, followed by the slam.

FORTY

Sarah

WHERE IS THE DAMNED orange juice? The door creaks again, and my heart betrays me, jumping for joy at Nick's return. I spin around to find Siobhan.

"What the feck? Ryan brings the wrong wine, and Nick's moping like someone just chopped off his left nut." She must notice the stony expression on my face and lays a hand on my shoulder. "If this doesn't smell like trouble, I don't know what does."

I open my mouth to answer, but what can I say that hasn't already been said? Siobhan's heard everything. Heard me crying over Shawn, crawled into bed with me without a word and held me. Raged with me when Shawn turned out to be Nick and threatened my future with the Starlight Foundation. Sipped tea as I gave her the highlights of Nick's confession in the car and spilled my fears.

"What did the tosser do this time?" Siobhan perches on a crate.

My emotions are killing me. Not slowly. They conspired to prove I'm in the wrong, insecure for no reason, and maybe I am. This is déjà vu, one I don't want. But I'm an adult. I'm not listening to the disappointment scratching at me with its hungry claws.

"Lied." My brain is trying to sort out the conversation. "I think."

"You think. Either he's acting the maggot or not."

The clickety-clack of the tips of my fingers on the lid of the box of organic pretzels might as well be the accompaniment to my racing pulse. I straighten my back and glower at my friend. "Ryan found out he has, no, had a criminal record."

"Okay. Putting aside how the feck does Ryan find this shit out, I'm confused. He's a criminal? Like behind bars?"

"No. He screwed up as a kid," I say. Siobhan's face twists and I plop next to her on the crate. "Nothing bad. Wrong place, wrong time. Actually, he was trying to help. Because he was under eighteen the record was sealed."

Nick tried to help, and he got punished for his act of compassion. My heart thumps. Life hit him hard as well. He's doing his best in a bad situation. Shit, there I go again, making excuses for him.

"Sounds like the wanker."

"Everyone has flaws." I lay my head on her shoulder. "You and I just never stick around long enough to discover them."

Siobhan steps away and leans against the glass of the refrigerator. "Can you live with Nick's flaws though?" Her gaze catches mine.

"He's not a bad person." My voice cracks.

My friend makes a dismissive sound but doesn't share her opinion, for once.

"He's not." Am I defending Nick to her, or to me?

"If you say so. You know him best."

"I thought I did. But now I'm not so sure. What if there's more?" The pain between my ribs returns. I don't think I could take any more deception.

Siobhan kneels in front of me and cups my cheeks. "Yeah. But is he worth the risk?"

I shrug.

"If he went back to Chicago tomorrow," her thumb traces the moisture below my eyes,

"and you never saw him again . . ."

Her words cause icy crystals to form in my veins. Never see Nick again. "Not fair."

"You and I both know life isn't fair." She tilts her head to the side and holds my gaze. "It's up to you. You. You have to decide."

Forty-One

NICK

Through the window of the control booth that separates me from the girl whose hand I want to hold, I stare at the back of Sarah's head—the only part of her visible to me in the dark theater. A week without talking to her when she's in the same city as me, when I know exactly where to find her, drags longer than the months between seeing her get into the taxi on Valentine's Day and the sight of her smile the first day of the Starlight competition. A week of checking my phone, hoping for a text saying she wants to talk to me, a week of nights interrupted with disjointed dreams of her and days finalizing the movie she is an integral part of. Now she's in the same room with me. A small movie room with a wide screen on one end, ten rows of red chairs in the middle, and me at the booth in the back showing the team what we've accomplished.

The people in the room tonight might not be the judges who'll decide the next steps in my career, but they're the ones whose reactions matter the most to me. A group of strangers who came together and created magic. Plus a few guests who helped. Sarah arrived late, but she's here. Everyone's here to watch the director's cut of *Indigo*.

Nausea hits me as the credits roll, and the room bursts to life with chatter. I press my palm to my chest and turn the knob. The pot lights in the ceiling increase in intensity.

In the front row, Siobhan jumps up and claps. More join her: Wil, El, her bodyguard Sven. I think that was his name. He fits the Viking vibe his name conjured. The others follow. From my vantage point, I watch them pop up like the classic game we used to play at the Chicago State Fair: whack-a-mole. Sarah stands beside Bri, her head away from the screen. I am the object she's studying.

Our eyes meet.

My stomach gurgles and reminds me a cup of black coffee is far from ideal fuel for a busy day. The acid burns a hole in my middle, but I don't drop my gaze. She's the first to shift and whisper something into Siobhan's ear.

I wasn't nervous about the showing of *Indigo*—that's in the bag. Our movie, the one born of Sarah's words, is a winner. I feel it in my bones. Sure, there are things I still need to fix. The story has a few weak moments. The scene where Rudo quotes the line from Shakespeare has a bit too much cheese factor, but overall, the movie is "Bloody brilliant," as Wil would say.

It's what comes next I'm scared about. My mouth goes dry.

Scared. Excited. Hopeful.

Our Christmas Eve rewrote my future for the better: that is a moment in time I'll put on my top ten list. But my number one? Hands down my last two months with Sarah, not the euphoric high of the epic first night we met. That moment was earth shattering but it can't, shouldn't always be like that.

My world shifted when we met, but the amazing part is . . . life keeps shifting every time I see Sarah, work with her, share my mind, learn hers. The buzz of being with her, hearing her laugh, surviving her jabs, watching her flourish, listening to her complain, and having the privilege of doing my best to make her life better. My heart takes off like a forward charging the net.

From the moment our hands touched atop the hill overlooking this city of lights, I knew Sarah was the one. I leave the booth and take measured steps to the empty space behind the last row. For months I created a fantasy of finding her again, never considering she'd not fall into my arms. I didn't think I could survive being imprisoned in the friend zone when we finally met again, but I had.

I lean against the glass of the booth. After Ryan blew my almost-reconciliation with Sarah, after I got a taste of what Sarah pretending I don't exist is like, fixing this is the only option. A muscle ticks in my jaw. I will make things right again. I want her back. I want her to understand. I want her to trust me.

Riyaz joins me at the back of the room. "Eight out of ten."

For the man of few words, this praise is the equivalent of a third encore at Rocker's concert.

"Team effort." I survey the *Indigo* crew: the winners who made this happen.

Riyaz who silently, stoically, found the perfect backdrop for each scene, raising hell the one time I was wrong and insisting we film at sunset. I sigh. We didn't spend a penny on our locations. Props, transportation—yes, but he managed to get us not only the right spots, but the free spots.

Wil and El, whose original song *Our Lines* became the final puzzle piece to the soundtrack of the movie. Their words and music gave the pivotal separation of our two lovers' scene a whole other layer of meaning. I scroll through *Indigo*'s playlist on my phone. El's haunting voice offers Isabel and Rudo both the pain of farewell and hope for the future.

Bri snaps pictures with the souped-up camera on their phone. The irritating habit is the source of the many captured memories they spam our Discord channel with. I shake my head and grin. They're more than the cheerleader of our team, taking photos of the people around them. Bri scoured secondhand shops, begged, borrowed, and stole for the nineties vibe needed to set the tone of the movie: checkered Vans shoes, slip dresses, and vest jackets, flared jeans with a chain belt I used to define the bond between the actors.

And Sarah. The inspiration for this story. The theme of sacrificing for love, doing what needs to be done for the one you care for, even if the choice hurts you. The stupid organ beneath my breastbone burns. I get it now. I thought her script was just a story, but support and commitment are her way to live.

I'd sacrifice for her again and again. The heel of my shoe kicks against the wall. Anything to make her happy once more.

Someone clears their throat, and I tear my eyes from the back of Sarah's head, her body engulfed in a hug from Siobhan. El stands before me, Wil right beside her.

"The film's beautiful." Her face glows, and my hand flies to my chin. Her praise stirs up the impostor syndrome rather than pride. She's just trying to be nice is all.

"I had my doubts about you, mate." Wil slaps my shoulder blades. "But you showed us all. You'd almost think a group of professionals made this thing."

The back of my throat hurts. For years I've been starved for approval, chasing after the tiniest morsel from Dad, Mike, even Mom, after I screwed up. The only way to get praise was to do what others wanted: to lie about my dreams. To others. To myself. I suck in a breath. I could never compare to my big bro's perfection, but I suppressed the real me in the hope that pleasing others could be a better feeling than catching their disappointed stares and words.

This competition, this film—it's not all mine. Took a crew, but I was part of the process, and the process was me. The essence of Nick Stavros is in every frame. Not my original vision, but a better, truer one. The bones of Sarah's story, the flare of Bri's costumes, the visuals of Riyaz's locations, the audio of Wil's soundtrack: the pieces shuffled and ordered by me. I rub my chest. My life impacted this movie. My world no longer viewed through a camera lens, but prescribed by it.

The *Indigo* team morphed, and grew, and transformed through me. I push away from the glass of the booth. My first collaboration with other creatives. I stretch to my full height. My first time trusting others to see my vision: the me I long to be. And they did. *And* people like the results. Like *me*. Pride diminishes the ache in my chest. The real me.

"What you did with the song"—El puts her hand over her heart—"it's like nothing I could've dreamed."

"You did the hard work, what with the writing and singing." I glance at Wil. "Wil did his magic in the studio. With talent like yours, we're sure to win the competition."

El's eyes are puffy, and the shine in them might be tears, but I choose to interpret them as joy. Wil's face softens when she regards him. Their love came through in a song, and anyone who spends more than a minute with the unlikely duo would get a lungful of the pheromones these two emit around each other. I scratch behind my ear. He's head over heels for our singer. Does he know yet?

"I wish I could stay, but my . . ." El surveys the room and finds her Viking look-alike by the door. "Curfew. You get it."

"Yeah." I don't really understand. Her schedule is more restricted than mine's ever been. I open my arms for a hug but reroute them into my pockets. Sarah told me El's not much for hugs. "Thanks for coming. And thanks for, well, everything."

She heads for the door, Wil trailing behind like the only oxygen in the room is around El.

Now or never. I straighten my shirt, wipe my palms on my dark blue jeans, and step closer to the group. "Everyone. Need a moment here." Eyes settle on me, and a bead of sweat trickles down my brow.

"You made a bloopers reel?" Bri claps and waits for my confirmation.

"There's something else. Can everyone sit back down?"

Out of the corner of my eye I check on Sarah. She doesn't need to know that her reaction would either rip my heart to pieces or set the world right again. Her forehead is creased. Is this confusion? Irritation? Surprise? She returns to the seat where she watched *Indigo*, and Siobhan plops beside her. I flick the lights off, and the room sinks into silence.

My hand trembles as I hit play on the board. The screen comes to life, and my mug fills the wide frame.

I spent hours painstakingly writing and recording, rewriting, and re-recording my confession. I don't understand how Sarah comes up with the right words to have the actors say, expressing in a few eloquent lines what the audience needs to hear. I didn't come near her level of articulateness—that can't be a word—but I did my best.

"Hi. I'm Nicholas Theodor Stavros. But I prefer Nick." My hands on the screen don't shake, but the ones on the board in front of me do. "You might wonder what's this about. Well, it's about me. More accurately, the things I don't tell people about. The ones I'm not proud of."

I can hit pause, ask everyone but Sarah to leave, but I want her to recognize I have changed. These things made me who I am today. Not a crowd pleaser. A guy who made mistakes and owns up to them. My giant head blabs everything. From my first crime, stealing Mike's transformer action figure, breaking the right arm, and then blaming the carnage on the dog, to the bigger things. Everything I've ever done wrong. Everything I could think of that I've ever done wrong. I exhale through my nose.

At first, my script earns a few tepid laughs at the cute mishaps of an errant child. As the crimes grow with me, the laughter disappears. Riyaz stares through the glass of the booth around me.

In the dark, I don't watch my confession. I watch her.

Sarah doesn't stir, the back of her head frozen, her shoulders rigid. The muscles around my ribs seize.

The screen goes dark, and this time there isn't any applause. Siobhan doesn't stand. She whispers into Sarah's ear. I'm frozen, unable to draw a breath, silently begging Sarah to turn and look at me, show me I did the right thing.

My girl gets up and brushes past Wil, who is just stepping back into the room. Sarah's gone. Somehow my heart starts beating again, air rushes into my lungs, but aching disappointment laces every beat, every breath.

Sarah didn't spare me a glace, but everyone else's eyes land on me. Wil surveys the whispering figures in the dark. "Who died?"

Me. My heart. I failed. My chest cracks into two. I'm not worth a second chance.

FORTY-TWO

Sarah

Heat prickles behind my eyes. He didn't have to do this. I know how private he is, how he doesn't want the world to scratch beneath the surface of his skin, see his inner pain, see him.

My tears are for the Nick of today and for the little boy who learned from people around him that hiding and lying is the way to survive. I wipe away the salty liquid that seeps through the cracks in my own shell. My barrier. We are so different, yet so alike.

I run up the stairs to the desk where the security guard is working on a crossword puzzle. He glances up as I skip across the lobby. "Sarah?"

"I need the bag I gave you."

An expression of confusion breaks across his face. "On your way out already?"

"Change of plans." My heart is racing, my brain, too, trying to process what just happened. I constantly complain about life sucker punching me, sending the loser men my way. I tried to convince myself Nick's nothing more than another loser in a long line.

But I know better. He's better. Better than any guy I've met before. Better for me. I pull in a deep breath. The plan was to pretend I forgot something when we left the building, force us to go back to the room. Siobhan was to distract the others so I could do this in private.

Frank pulls out the bag containing the stuff I collected for tonight, including the one item harder to find in LA than the distinctly Canadian butter tarts I tracked down for Wil last month. "Thanks."

I dash down the stairs, along the hall, and back into the viewing room. The crew and our guests are there, even Wil is back, but not Nick. Goosebumps run up the back of my neck.

"Where is he?" I ask everyone, no one in particular. "Where's Nick?"

"Boyo's in there." Siobhan points to the closed office door off the auditorium. "Looked a little green when he slammed the door shut."

Shit. I didn't think, my mind on the bag. He must've decided I left. Shit, Sarah, shit.

I don't knock but push the door open and shut out everyone but us. A low light on the empty desk illuminates the tiny room. In the gloom, Nick sits in an office chair, elbows pressed against his long legs, head in his hands, shoulders shaking. My heart lurches into my throat. Shit. Shit. Shit.

"Nick?" I take the couple of steps needed to cross the tiny room, land on my knees beside him, and touch his arm.

He wrenches away and twists his face. "I get it." His voice is off: nasally and rough. "Just leave me."

"No."

"I won't bother you again. Once the competition is over we"—his Adam's apple bobs as he swallows—"you won't have to see me ever again."

His words make my heart feel like a punching bag, each one a jab I doubt I could survive. Never seeing him again being the worst. "Nick, look at me."

He shifts farther away.

My heart wrenches. I open the bag and pull out the knit toque, gray and red with the band of black, white letters spelling out Chicago. Nerves tingle in my fingers, up my arm, and to my heart as I hold the fan favorite out to him. "Please, I need you to see this."

I catch his hand and place the hat in his palm. His fingers curl around the material, but otherwise he stays still.

"Remember my hat? The one you found? Kept?" I talk to the taut muscles of his neck, the tendons thick with tension. "My grandfather, Alain, gave it to my grandmother, my namesake, Sarah Côté, as a token of his love for her. He had her name embroidered on the inside. Remember? You thought it was my name."

The muscles in his neck distend. Head down, he eyeballs the hat. "Look inside. Please." I roll back the hem to reveal the stitching I paid extra for them to rush.

Black letters spell out Nick Stavros.

Nick shudders.

I lay my head on his arm. "She wore my grandfather's hat as a symbol of her love for him, even years after he died."

"I don't understand." Nick's voice is barely a whisper. The hope lacing the three words stabs at my heart.

"My grandparents had an epic love story. My mémère told me I would find a man as amazing and wonderful as she did. I didn't believe her. Until I met you." I shift, bracketing his long, goofy face with my hands. I stare up and encounter those deep velvet eyes I can make out even in this darkened room. "You're my epic love story, Nick."

"I thought I blew it with my confessions."

"You blew me away. And I have one of my own to make."

"A confession?" His face is so serious, my heart aches.

"Here it goes." I try not to grin. "I will always be a Leafs fan. No matter how I feel about you."

Nick smiles, a tiny underpowered thing. But he appears less desperate. "I knew that."

"But." I rifle through the bag. "Here's as far as I'm willing to go. Take it or leave it."

Nick accepts the two tickets for the LA Kings vs Chicago Blackhawks game. His eyebrows knit. "These are for two months from now."

"Yes." I run my knuckles along the gruff stubble of his cheek and stop at the small scar where the hockey puck hit him. "I'm warning you, I'm going, but I refuse to wear any Chicago attire. Can't betray my beloved Toronto Maple Leafs, even for you."

"You're coming . . . with me?"

"Well, you don't have to take me. But—" The force of his arms squeezing me knocks the air out of my lungs. He buries his head in the crook of my neck. I can't really move, but I manage to thread my fingers through the belt loops of his jeans.

"I want to take you." The words dance on my skin, his lips close and hot. "Everywhere."

"Well, let's start with the hockey game. See how that goes."

His embrace gets tighter.

Guess it's too early for my sarcasm. I find his ear. "I want to go everywhere with you."

He nuzzles my hair. Such a small token shouldn't set my scalp on fire, but then nothing about me works like it should around him. Like a layer of my skin was stripped, and every interaction hits with raw abandon. I shouldn't like the lack of safeguards in my reaction to him. That's how hearts get hurt. That's when the pain becomes real. But his touch leaves me wanting more. Always more.

"I won't let you down." His promise is sincere, but this is a lie he doesn't need to tell me. One I can prevent.

"You will." His soft curls brush against my neck in his protesting head shake. "But that's okay. You don't have to be perfect. Not for me. Not for anyone. I"—can I say it?—"I like you. All of you. Just the way you are."

His fingers dig deeper into my skin, and a small sound like a moan reverberates against the hollow space underneath my earlobe. I feel his upper body expand and contract. "Same." His word screams true.

And this is the truth I'm not afraid of. I open my heart wide. He's nothing like what I imagined Shawn Rosstav to be. He's better because he's true. His lies were true. His apologies are true. His care is true. His feelings for me are as true as mine are for him. And I'm done protecting myself. Whatever comes next for us, I'm feeling it all. Living it all. Starting now.

I lean back long enough to find his lips. Third time is the charm? Better be. Softness first. The sensation holds me, welcoming and sweet. I bite his fullness, and he tastes of strawberries. Crazy. Impossible. I bite again, and the summer heat blooms between us. He fills my pause with pressure. Gentle but also not. His turn to savor me.

Nick's teeth draw small breaths out of me. They stammer when his tongue touches mine, and I know. Third time *is* the charm. Bullseye. I'm living the dream, and it's not a nightmare. It's the answer to my most secret desires. I surrender to the feel of Nick's mouth on mine.

The world comes back into focus when I take a fourth deep breath through my nose and force the air out through my mouth. We can't keep sharing breaths. Not in this cramped room. Not with our teammates on the other side of the door.

"Hey." Not the dumbest thing I could've said, but close.

"Sarah." His palm touches my cheek, and I press into the rough skin.

"This feels right, right?"

Nick's thumb runs along my lower lip. "The rightest. We had to end up together."

"Why?" I know my reasons, but I want to hear his. Why me? Why now?

"I don't understand it myself. You challenge me, yet you support me. We don't have to always agree. Sometimes I think you know me better than I understand myself. And I want to grow and learn with you. I can't imagine a better partner." He smooths my hair, pushing a strand behind my ear. "When we found each other on Christmas Eve, it was like a miracle. Our miracle. I thank my lucky stars for you."

FORTY-THREE

NICK

IT'S HOT. SARAH'S APARTMENT is great and all, but the lack of the air conditioning makes me take two showers a day. The heatwave became a heat month. I wasn't prepared for the scorching weather to last so long. Back home in Chicago we get a blistering August but by September a cool breeze blows off the lake.

But Chicago isn't my home anymore. LA is. And LA's weather in September has one gauge: hot.

The drawback? Can't wear my new hat.

The benefit? Sarah is still wearing shorts as she sits beside me.

I'm not complaining. I put my hand on her thigh, her bare skin warm. My heart expands. What's most important is the fact I can touch her whenever I want. We left the friend zone behind. Every day I discover what it is like *not* to be Sarah's friend. Or *not only* a friend. No matter how slow we're taking things, every new inch of her I get blows my mind. Nothing like this ever happened with Mackenzie. I'd prefer a PG-13 night with Sarah to any of the mature ones Mackenzie and I shared.

This is what attraction is supposed to feel like.

Not the best time to be living on Dad's couch, especially when leaving Sarah for the night gets harder every day. I take her hand in mine. Maybe I can stay here tonight again. Or better still, I need to find a place to rent, preferably without six other guys sharing one bathroom. Wil might have a lead on a place. He better give me his answer soon.

But then again, maybe not. My lack of a permanent home is a great excuse to stay here with Sarah in the few moments we can grab together and make use of the few calm days now that the movie is finished, submitted, and out of my hands before school starts.

Our film. I think it's good. No, I know it's good. We have a real shot at winning.

The only thing left is to sit and wait. I draw Sarah into me. With the end of the Starlight program comes the end of the stipend, yet no one cancelled food, bills, and transportation costs. That means work.

I circle my thumb over the soft skin of her knee. "When do you have to go?"

Sarah's been pulling doubles several weekends in a row. The Diamond Club is booked to capacity with everyone squeezing in a final getaway this Labor Day weekend.

Sarah's gaze flickers from her phone to me. No pain in them anymore as her eyes meet mine. "Not yet."

I finished my six-to-one shift. Working at Blend over the summer left me in the perfect spot: I'm Harold's only decent choice for the recently vacated assistant manager position. Weekend and morning shifts are ideal for the afternoon classes I start in a couple of weeks.

"There'll be traffic." Siobhan doesn't take her eyes off her sketch pad. The other day when she was in the shower, I peeked at her drawings. Colors and fine lines created intricate designs I have no idea what she's going to do with. But they were cool.

"So soon?" I sound like a kid whose mom is threatening to take away his favorite toy.

"What are you gonna do with your last afternoon of freedom?" Sarah puts her hand on mine, and I'm still not used to the tingle from her fingertips rushing through my skin, across my chest.

I shrug. "Sleep."

Sarah rolls her eyes, leans in, and kisses my cheek. "Lucky you."

Don't I know it. I'm not quite sure what changed Sarah's mind about me. She says it was a choice, and she chose me. Chose to believe the good in me.

Someone believes in me. The concept settles on my shoulders like my favorite hockey jersey. Still getting used to this as well, but much easier to get used to the idea she feels the same way I do about her. Our connection was not only in my head. What we have is real, and solid, and forever.

"Can I stay here while you and Siobhan are at work?"

Now Siobhan rolls her eyes.

"Sure." Sarah puts her head on my shoulder, and even though this apartment is like a million degrees already, I bask in the heat of her body against mine.

"Nick." Sarah squeezes my hand and sits up, her eyes glued to her phone. "*Indigo* got nominated for Best Picture."

"What?" Siobhan and I say at the same time, our attention on Sarah.

Sarah bounces up and down, cutting off the circulation in my fingers. "You're nominated for Best Director." She tilts the screen of her phone my way.

Air whooshes out of me. There it is in black and white:

Best Director

Megh Eaton: *The Sun Will Rise Again*

Aleksey Til: *Jupiter Sinking*

Nick Stavros: *Indigo*

I can't believe what I'm seeing. My pulse races as the reality of what this nomination means sinks in. Someone else sees my talent. Someone else has faith in me.

Sarah beams at me, and the words on the screen lose their shine. That's the prize right there.

I snag her phone and scroll, and scroll, and scroll.

"Explain for the eejit in the room." Siobhan forgets about the pen and paper on her lap.

Sarah faces her friend. "The Starlight Foundation, at the end of the competition they do this big gala event. It's like a mini-Oscars."

"Is there a red carpet?"

"You bet. And movie stars. And studio execs."

"Timothée Chalamet?" Siobhan is squirming in her seat.

"He might be busy, but movie stars for sure. The people who win are often headhunted by studios. This could mean a real job in the business."

The screenwriters are the last to be listed. I hold my breath as the names appear. And it's there.

Sarah Connor: *Indigo*

I grin. "You're nominated too."

Sarah stops bouncing. I show her the phone, but she doesn't take it.

"It can't be."

"I promise you. I'm very good at reading. And I don't think there were any other Sarah Connors in the competition."

Her eyes swivel between the phone and me. "Pinch me. I need to know I'm not dreaming."

I can do one better. I put down the phone, bracket her face with my hands, and gently bite her lower lip. Sarah's pupils dilate. "You're brilliant. *Indigo* wouldn't exist without you." Out of the corner of my eye I see Siobhan watching us. "This is only the beginning. Soon every producer in this town will line up and ask Sarah Connor to write their movies."

Sarah's smile morphs from small and unsure to a wide grin.

"You're gonna be famous." Siobhan lunges for Sarah, wrapping her arms around her and joining us on the couch. "I'm so living with you, when you have a Calabasas compound of your own."

"Deal." Sarah croaks and slides off the couch. "But our current living situation is a more immediate problem." She pushes Siobhan off the couch and back toward the kitchen. "We gotta find someone to rent out Claudia's room, or we aren't going to make next month's rent."

Sarah lands on my lap and the blood in my brain rushes to the spot where she sits. She brushes my bangs out of my face and bites the spot my teeth left a minutes ago. "I think I have an idea where we might find a decent roommate."

"Oh, really." Siobhan opens the fridge and pulls out half a watermelon. "Are they reliable?"

"Very." Sarah runs her fingers through my hair, and I lose concentration for a millisecond.

Siobhan takes the biggest knife from the magnetic strip under the cabinets; the afternoon sun glints off the metal. "Do I know her?"

Sarah tugs on my ear. "Him."

Is she suggesting what I think she's suggesting? I sit up.

"Oh, no fecking way." The knife crunches through the juicy flesh and hard rind. I'm concerned for Siobhan's fingers. "It's bad enough he stays here all the time."

"Exactly. He's here already. And he's not going anywhere." Sarah stares into my eyes. "Right?"

"Right."

"So, don't you think he should start paying rent?" Sarah addresses Siobhan, who is attacking the watermelon, cutting it into smaller and smaller chunks. Is Siobhan imagining the fruit in front of her is me?

She puts the implement of death down, sinks her teeth into the pink flesh, and sucks. "Rent is due on the fifth of the month."

And that's how I know everything is right with my world. I hum the chorus of *Our Line*. I'm moving in with Sarah. Putting the carriage before the horse? Maybe. But I'd much rather do so than pretend for propriety's sake that I don't constantly want to be near her.

FORTY-FOUR

Sarah

IN SOME PROPHETIC STROKE of luck, Ryan and I haven't had a shift together in over a week. Eight days without talking to my friend. I'm not sure we've spent this much time apart in over a year. Siobhan says he's switched shifts to morning hours and got Layden, the wannabe actor, to cover the rest. Six months into this job and Layden remains as useful as a cardboard prop, his dazzling teeth the only point of attraction. Ryan is well aware I'd much rather work alone than with Layden. I underline the last drink order in my notepad. If I didn't know Ryan better, I'd say he's avoiding me.

"Two Buds, a strawberry daiquiri, and gin and tonic, right?" The glare from one of the foursome's sunglasses blinds me as I recite their order back to them.

The first week of September means less than a month until we close the main pool, and the deck around the aqua water is packed. LA natives and tourists alike are under pressure to squeeze every drop out of the remaining pool season. The last long weekend before back to school, back to work, and back to the everyday.

I beeline back to the bar where Siobhan wipes at the beads of sweat clinging to her forehead. "Feck me it's a stinker today."

"Tell me again why we don't have jobs with air conditioning?"

"Because the tips suck at Applebee's." Siobhan's had quite a few careers before she found The Diamond Club; the last was as a server at the popular restaurant chain. She hated every minute of it. "And it's full of kids."

"One positive about here." My gaze takes in the crowd—designer bikinis, expensive watches, diamond earrings, and platinum credit cards. No children marring the adults-only vibe. The youngest folks in the crowd are at the table I just took orders from, and they crossed twenty-five off their calendars several summers ago.

"Were you serious about Nick?" Siobhan bends to get the daiquiri mix.

The image of Nick's ridiculous grin earlier today makes my heart leap. All I did was ask him to pay rent and move into the vacant bedroom down the hall. Not like we'll be sharing the same bed. Now I'm thinking about Nick in my bed. Dangerous. I've never slept better than the night we fell asleep talking and I woke with my face pressed into his broad chest, his arms surrounding me. I want more of that. I want more.

Taking things slow has never been my style. Three kisses in nine months? No wonder I turned into a freaking glacier. But in the few days since the *Indigo* screening Nick has been thoroughly thawing me. Making up for time. Heat radiates through my chest like after a shot of top-shelf whiskey. I'm not longing for the future. For the first time in a long time, or ever, I live in the present.

I savor every kiss, every touch of his hand, every minute our bodies are squeezed into my bed, talking the night away. The time we have together plays at half-speed. The reason we gave ourselves for taking it slow was me not sleeping with my boss. Deciding that nothing happens between us until after the competition ends with the Starlight Gala was easy. Keeping that promise is getting harder every day. I pull on the collar of my uniform. Now I go and ask him to move in. Really, Sarah, what is he going to think about that?

Is this what dating a younger man feels like? Geesh, am I gross for dating a nineteen-year-old? He won't be able to drink for another year and a half. Three years between us might as well be ten.

"I'm always serious about Nick." I pinch Siobhan.

Siobhan pretends the glass she's filling deserves her full attention. I pinch her again. "Is that a problem?" I wait for a litany of snickers and jabs from my usually verbose roommate.

Her hands pause, the ice in the scoop frozen above the bulbous glass. The cubes rattle as they hit the cup. "Is he good? Trustworthy?"

It's not about money. I understand what she's asking. Making ends meet might be a constant concern, but at the end of the day, we care about each other's happiness the most, and she doesn't want to see me hurt. Love for Siobhan is a warm bright blanket adding to the blistering heat of the day in the best possible way.

"He is. I promise." I slip an arm around her waist and squeeze.

"Sarah." Ryan's voice jerks me out of the smoldering fire of Siobhan's worry for me. He's standing on the other side of the bar, palms pressed together.

"I thought Layden picked up your shift today."

"I . . . Can we talk?"

"Bit busy here." I wave at the throng of customers.

"I've got this covered." Siobhan grabs my tray of drinks and heads to my table. She's been hinting at how bad Ryan feels about causing the rift between Nick and me. I never thought Siobhan and Ryan would end up friends when he joined The Diamond Club's staff. Yet we've been a crew for a while now, watching each other's backs, in the trenches together, always in sync. I get why she doesn't like Ryan and me not talking. It's like we've lost a limb.

I roll my eyes. "We might as well get this over with." I abandon the busy bar and walk down the path to the storage shed. Do I want to yell at Ryan? Tell him to mind his business next time? Yes, except there better not be a next time. The reasonable side of me insists I should let Ryan explain first. Let's see which side of me wins.

The door squeaks, protesting the force of me shoving the metal open. The hinges quiet as Ryan holds the heavy slat contraption and follows me.

"I'm not sorry," Ryan hurries to say before I have a chance to make up my mind about yelling at him.

Well, this is a good start. I park my butt on a stack of Belgian Pale Ale, hold my tongue, and wait.

The shed isn't wide, and Ryan crosses the floor twice in only a few steps. Halfway through the third repetition he stops; his gaze finds mine. He holds it, opens his mouth, closes it, and presses his lips together like he's trying to hold in his words.

Ryan is a conundrum. Man of few words is what most would say, but I know different. On the surface he's shy and shuts down when he gets jittery. If he cares, or once he has a few too many drinks, he loosens up and can talk your ear off. Right now, he appears downright terrified. My heart goes out to my friend.

"Just spit it out," I say.

"Are you familiar with the concept of cognitive dissonance?"

I was not expecting that. "Missed that day in class."

"It's a concept in social psychology first pondered by Leon Festinger where a person holds conflicting beliefs, and the conflict causes certain unusual behaviors. The condition can manifest in mental and physical ways such as anxiety, depression, feelings of guilt, and shying away from difficult conversations if allowed to fester." His hands are flying around, and he resumes the pacing. "Of note, the word fester doesn't come from Festinger himself. The word has routes in a fourteenth century old French word *festrir* meaning small sore discharging pus. Probably originates from the Latin word *fistula*—"

"Ryan." I raise my voice over his mumbling. At this rate, we'll never get to the end of this blatant attempt of Ryan's to *not* apologize. "Is there a point?"

He glances at the ceiling. "Right. Yes. My point." Ryan plants his feet by the shelves with paper goods. He straightens the package of napkins and adjusts the bag with breadbasket liners. It's not like I have hours to wait for him to gather his thoughts. Maybe we need to try another time. Siobhan can't manage the crowd by herself for much longer. "I had two conflicting beliefs. One—Nick makes you happy. The other—he could hurt you. Him hot-wiring Betty planted a seed that there was more to his past, and I couldn't leave it alone. I had to find out."

"Not really any of your business." I jiggle my foot.

"It was. Because you are my friend, and I protect my friends."

"I don't need your—"

"I know you don't; you're completely independent and don't need anyone to fight your battles for you." Ryan steps away from the shelving unit. "But your friends want to be there for you. Not just in the good times, not just for the Fun-Sarah. You are important to me. You . . . I . . ." He throws his hands up. "I won't regret looking out for you. You deserved the truth."

"This definitely doesn't sound much like an apology. What if Nick and I split up? Would you've apologized then?"

Ryan edges closer. "Why? I would've been right. He wouldn't have been good for you if he could've left you without talking things through."

"What if I hadn't accepted his explanation? What if I would've booted Nick out of my life?"

"You're too generous. Care too much."

I pop off the cases of beer and jab Ryan in the ribs. "You're trying to talk me out of being pissed at you by complimenting my overabundance of care?"

He gives me his half a grin. "Is it working?"

I roll my eyes at him. "Maybe. Your heart might have been in the right spot." He opens his mouth, but I cut him off. "But you went about it all wrong. Next time you're concerned about me, talk to me before you go behind my back and launch into your super spy stuff."

"Okay. I can do that."

"Promise?"

"Promise."

"Good." I feel lighter now that the anger has dissipated. Ryan opens his arms, and I dive in. "But you're not off the hook."

"How about I owe you a favor? For the trouble I caused. Even though I wouldn't take it back."

"How about apologizing to Nick?"

"Already did that earlier."

"What? You went to Nick first?"

"Nick was easier. He cares about you too."

"Fine. A favor it is. But I'm going to make it a huge one. You're gonna work for your penance."

"For you—anything."

I push the door of the shed open. The hinge's tired noise sounds like a grunt of approval. I'd hate to lose a friend over a boy. But I'm not afraid of choices anymore, and I'll fight for the people I love, for the things I believe in. I'm stronger than when I got to LA. What doesn't break us, makes us stronger, right?

LA made me hella strong.

FORTY-FIVE

NICK

MOVING IN WITH SARAH solves so many problems: the rent is manageable, so I still have enough money to buy a car. Soonish. Public transportation is available to get me to campus until the car situation is resolved. I dance my way to the couch and plop on the middle cushion. I'll be in the same apartment as Sarah. Every day. This is the biggest positive. The negatives are there too. Siobhan. Siobhan isn't my ideal . . . anything? But I can cope with her attitude. All for Sarah.

My skin sticks to the leather of Dad's couch. I'm sweating for a different reason now, working up the nerve to Facetime with Mom.

I have to tell her about Sarah. No lies. And why should I lie? I'm proud of having Sarah as my . . . future roommate? I cross my feet under the coffee table. Not a lie, but that's exactly how I got into trouble before. Girlfriend? I uncross them. We haven't put a label on it, but maybe we should. Who am I kidding? I'm dying to put a label on it. I want to shout to the rooftops and tell all seven people I know in LA and anyone else who'll listen, "Sarah is my girl."

But first, Mom.

"Nicky?" Mom's face blooms. Her smile takes up half the screen. Photos of her, me, and Mike peek from behind her in the fancy silver frames my brother and I spent hours hanging. Mike still thinks they are crooked. "Your hair is so long."

Having a hairdresser for a mom has its perks, but two months without her skills and my curls almost reach my shoulders. "Plenty for you to work with."

"About that. I'm coming to LA in a couple of weeks."

"Oh." I lean my elbows on my knees. I wasn't expecting to see her until Thanksgiving.

"I'm going to bite the bullet and spend the money on the conference. The hotel stay will cost me more than the flight. But my clients will thank me."

"Great." I grin. About time she started doing things for herself. She gave up so much for Mike and me. "When you get here, you'll have to come visit me in my new place."

"You're getting a place of your own?"

I look over the top of the phone at the boxes stacked in the hallway. "Not quite. An apartment with two roommates. But there's access to a shared roof deck, and it's close to the beach."

"I knew you were hunting for one, but this is—"

"Sarah asked me yesterday. I don't have much, so she's helping me move today."

Less than three months at Dad's and on top of Mom's old suitcase, my hockey duffel, and the backpack I came into this apartment with, I have three more boxes of stuff I don't remember accumulating.

"Sarah? The screenwriter?"

"Yes. She . . ." My pulse takes off. How do I segue this into the girlfriend conversation? Might as well rip off the Band-Aid. "We are sort of together."

"Sort of? And as of when?"

I feel like it's the first day of school, and she's asking me if I made any friends. "It's . . . complicated. But you'll love her. She's amazing."

"Complicated is not what I want to hear. She's the petite blond one, right?"

"Yeah. How?"

"I'm on Instagram too. Thanks to Bri, I get a glimpse into your life in LA and your friends. Bri's photos are of actual people, unlike your account. If I relied on you, I'd think LA is full of street corners and alleys. Why did you take a picture of the garbage can yesterday? Why post it? I want to see your handsome face, not a garbage can."

"Mom." I groan. "It's art. I'm trying to establish my brand, show potential agents I have an eye for directing."

"But would it kill you to post a selfie once in a while?"

"No one wants to see my mug."

"I do." She presses her hands into the frilly top of her blouse. "I want proof you're alive. Your dad says he barely sees you."

Not my fault we're on different schedules. He'll be seeing me a lot less. I'm not sure what I was expecting of him when I came here, but Dad last December when he showed back up in our lives and Dad now aren't the same person. I'm not sure if Mike's right and last year's version was an act, or he's forgotten what it's like to have a kid. I want him to be the dad of my dreams. I'm still holding my breath for the man I remember to reappear.

My phone buzzes, and Sarah's message pops up on the screen.

Sarah: Parked at the loading dock. Coming up.

"She's here. I better go."

"Nicky, hold on." Mom licks her lips and takes a deep breath. I thought her visit to LA was her surprise. What is she nervous about now? Does she want me to put Sarah on the phone? Shouldn't Sarah's parents be the one asking me about my intentions, not the other way around?

"Mom?"

"With you out of Theo's place, maybe, I thought, and I will have to ask him first, but I have this idea . . ."

"Just tell me." I glare at the ceiling.

"Since you won't be there, I might ask Theo if I can stay with him. It'll save me a ton on the hotel, and I can maybe change the tickets and stay an extra night so you and I can catch up? I'll give you a haircut. You could introduce me to Sarah?"

Mom's not normally the person to ask for my or Mike's permission. "You want to stay with Dad?"

"Is it such a bad idea?" She licks her lips again, and the proverbial lightbulb goes off in my head.

"I'm not a baby, Mom. Are you trying to tell me you and Dad are dating again?"

"Well, I . . . we . . . he and I . . . it's complicated."

"I coined the phrase first." Seems everything is complicated today. Not sure how I feel about my parents getting back together. For months after we moved to Chicago, I spent nights fantasizing about us being a family again. Everything that happened beat the hope out of me. Mike is going to hate this.

"Mike disapproves"—called it—"but I thought you would understand. Living with him, I thought you'd see how he's changed. Theo really was excited to have you in LA."

Was is the key word. His dream of a son was better than the reality he faced. "Can't say we've had much father-son bonding time. I'm not going to warn you to be careful. You were married to the guy for fifteen years before he went to jail." I look at the camera instead of the screen, so she knows I mean it. "I'm always going to be on your side first."

"I love you too, Nicky. You'll make some woman really happy one day."

Sarah. I'll make Sarah happy. And I plan to start now.

The doorbell rings. "Gotta go. Love you, Mom."

The angry buzzer repeats its demand to open the door. When I do, even behind the giant sunglasses, Dad's irritated expression is unmistakable. Fuck. He wasn't supposed to be here. "Can you let me through? The box isn't getting any lighter." He readjusts the black plastic tub with a yellow lid and walks past me.

The sunny smile I was hoping for appears at the stairs, and my stomach twists. The light of my life being sucked in by the dark hole of my life is exactly what I was trying to avoid. My brain tries to find a way to delay, reroute, stop the collision.

For a moment, my panic recedes as Sarah's lips find mine. "Hey, you."

"Hi." The hallway brightens. I don't understand how she does it, but when she's near, everything seems . . . possible. "Listen, my, um, dad, he's inside."

Her eyes widen. "Oh."

"If you don't want to meet him, we can get my stuff later." Maybe I can avoid this.

Her cute mouth forms a line. "Do you not want to introduce me?"

"No. Yes." Crap, I hate this. The truth. "He's in a bad mood." When isn't he lately?

"I get it. I'm on your side." Sarah's fingers entwine with mine, and she squeezes them a fraction. "We can come back if you want. But I'm not afraid."

I am. If Dad so much as throws a snarky remark her way, I might not be able to keep it together. Things are good right now, and I don't want to screw anything up with her.

"Did you drink all my milk?" Dad's voice booms from the kitchen.

I swivel in the doorway. My father stands there with an empty carton of milk in one hand. The fingers of my free hand ball into a fist. "No, Dad. You used the last this morning, remember?"

"Oh, right." He spins and bumps his knee against my stack of boxes. "Shit. Why's this crap here?"

"That's my dad," I mutter under my breath. I pull Sarah into the living room, holding her hand tighter. "Dad, I want you to meet someone."

"What's your stuff doing in the middle of the room?"

"Dad." I raise my voice, and his head snaps to me.

His mouth opens, and he points to my suitcase by the door when his gaze lands on Sarah. His whole body shifts. Gone is the grumpy miser. Dad morphs into the friendly schmoozer. "And who is this?"

"This is my . . . this is Sarah."

Sarah steps over and extends a hand to my father. "Hi, I'm Nick's girlfriend."

Sarah and Nick's romance story continues in

Passions, Hopes, & Us.

Turn the page for a sneak peek

WILLA DREW

PASSIONS, HOPES & US

Sarah

I CLING TO THE last shreds of my willpower and run my hand over the steamy mirror in the bathroom. The glass fogs. Again. Everything is out of my control. Again.

What will tonight hold?

When the nominees were announced weeks ago, I was thrilled Nick made the list for potential Best Director. *Indigo* as Best Picture and *Our Lines* as Best Song also made sense. My nomination came as a surprise, and while I've been trying to play it cool around everyone, this win would mean a lot.

The Starlight Foundation's awards gala has the potential to change everything, be the validation I need. If our movie wins, or if I win for best screenplay, job offers are almost a guarantee. If that doesn't happen . . . what will I do next? How long do I cling to my hopes before I accept I'm not made for Hollywood?

A win would prove to Mom I'm making the right choice staying here.

My towel slides off my head and releases the damp wave of my blond tresses. The sweet aroma of strawberry conditioner emanating from them reminds me of home and dulls the shards of anticipation coursing through my body. Mom's care packages always contain things I miss from Toronto, but the fruity conditioner Mémère and I found while roaming around Kensington Market is a must. I need to remind Mom to send me another bottle. I run the towel over my hair then wrap it around my body.

I open the bathroom door and slam into a broad chest.

"Thought you'd never get out of there." Nick's hands find my waist, and his mouth finds my lips.

I sink into the kiss. More calm. More comfort. More of the support I crave tonight. His body and mine press together, and I dig my fingers into the silky brown waves I love. Since his mother cut his hair last week, it's far too short for my liking, but the style accentuates his cheekbones and gives him a polished, professional look. Adding a tuxedo will be a dangerous combination. A different kind of anticipation washes over me. I can't wait to see him all dressed up.

Nick's hand heads south. He creates the perfect angle, and the kiss is no longer flirty: it's ambitious and beckons me to step over the line we've agreed not to cross. Not until tonight. Not until he's no longer the leader of Team Blue. With the Starlight Foundation competition complete, Nick will stop being the boss I have to work with. He'll be the man I want to be with. My boyfriend in every sense of the word. At last.

As much as I don't want to, I have to cool this down.

"Just a few more hours"—I twist away from his mouth—"and our pact is over."

Heat flares on my collarbone. I'm not sure I can hold out much longer. The way Nick presses his forehead against mine, I can tell it's getting near impossible for him as well. "Whose stupid idea was this pact, anyhow?" Nick's voice rasps against my ear.

"I believe it was you?"

He might not have been serious when he teased that I shouldn't sleep with my boss. But I didn't want to be known as someone who sleeps her way up the ladder. Not doing what I always do—jump into bed with the guy I like—seemed like a good idea at the time.

The front door slams, and Nick and I spring apart. I grab my towel before it reveals more than would be visible in a bathing suit.

"Oy, I'm home," Siobhan announces. She's so loud our neighbors above and below probably hear her. "Hands off each other."

Nick drops his hands but leans in and hovers his lips over mine. "Does she have a sixth sense for when I kiss you?"

He takes a step back, rakes my naked shoulders with his stare, and walks around me into the bathroom.

Heat floods below my navel. I should be grateful to Sio for halting Nick and me when she did. The only reason we haven't broken our self-imposed pact is that between Nick's new responsibilities as morning shift manager at Blend, my late hours at The Diamond Club, and our ever-present roommate, Nick and I have barely had a moment alone together in the apartment. I wanted to rent a hotel room for tonight but neither of us can afford one. Hopefully I'll have a screenwriting job by his birthday. Extra money for a night alone would be heaven.

"You're never going to believe this." Sio strolls in holding an extra-long garment bag.

"What's that?"

"Mrs. Marino lent me a dress for tonight. Look at this stunner." Siobhan runs the zipper down the black cover to reveal a swath of gold beaded material. The owner of The Diamond Club and Siobhan are the same height. Tall. Well, everyone is tall to me, but either of them could've been a model. "It has a thigh-high slit. Move over, Angelina Jolie. This is my opportunity to show some calf candy."

"The dress is beautiful. Can't wait to see you in it."

"Let me wash off the grime of old men drinking scotch first—"

"Totally." I wince. "But Nick's in the bathroom."

"You have to tell him to stop steaming it up. It's like I'm back in Ireland sharing with my brothers. Do I have to remind the Prom King about the five-minutes-per-shower rule?"

I nudge her shoulder. "Be nice."

Chimes bounce off the walls of the open-concept living room and kitchen.

"You gonna answer that?" Siobhan knows my mom's ringtone.

"I better." Mom won't stop until I answer so I hit the green button.

"Which dress did you decide on?" Mom's voice erupts through the phone speaker. No hello. That's my no-nonsense mother.

Right. I was supposed to send her a photo. This is not an emergency, but now that she's on the phone I can't not reply. "Hang on. I'm about to put it on." In my room, I switch the phone's camera off and change.

My dress is sparkling, short, and tight. The miniskirt makes the most of my legs, especially paired with the one pair of high heels I own. I spent a whole night's tips on the stilettos, but they give the illusion that I'm average height. Nick won't have to practically bend over to kiss me tonight. I turn the phone's camera back on and move it up and down. "What d'you think?"

Mom insisted this was the best of all the options I tried on at the second-hand store. It's both retro and back in style, and friendly to my budget.

"A vision in silver." Her smile is wide and genuine. "You'll need to put your hair up for it though."

"That's the plan." I set the phone in the holder on my dresser and brush my smooth locks.

Mom's face sours. "I'm sorry the family can't be with you tonight. Even though we're not there, remember, you always have us. A home, a job, and people who love you here. Win or lose." Tears are visible in her eyes.

Emotion from my mom is all or nothing. Today it's all, and the force of her words tugs on the longing to come home that always lingers in the background. It would be so easy to stop struggling in LA and go back to Toronto. "Mom, don't cry. I know you guys love me. I appreciate it. I really do. But this has been my dream for so long."

"I know." Mom wipes at her cheek. "We support you. Mémère would've been so proud of you for getting where you are." Her smile returns. It's a different kind, but better than watching her cry and not being able to hug her.

"I've been thinking about her all day." Mémère is never far from my heart. It's been less than nine months since her death, and I see reminders of her everywhere. When I pour a glass of sherry at work, when I shift Betty into fifth on the highway, when Nick laughs at my corny jokes.

"Wherever she is, she's thinking about you too." Mom's voice is wobbly.

"We're rooting for you." Dad appears behind Mom's back and kisses her on the temple. "Text us as soon as you know."

"Love you, honey," Mom and Dad shout in unison.

"Love you too." Their faces disappear from the screen, and I hunt for the clip I want to use to hold my hair up.

"Are you almost . . ." Nick's head pops into my room, his damp hair a contrast to the tux. With the silver tie loose around his neck he could be on the cover of GQ. Heat blooms in my stomach and obscures whatever thoughts I had. Nick's eyes drink me in from my head to my toes and back again. We might be on the same page because I read his desire to remove the dress I just put on. The fire spreads from my core and rushes over my skin. I need Mom to call me again or I'm going to make us late by peeling the suit off him.

I know I'm playing with fire, but I put my hand on my hip. "See something you like?"

Nick's pupils dilate and cover the brown of his eyes with the inky glimmer of desire. "Do I ever."

A silent conversation courses between us. This happens a lot these days. Like I can read his mind, and he can read mine. Both of us agreeing we want to act, close my bedroom door, and devour each other, but also agreeing we can't.

Nick lowers his eyes to the floor first and breaks the trance. "Who were you talking to?"

"Mom and Dad apologizing for not being able to make it today."

"Your parents are sweet." He leans against the door, not daring to cross the threshold. "Don't think I've ever heard my dad say I love you to me or anyone."

"He'll get there. You still have a lot to learn about each other. At least he's coming to the Gala. Is he riding in the limo with us?"

Wil opposed the limo idea, grumbling about the expense, but Nick never went to prom and never got the experience. I want him to have everything, so I arranged it with the company that provides car service at The Diamond Club. With everyone on the team chipping in, it wasn't too unreasonable.

He continues to scrutinize the faded herringbone design of the parquet. "You know Dad. He's not going to hang with a bunch of young people. He'll meet us there. We'll have plenty of time together at the Gala."

"Maybe this'll help you and him to get closer."

"You'd think spending two months on his couch would be enough." He pushes off the doorframe. "But I'm not going to complain. He's in my life. And that's more than he's done for ten years." I have trouble grasping what it's like to not have a father around. His older brother Mike played the role and from what I gather, he was good at it. "I've always wanted a dad. A dad who wants me. Who's proud of what I'm doing with my life."

"Nick." I wait until his gaze finds mine. "I think Theo is. He's just not great at showing it."

"Your parents are the best. Can't wait to meet the legends who inspired our movie."

"A few more weeks." I was nervous asking Nick to come home for Thanksgiving in October. Flights to Canada from LA are expensive, but the way his eyes lit up and the instant yes erased all doubt. "Now shoo." I wave my hairbrush at him. "Let me do my hair or we'll be late."

NICK IS HOLDING MY hand under the table. My shoulders relax, and I'm grateful for his strength. I need a little too much of it tonight in this ballroom abuzz with Starlight Foundation winners and hopefuls. I'm in the hopeful category.

"You've got this," Nick whispers in my ear as the crowd's attention moves to the stage where a buff guy in a classic black tuxedo is reading the list of my fellow nominees. Adrenaline spikes, and my tapping on the chair leg resembles Mémère's whisk hitting the bowl of cream she preferred to whip by hand. Nick pushes with our joined palms on my knee, and the weight holds me in in place, fusing us together.

"And the Star goes to . . ." Butterflies the size of elephants swirl in my stomach. As if looking at the presenter might jinx me, I close my eyes and hold my breath. Please, let it be me. Nick crushes my hand in a silent 'you got this,' and I squeeze back, a silent 'I got this.'

"Karina Appleton."

What? Applause erupts, and I unwind my fingers from Nick's. Following the expected routine, I clap for the winner and take a sip of champagne, but the taste of disappointment overrides the fizz and sinks into my stomach like an oversized ice cube. I didn't win. No marker to validate I'm worthy. I can practically sense the job offers drying up.

I track Karina, who looks dazzling in her blush-pink off-the-shoulder gown that complements her light-brown skin. Her teammates shout their congratulations as she makes her way onto the stage. I try another mouthful of the bubbly alcohol, but it only irritates. The applause, the lights, everything is irritating. I should be happier for Karina. For my friend. Because she is my friend. Alongside Sio, Ryan, and Nick, Karina made her way into my very selective friends category.

These last few months of laboring together over our scripts during the competition, I found first the critique partner I enjoyed working with, and then a friend whose company I loved. But Karina already has a position as junior writer with a small studio. I have nothing connecting me to the career I want. No fallback plan. I needed this. Nausea hits me. Partly because I struggle to imagine what's next for me. Partly because I hate to be a person who's jealous of a friend's success.

From the stage Karina thanks her parents, teachers, and friends, and her smile is infectious. It melts the ice of my disappointment. I swallow my defeat and rise to join in the applause.

Nick follows suit. He towers over me, standing close behind. The heat from his body seeps through. I lean my back against him.

"It should've been you," he says.

I shush him as I nudge his shoulder. I want to kiss him, take solace in the lips that always make me feel better, but we have a strict no PDA rule. For now. We take our seats. I interlace my fingers and tuck them under my chin, resisting taking Nick's hand again. I don't want to be too needy. He slings his arm over the back of my chair, and I take in a lungful of his aftershave. Nick's scent, touch, and presence calm me. And I borrow from him the strength I lack. My pulse is pounding in my ears, and I'm willing it to slow down. I can figure something out. Our movie can still win. There still might be job offers. It's not over.

Karina's back at her seat. She's breathtakingly happy. The only thing I can do is step over my jealously and guilt and go talk to her. "I'll be right back."

I tug at the short hem of my dress as I wind my way through the tables. Karina's face is glowing when I reach her. She catches sight of me, and her grin widens. "Can you believe this?" She holds up the trophy.

"I can." I wrap my arms around her and squeeze. Her joy swirls around us, and I smile into her shoulder, for the first time truly happy for my friend. "Congratulations."

"I couldn't have done it without you."

"Me? I doubt that." I keep my hands on her and fight the tears that threaten to ruin my makeup. I'm not crying for myself. These are for Karina, her success, and her talent.

"No, I'm serious." Her deep brown eyes implore me to believe her. "You're the perfect sounding board. You pushed me to cut out all that dialogue in the spacewalk scene and let the camera do the talking."

Karina and I do work well together, and I don't want this to be the end. "Well, there's more where that came from. I'm always here to lend my judgy eye." I wink at her. "But today is not about working. It's a celebration."

"I'll drink to that," an unfamiliar man's voice says behind my back.

I spin to find a man in his early thirties, jet-black hair tousled a little too professionally, one curl begging to be tucked back into place. "Sarah, this is my boss Rod Varma. Rod—Sarah Connor. She was also nominated tonight."

Rod extends his hand. "Karina mentioned you were the one to beat."

His hand is clammy, but his grip is firm.

"Apparently not." I shrug.

He chuckles at my joke, releases my hand, and offers Karina a quick hug.

"But if it had to be one of us who won, I'm glad it was her," I say.

Rod smirks at Karina. "Don't let this win go to your head. We still need you in the writers' room bright and early tomorrow."

"I'll make it a triple espresso then." Karina pretends to write a note on her palm.

Rod tilts his head to address me. "This one cracks me up. I need it after today's session." He regards Karina. "The execs want a big action-packed scene for episode eight, and every idea was complete and utter shit." He glances at the ceiling. "What I wouldn't give for an original idea."

"They say there are no original ideas." The words fly out of my mouth. "Only different twists."

"True." Karina backs me up. "Aren't there like only seven storylines and three motivations: love, hate, and money?"

"Someone's done her research." Rod crosses his arms. "Listen to a lot of podcasts on writing, do you?"

"Sarah's big on research. You should see the detail she went into for her movie. It took place in the '90s, and she figured out what kind of security system a car of that time would have." Karina wraps her hand around my waist and pushes me a little bit forward, as if she wants Rod to pay attention to me.

"Not that hard. I've always been into cars." I offer him the everything-is-great smile I've perfected in my years of bartending. Rod's gaze is intense, and my cheeks flush, like I'm being inspected. A new flock of giant butterflies is wreaking havoc in my stomach. I scramble for something to break the tension. The stupidest joke my dad told me last week springs to mind. "What type of car does a dog hate?"

His eyebrows rise, and I'm sure he thinks I'm an idiot. "I don't know. What type of car does a dog hate?"

"A Cor-Vet." I mentally add the cymbals crash. There's a moment of silence. What is wrong with me? This guy must think I'm drunk or something.

"Cute." His lip curls to the side. "Corny but cute."

"Sorry, I have a million car jokes." Now my cheeks must surely be blazing. "It's a competition between my dad and me to one up each other."

"Well, should I ever need a bad dad joke, I'll know where to look." He nods at Karina. "Glad we have another award-winning screenwriter on our roster, but I need to get back to my table. This event is about schmoozing just as much as about the winners."

I give Karina another hug. "I better get back too, before Nick sends out a search party." Though I might not have won the trophy I came here for, I'm taking home the grand prize. A wave of longing crashes from my heart to my belly as I make my way back to Nick. I'm not going to be Team Blue for much longer, but after tonight I'll be Team Nick for a long time.

Passions, Hopes, & Us

Out Now

Wait...there's more.

Sarah originated as a side character in DL's hidden identity contemporary romance, Ruby Red, which takes place the summer before Sarah meets Nick on that fateful Christmas Eve. Ruby Red tells the story of Ali and Sam, who you briefly met in Part 3 of Kisses, Lies, & Us.

Enjoy this excerpt from Ali and Sam's story where DL's readers met Sarah for the first time.

An excerpt from

RUBY RED – HIDDEN HEARTS BOOK 1

by DL Croisette

Sam arrived early for his evening shift at the resort. He convinced himself it was because he'd been bored hanging in his sad little apartment. This morning had consisted of an extra-long jog, trying to blow off his pent-up energy. The ploy had worked for a bit, but he found himself jittery again now. He considered dusting off his camera and exploring a new part of LA, but the Nikon stayed in its case. What he truly wanted was to bump into the woman he'd spent last night dreaming about.

Disappointment burned in him at her absence. Did he reckon she'd be sitting there waiting for him? Well, he could dream.

His actual dreams last night had been full of Ali. Her soft skin had wreaked havoc on his mind and body. Cold showers were never fun, yet one was necessary after a night aching for what he didn't get to sample in the cabana.

Ryan wasn't behind the bar tonight. Instead, there was a girl Sam hadn't met before: a petite blonde with tanned skin similar to his and a slight athletic build underneath the resort uniform.

"Hi, I'm Sarah," she said, introducing herself with a peppy attitude he was sure garnered her big tips.

"Sam. The new guy."

Sarah's mouth split into an enormous smile as she shook his hand. "Nice to meet you. Should be a good crowd a little later. A few VIPs coming in."

His gut told him they were going to get along. She had a confidence surrounding her, and he bet anyone would find her easy to talk to: an essential quality in a bartender.

They got down to work. Sarah showed him what was still left to be set up after the rush of the afternoon crowd, and he surveyed the bar area for any sign of Ali.

An agonizing hour later, Ali walked in. Well, "walked" wasn't the right word. She promenaded onto the patio, reminding him of the queens he'd studied in history class.

Dressed in a skin-tight white dress, with a neckline plunging so deep Sam might have been able to make out her belly button, she turned the heads of men and women alike when she passed the bar. He briefly forgot how to breathe. Without thinking, he started toward her.

Sarah yanked on the sleeve of his uniform. "Whoa there, big fella." She laughed and adjusted her shirt. "Remember how I mentioned VIPs? This is the biggest. Let me handle her table. She requires...a certain set of skills. Lots of rules with this one."

Every cell in his body screamed to go to Ali. Somehow, somewhere, he regained a degree of control and stood his ground. She selected the finest table in the place, one where every patron in the room would have a stellar view of her. He wondered if the move was strategic. Sarah greeted the dark-haired goddess with a tall glass of champagne, and Ali responded with a polite smile. He envied his co-workers' proximity to her as they briefly chatted before Sarah returned.

"Eyes back in your head, man," Sarah teased him. "You'll want to be on your best behavior. The boss is on her way down. They're having dinner together tonight."

This confused him. The patio didn't serve dinner. Sarah read his mind and explained that for Ali Stinson, the rules were different. This guest preferred to eat outside, and it seemed Ali got what she wanted.

"'Under the stars,' Ms. Stinson calls it. And when you're good friends with the boss, you get little perks like that. I'll get to play server and bartender tonight, so you'll be busy. They are my first priority, but I'll help as much as I can with the rest of the guests. You okay with the arrangement?"

He nodded. Not as if he had a choice. Besides really needing this job, he was quickly discovering he also wanted it. The position had certain perks, making it oh-so interesting.

"Good. I'll split some of the tips with you. I'll say one thing about Ms. Stinson; she's the best tipper in town. She demands a lot, but she makes the effort worth your while."

A strange kind of satisfaction washed over Sam. He'd spent a lot of time around the wealthy and invariably had found the more money they had, the less they tended to care with regards to those who didn't have much. He'd witnessed countless times when those in the service industry, working on minimum wage, had gone above and beyond for VIPs, only to have those VIPs be stingy when it came to showing their appreciation.

He now valued those tips, realizing they were an important part of any service industry worker's income. They meant the difference between paying rent and eating or doing both. Somehow, his gut said Ali Stinson would be different.

Sarah pointed to Mrs. Marino, who headed straight for her friend, ignoring the bar staff. Would it kill her to say "hello"? He thought better of the notion. Maybe she would recognize him from the cabana the other day. This would not be good for him.

Memories of the cabana and what could have occurred, had they not been interrupted, bombarded him. He had to keep this job—find a chance to get Ali alone in a room again. Taste her luscious lips. Again.

Sam shook his head to dislodge those images.

Over the next few hours, he did his best bartending with one eye. The other was always on Ali.

From his vantage point behind the bar, he'd noticed most of the male patrons glancing or outright staring at her. She ignored them all like they were merely mannequins in a window of a store she wasn't interested in buying anything from. His breath had frozen when one had summoned the courage to approach her. Exactly the type of man Ali should be with—rich. The prick must have plenty of money to give her anything she could ever desire.

Within moments of the man nearing her, it was as if an invisible armor enclosed around Ali. Her shoulders straightened, her chin stuck out, and her features hardened into ice. A cold rebuff pushed the man away, and he made a face as he returned to his drinking companion. Sam was confident she was anything but cold. No, she was warm and affable. In fact, his fingers still tingled from her warmth.

His boss eventually joined her, and they chatted and laughed with their heads close, making their way through a bottle of champagne before their other guests arrived.

When Ali stood to greet the newcomers, he thought she was smiling his way, an open, warm act that softened her features and made his heart skip a beat. He almost waved like a little boy until it dawned on him that the smile was meant for her company, not him. Instead, he concentrated on mixing an old fashioned for the gentleman seated at the bar, laughing at himself for acting like a teenager.

When the night wore on and the meal was well over, Mrs. Marino left the table. As she passed by the bar, she pulled Sarah aside. He moved closer to listen to the conversation.

"...anything she wants."

"Yes, ma'am," said Sarah.

"Don't charge anything to the house. I want everything run through my personal account. Make sure there's a note on the system. All the staff needs to be made aware. She's not to pay for anything until further notice."

"I'll personally see to it, Mrs. Marino," chirped Sarah.

"Thank you, Sally." With the wrong name, the older woman walked away.

Sarah turned to Sam and rolled her eyes. "She never remembers anyone's name. It's a running joke around here."

He laughed with Sarah, relieved his boss seemed more forgetful rather than too self-important to take the time to remember employees' names. He secretly hoped the same trait applied to faces.

"You catch all that?" Sarah demanded.

Had he been obvious?

He reiterated the manager's request for Ms. Stinson. "What's it all about?"

Sarah wiped her hands on a bar towel. "Darned if I know. I can't figure what drives these women. Probably lost a bet on a horse race." She grinned at her own joke. Sam nodded with her even though he didn't share her sentiment. In his gut, he sensed something else was going on.

Soon after Mrs. Marino disappeared, the other guests also departed, leaving Ali alone at her table. She didn't make any effort to move. Sarah brought her another flute of chilled champagne but returned with the glass still in hand.

"Here we go," griped Sarah. "She's moving on to the martini phase."

He regarded her, puzzled. "What does that mean?"

"It means she's sticking around all night. Martinis mean she's getting serious. 'Drinking to forget', she calls it. Although I don't get what a woman like her wants to forget."

He glanced at her solitary figure, and a sense of sadness settled in. She was all alone. Rapunzel in her tower.

Sarah echoed his notions. "If it were me, I'd be with my friends, hitting the clubs, having the time of my life instead of wasting my night hanging with this lame crowd. I mean, look at her, she's got it all. Still young; all the money in the world. Doesn't have to get up for the 7 AM shift tomorrow."

Out of politeness, he agreed with Sarah, but his mind drifted toward theories about why Ali was drinking alone. He supposed being cheated on couldn't have been an easy thing to get over. The whole "once bitten, twice shy" theory came to mind. It would take time for anyone's heart to heal. Maybe she simply needed to meet the right person to convince her she could love again.

Maybe he could be that person.

"Oh no." Sarah invaded his musings. "She's coming over here."

He turned to find Ali sauntering toward them. With the way she ambled, he had an inkling that her movements were a little less the seductive sort and more trying to keep steady while being slightly inebriated. Still, she was like a model making her way down the runway. He swallowed in anticipation of her arrival.

She took a seat at the opposite end of the bar, placing her purse on the stool beside her to create a cushion as Sarah delivered her martini. Ali thanked her for the drink and took a long, leisurely sip. Sam found himself insanely jealous of the glass.

Shot glass in hand, he attempted to inch closer without being too obvious, hoping to draw her attention. However, Murphy's Law applied its powerful pull, and the bar grew busy again and he became engaged in mixology 101.

When they ran low on pineapple juice, Sarah ventured off to get more, leaving him alone to tend the bar. He granted the last patron's request and was screwing the cap back on a top-shelf Scotch when a woman's voice cut through the air.

"Excuse me." The words were slow and sultry, yet the honeyed tone was different from the day before, when it had been charged with sexual tension. Now, the sound was blunted by alcohol. Still, her voice sent a thrill through him, and he walked toward the siren.

"I'll have another." She shook the now empty glass. "Please. A——"

"A vodka martini with a slice of lemon," he finished for her. He had paid careful attention to what Sarah had made for Ali the first time.

The bombshell rewarded him with a tiny smile. "Yes, that's right."

With studied practice, he poured the ingredients into the shaker. This was it. He set down the drink before her and gripped the edge of the bar. This was the moment he'd been waiting for all night. Now she sat before him, and he found himself mute. He racked his brain for some charming comeback, or even something funny, to try to take the sadness from those cheerless eyes, but he came up completely blank.

He was blowing it.

Ruby Red – Hidden Hearts Book 1
by DL Croisette
OUT NOW

SERIES BY WILLA DREW

SECOND CHANCE BILLIONAIRES

The Second Chance Billionaires series follows five lifelong friends—a grumpy CEO, a charming playboy, a retiring hockey pro, a British aristocrat, and a sci-fi author—from college roommates to billionaire boardrooms as they each get one more shot at love.

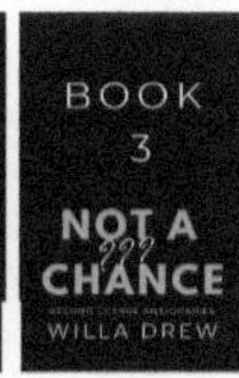
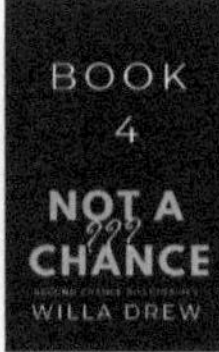

AND US

Watch movies and real life collide with Sarah and Nick in a right person/wrong time, hidden identity, new adult romance. One year, five parts, six major holidays, many twists.

Kisses, Lies, & Us

Passions, Hopes, & Us

Distance, Love, & Us

or binge the complete series with bonus scenes in
Friendzoned By My Crush

FALLING FOR THE ROCKSTAR'S DAUGHTER

An upper young adult, friends-to-lovers, slow burn romance featuring a reluctant collaboration between two musicians.

WE Blend

WE Breathe

WE Balance

ANDERS INVESTIGATIONS

Meet the men of Anders Investigations, a new contemporary romance series with a romantic suspense element.

Taming the Grumpy Bodyguard

Loving the Grumpy Bodyguard

FALLING FOR THE MOVIE STAR

If you like an age gap, brother's best friend romance featuring
LA's red-carpet glamor, Irish charm, and a reunion written in
the stars,

Siobhan and Asher's story is for you.

Acknowledgements

Kisses, Lies, and Us is the very first story we wrote as a duo. Before *WE Blend*, before *Star Struck,* it all started December of 2020. Stuck at home over the winter break Gala reached out to DL and suggested we try writing together. DL said, yes please.

But where to start? We each had stories of our own (we met on Wattpad) and decided to merge worlds.

The stars aligned as Sarah, a side character in DL's romance Ruby Red, and Nick, the brother of the main character in Gala's Love Strings, both happened to be in LA for Christmas.

Sarah, 22, and a bartender, and Nick, 19 and about to go to college in LA, needed a meet-cute. How would a nine-teen-year-old get into a bar? With a fake ID, of course.

The truth is—I tell lies all the time, what's one more?

This line from *Kisses, Lies, and Us* was one of the first things we wrote together.

Our friends from the Sweet and Sassy Writers' Squad read the story and asked, "What happens next?" So we wrote. . .four more books and completed the *And Us* series by telling Sara and Nick's love story over five holidays throughout one year.

Sarah and Nick were not the only ones destined to meet. This story wouldn't be the best we could make it without the vigilant eyes and guiding hands of our wonderful editors Julie, Kay, and Victoria.

Shout out to our ARC readers, Street Team, and group who keep us entertained (with pets, kids or reading recommendations), make us laugh with their reactions, and talk up our books better than we ever could. Hop on over to for previews, sneak peeks, and new friends.

And to the original match-made-in-heaven: our families. Thank you for supporting our writing careers despite the holidays we spent holed-up in our writing caves. We love you to the moon and back.

Two authors. Two countries. One obsession with love stories.

Willa Drew's contemporary slow-burn romances are full of feels, playful banter, and high-stakes emotions. Their globe-trotting characters fight for love as they discover who they are and where they belong.

Willa, a proud Canadian and devoted Leafs hockey fan, and Drew, a Russian-American with a lifelong love of languages, always search for the perfect words to capture heartbreak and connection.

Their books guarantee swoon-worthy kisses and happily ever afters.

Come hang out with them
@willadrewauthor
willadrew.com